MW00560409

CassaFirE

Also by Alex J. Cavanaugh:

CassaStar

"...calls to mind the youthful focus of Robert Heinlein's early military sf, as well as the excitement of space opera epitomized by the many Star Wars novels. Fast-paced military action and a youthful protagonist make this a good choice for both young adult and adult fans of space wars."
- Library Journal

Alex J. Cavanaugh

DANCING LEMUR PRESS, L.L.C.
Pikeville, North Carolina
www.dancinglemurpress.com

Published by Dancing Lemur Press, L.L.C.
P.O. Box 383, Pikeville, North Carolina, 27863-0383
www.dancinglemurpress.com

ISBN: 978-0-9827139-4-5

Printed in the United States of America

Cover design by C.R.W.

Publisher's Cataloging-in-Publication data

Cavanaugh, Alex J.
CassaFire / Alex J. Cavanaugh.
p. cm.
ISBN 978-0-9816210-6-7 (pbk.)
ISBN 978-0-9827139-3-8 (e-book)

1. Space travel —Fiction. 2. Outer space—Exploration—Fiction. 3. Teleportation—Fiction. 4. Psychokinesis—Fiction. 5. Science fiction. I. Title

PS3553.A964 C38 2012
[Fic]—dd22 2011937168

For my three awesome friends
who guided me on this journey -
Rusty Webb
Jeffrey Beesler
Anne Gallagher
I couldn't have done it without you!

Chapter One

Damned sloppy work!

Byron scowled at the cargo. Twenty years ago, I helped end the Vindicarn War, received the fleet's highest honors, and was given the freedom to pursue any position worthy of a pilot of my caliber, he thought, grinding his teeth. Today, I'm supervising the loading of luggage. Damn, this is wrong!

Pulling on the straps, Byron tightened the latch one more time. The men who'd loaded his shuttle knew nothing about proper cargo storage. They had not even checked the restraints. It wouldn't do to have the bins break free during flight. He was responsible for the cargo's safe arrival on board the Rennather.

Satisfied the crates were secure, he returned to the shuttle's central compartment. His boots echoed off the metal floor. One section squeaked in protest, but it was a comforting sound to Byron's ears. He'd piloted this particular shuttle for over twelve years and knew every rattle and groan. Only his knowledge of the Darten rivaled that intimacy, as twenty years in service together had bred a certain amount of familiarity with the tiny fighter.

Pausing at the open hatch, Byron scanned the encampment. The temporary structures, awash in pale blues, stood out against the green of the forest. With the cargo in place, all he lacked were three passengers. Last time Byron had seen the men, they were gathering personal equipment. Considering the urgency of their orders, he wished they'd speed up the process. Commander Korden wanted to reach their next destination in two days.

Noting three men ambling toward the shuttle, he continued forward and entered the cockpit. Judging from their pace, he had time to perform a systems check.

His fingers raced across the control panel, their movement automatic. Byron possessed more than enough experience and skill to fly an exploration shuttle. For twelve years now, the Rennather's commander had reminded Byron of his qualifications and eligibility to transfer to any ship he cared to pilot. Claiming contentment with his current assignment, Byron saw no need to seek other opportunities. Byron's outstanding skills were a luxury in his position. Despite moments of monotony, he found ways to challenge himself and avoid complacency in his position. Besides, he'd made a promise to a friend many years ago. Byron could not justify breaking that pact just because he was bored. Besides, Cassans lived long lives. He still had time for another career change and was in no hurry.

There were moments of excitement on the Rennather, though. Byron had seen more regions of space than even piloting a Cosbolt fighter would've provided. Exploration ships traveled beyond the allegiance borders, meeting new races and strengthening relationships with potential allies. Politics didn't interest Byron but flying on the edge of known space held a certain mystique.

A door sensor alerted him that his passengers were boarding. Pressing one final button, he turned from the controls. Byron stood and placed himself between the cockpit and main cabin. Crossing his arms, he leaned against the wall and focused on the three scientists strolling up the ramp. The third man crowded the first two, pushing them forward.

At least someone understands the importance of our next mission, Byron thought.

"Officer Byron," the first man stated, pausing to stand at attention. His voice was as thick as his midsection.

Byron nodded an acknowledgement, fighting to conceal the smirk that tugged at his lips. He recalled Vorsan's presence on previous flights. The science officer didn't handle space flight well.

"I hope your meal was light," said Byron.

Vorsan's eyes narrowed, but he offered no answer. Byron wondered if he dared taunt the man today with a demonstration of his flying ability. The science officer was a dour sort. Byron might as well have some fun.

The second man hailed a greeting. His shrill voice matched his tall, lanky frame. He joined the first, stowing his gear in the empty compartment. Byron followed their every movement. Although science officers were precise by nature, they tended to forget those habits when traveling. More often than not, stowed gear required adjustments.

Aware that the third man had paused, Byron's attention shifted to his final passenger. Wide eyes greeted the pilot, and the dark orbs appeared ready to pop out of their sockets. The lad's expression mirrored the stunned recognition that arose in his thoughts. Byron frowned. Remote exploration assignments were assigned to those with experience. This boy was far too young.

As if sensing disapproval, the young man altered his expression and straightened his shoulders. "Officer Byron?" he gasped. The pitch of his voice confirmed his youth. The boy's thoughts continued to project amazement and were filled with adoration.

While telepathic courtesies might be beyond the lad, Byron did not want his own mind exposed. Locking his mental shields into place, he nodded and gestured for the young man to join the others. He'd long grown weary of the recognition. The Vindicarn War was many years past now, and Byron wanted to curtail any further comments regarding his war hero status. He'd lost his closest friend during one of those battles. He didn't want, or need, to be reminded of the tragedy that had changed the course of his life and career.

Byron sealed the hatch and returned to the controls. Engaging the engines, he listened with pleasure to the deep resonating roar. Connecting to the ship's teleportation device with his mind, he confirmed the unit's full strength. The teleporter's force echoed in his chest and he smiled. Even if the device's power were to fail, he could still jump the ship. Very few Cassans possessed that ability.

"A smooth flight this time, Officer Byron," Vorsan called from the main compartment.

"Last one a bit bumpy for you?" Byron asked, lifting the ship from the ground.

"I nearly lost my meal, damn it!"

Guiding the shuttle over the encampment, a sense of mischief crept over Byron. Yanking hard on the throttle, he pushed the engines to full capacity. Within seconds, the shuttle's position changed from horizontal to vertical. It ascended skyward at a rapid pace. The engines screamed as they fought the planet's gravitation. The sudden acceleration pressed Byron into his seat. He delighted in the sensation, despite the cries of dismay radiating from the main cabin and echoing through his mind.

"Byron!"

Ignoring the protests, he continued their steep climb. The ship shuddered in protest of such rough treatment, further rattling its contents. The thundering noise, coupled with the engine's roar, drowned out all other sounds. Eyes focused skyward, Byron's heart beat with exhilaration. He felt as one with the ship.

Sensing his passengers' discomfort, he leveled the craft. Relieved moans resonated from the main compartment. Before any of the men could chastise such rough treatment, Byron selected a location within proximity of the Rennather and teleported the shuttle.

For a split second, a silent darkness enveloped the ship. As the shuttle reentered space, the sight of the exploration vessel filled the view outside the cockpit. Without slowing his pace, Byron communicated his intentions to land and steered the ship toward the open bay. The landing bay loomed closer, threatening to engulf the shuttle. Slowing his speed at last, he glided into the opening and brought the runners down without so much as a single jolt. Byron eased the ship into position with a steady hand. He then powered down the vessel as it was towed into the central hanger.

When the shuttle ceased its movements, Byron turned off the remaining systems and arose to open the hatch. His passengers were fumbling with their harnesses. He sensed a great haste to exit his ship. Byron grinned at the ashen complexions, noting drool on Vorsan's chin.

"I hope you enjoyed your flight," Byron said, releasing the hatch.

"Damn it, Byron," the man exclaimed, wiping his face. "The ship's commander will hear about this."

Byron straightened his back and met the man's gaze. "I'm sure he will," he offered, "and that's Senior Officer Byron to you, Officer Vorsan."

The man hesitated as he reached for his pack. Pressing his lips together in resignation, Vorsan nodded. Yanking his bag free, he stormed out of the craft. The other two men gathered their items and followed at a slower pace. However, the youngest man paused before disembarking.

"Is that how you used to fly your Cosbolt, sir?" he asked.

Sensing admiration rather than malice, Byron allowed a grin to tug at the corner of his mouth. "No, if this were a Cosbolt, Vorsan would've thrown up."

The boy's broad face broke into a smile. "I'd like to hear about your adventures sometime, sir."

Byron's chest tightened. "Perhaps."

The young man trotted down the ramp, his step light and hopeful. Hanger personnel appeared to retrieve the crates. Byron supervised the process while the crew emptied the shuttle. Relieved of all cargo, he made one final sweep of the ship before exiting his craft. The Rennather would remain in orbit, conducting system checks, until the middle of the night. He intended to take full advantage of their stationary position.

Approaching the hanger chief, he requested permission to take out the Darten. The man gestured toward the tiny fighter and announced he would inform control of Byron's flight.

Byron conducted a visual inspection of his ship, running his hand down the sleek, metal surface as he circled the vessel. Slender by design for mobility, the Darten was the smallest fighter in the fleet. Completing his task, he mounted the short steps to the cockpit. Wiggling his body into position, Byron found his tall frame enveloped by the small compartment. Some men found it claustrophobic. Over the years, he'd grown accustomed to the cramped quarters. It paled in comparison to the spacious Cosbolt he'd once flown, but that fighter was no longer a viable option.

He ran through the pre-flight checklist before donning his helmet and lowering the canopy. Flashing an "all ready" thought to the hanger crew, Byron waited as the Darten was towed into place.

Launching from the Rennather's bay did not hold the same thrill as speeding down a narrow launch tube, but he still experienced a surge of exhilaration as the fighter raced toward space. Once clear of the opening, he banked left and circled around the ship. As instructed by the commander, a visual inspection of the Rennather was required whenever he took the Darten out for a run. Byron circled twice, his eyes scanning for minor damage or debris caught in one of the vents. Satisfied everything appeared to be in order, he steered away from the Rennather and out into space.

The small fighter saw little action these days, but Byron wanted to keep his skills sharp. He ran through several drills, executing each maneuver with precision. The Darten handled tight turns with ease, even better than the Cosbolt. Byron preferred the strength of the larger fighter, though. The Darten made up for its lack of engine and firepower with incredible maneuverability and speed. However, at the moment, its limitations meant nothing. Byron simply enjoyed the responsive controls and rapid flight.

Arcing to the left, Byron dove, sending the Darten racing toward the Rennather. His breath grew shallow and he pressed the throttle forward, increasing the vessel's speed. Byron's mind reached out for the ship's teleportation device, located behind his seat and secure within the hull of his vessel. The unit's hum was inaudible to the ear, but the sonic vibrations reverberated in his head, sending a rhythmic pounding down his spine. Locking his thoughts on the surging energy, his mental powers increased to match the power level of the teleporter. If the device's energy failed, Byron was prepared to replace it with his own charge.

The hull of the Rennather loomed closer, filling the view. The Darten's speed ensured no evasive action would prevent impact. Not even a pilot with Byron's skill could avoid collision now…

Jump!

The blackness of space enveloped his senses. Byron spun the ship around, whipping the Darten with such force that he was jostled in his seat. His forward progress halted, he gazed in triumph at the view outside his cockpit. The Rennather's massive engines filled his vision. He'd timed his jump perfectly.

A smile crossed Byron's lips. His stunt had probably unnerved the newer crewmembers on the bridge, but the commander never voiced concern. Byron only performed maneuvers he'd mastered this close to the ship. This jump pushed his limits, but that's when Byron felt most alive.

He returned to the Rennather, tired and ready for a decent meal. Voices reached his ears even before Byron entered the dining hall. He scanned its occupants before retrieving a tray of food. Most of the short tables were occupied. Byron spied an empty seat beside Garnce, the ship's other small craft pilot. The man's gruff nature matched his grizzled appearance, and his apathetic attitude surfaced at every opportunity. Byron had grown used to the abrasive words that often tumbled from his lips. It was the man's lack of ambition that really annoyed Byron, but he could do worse this evening than Garnce's company.

The pilot noticed his approach, offering a curt nod. Byron glanced at the other occupants as he circled the table. He realized the young man from the shuttle occupied the spot across from his empty seat. The lad met his gaze before Byron could look away. Straightening his back, the boy sat at attention. Unable to retreat without raising suspicion or implying offense, Byron set his tray on the table.

"You take the Darten out for a spin?" Garnce asked, still gnawing on a fruit core.

"Thought I'd take advantage of the down time," said Byron, sliding into his chair.

Their exchange caught the attention of the scientist. "You fly a Darten too, sir?" he said, almost dropping the food on his fork.

Byron reached for his drink. "I have for twenty years."

"But before that you flew Cosbolts, correct?"

"Just one," he answered, hoping his casual reply would squash further questions. Byron just wanted some food in his empty stomach.

Fortunately, Garnce intervened. "Mevine here was telling us about the new discovery on Tgren," he said, gesturing to the young man.

The boy's face grew radiant. He grinned with obvious enthusiasm, which echoed from his unshielded thoughts. Byron took advantage of the distraction. He shoved a forkful of food into his mouth and gestured for the science officer to elaborate.

"A recent excavation revealed an ancient underground facility," Mevine explained, his voice quivering with excitement. "Four days ago, a team gained access to the interior and found what they believe is the control room. The technology is so advanced, it's beyond anything we've previously discovered. Why, the possibilities of its application are endless!"

The young man's voice had risen as he spoke, accompanied by frantic hand gestures. The opportunity to dissect alien technology seemed to excite Mevine, but experience had taught Byron caution and a healthy respect for the unknown. He glanced at Garnce, who shrugged with indifference.

"Sounds dangerous to me," the pilot replied, crossing his arms across his broad chest.

"Not necessarily," protested Mevine.

"What do they know about it?" asked Byron. Despite Garnce's apathy, he was curious. A little danger sounded appealing, especially after months of routine assignments.

Mevine pulled his dark brows together, his shoulders sagging. "Very little at the moment. They've been unable to translate the language. Of course, no one stationed on Tgren specializes in alien script. I'm hoping to receive an upload from the team before we break orbit, so I can get a head start."

Byron regarded Mevine with surprise. "You're a linguist expert?"

"Yes sir, I'm trained in alien dialect, print, and code."

Garnce offered a skeptical guffaw. "You're rather young for deep space exploration," he observed, frowning as he reached for his glass.

"I'm twenty-three," Mevine announced, straightening his back and dropping his hands to his lap. "And I completed training at the top of my class." Indignation flashed through his thoughts before the lad abruptly shielded his mind.

"What he means is we don't see many men your age out here on the edge of space," Byron offered in an attempt to sooth Mevine's agitation. "You must be damned good to finish your training so quickly and acquire this assignment."

Mevine nodded, his wide eyes fixed on Byron. "You were young when you began active duty, sir.," he observed. "I understand you were one of the best pilots to train on Guaard."

"I suppose."

"Is that why you were assigned to the flagship Sorenthia?"

Byron shoved the last bite of food into his mouth. "One of the reasons," he said, swallowing without chewing. He sensed the conversation's direction. Byron wanted to escape before it drifted too far.

"Wasn't your navigator accomplished as well? I forget his name..."

The boy's question, while innocent enough, sparked anger in Byron. He'd grown accustomed to deflecting questions regarding his involvement in the Vindicarn War, but inquiries involving his navigator cut deep. That Mevine couldn't even recall the man's name was an affront to the senior officer's memory.

"Bassa was the most decorated navigator in the fleet and a true legend," he replied, rising quickly to his feet. "Now if you'll excuse me, I'd like to get out of this flight suit."

Mevine leaned away from the table, mouth open in surprise. Byron nodded at Garnce and exited the dining hall, his mental shields secure. He slipped into the first available telepod. Envisioning his destination, he transferred to the officers' level.

He began yanking off his flight suit the moment he entered his quarters. The fabric felt melded to his muscles as he peeled it from his body. Dropping into the room's only chair, he removed his boots, allowing the air to circulate around his warm feet. Byron dumped his suit into a bin located within the wall and retreated to the bathing room for a much-needed shower.

Dressed, refreshed, and hunger sated, Byron pulled the chair closer to his workstation. He updated the logs for both spacecraft, reviewing each one's flight recordings in detail. Neither revealed numbers outside of the safety parameters, although the shuttle's rapid acceleration had pushed the limits of the vessel's capabilities. Scanning the passenger list once more, Byron glanced at his personal record. Despite Vorsan's threat, no complaints were listed regarding today's flight. Byron smiled as he recalled the man's request for a smooth ride. Those words had almost demanded a response, and his fighter pilot instincts were too strong to pass up the opportunity.

Shifting his weight, he leaned back in his chair. Byron's gaze traveled to a photo resting beside his console. The dark metal frame showed signs of wear around the edges despite the durability of the alloy. Fortunately, the picture within was untouched by time. Over twenty years old, it was a memento of his days as Cosbolt pilot. His image revealed a much younger man, but Byron did not linger on that thought. It was the other man in the photo who held his attention.

You would've advised against my stunt today, he thought, recalling his navigator's views on discipline and proper procedures. However, Bassa had never denied his pilot the pleasure of an outlandish maneuver.

But, it would've amused you, Byron concluded, a smile tugging at his lips.

Mevine's comment returned to his thoughts. The boy had meant no disrespect. However, it annoyed Byron that the young man knew so much of his past accolades while Bassa's accomplishments were lost to memory. At one time, every man in the fleet knew the navigator's name and regarded Bassa as a living legend. Byron could not think of another man he'd admired more. He would always consider Bassa his closest friend and brother in spirit.

He reached for the photo, his hand lifting it with care into his lap. Byron stared at the figures leaning against the Cosbolt and felt a pang of regret. If only Bassa were alive to experience the life of exploration they'd planned. Byron had continued the course, but it was not the same without his friend and navigator.

Grasping his computer pad, Byron pulled up an image of Tgren. The planet looked similar to Cassa, although less water dotted her surface. The site of the alien ruins was clearly marked and situated next to a city called Ktren. He needed to read up on their next destination, but fatigue overwhelmed him and he could not focus on the information. Yawning once, his eyes returned to the photo in his hand.

So, what awaits us on Tgren? he thought, arching one eyebrow. The remains of a superior race? A weapon, perhaps? Think I might finally meet my match on this assignment?

No reply echoed in his mind. The silence was as complete as the day Bassa had died.

Byron sighed and returned the photo to his desk. Slapping his knees, he rose to his feet.

I guess we'll find out soon enough, won't we brother?

Chapter Two

By the time Byron awoke the next morning, the Rennather had broken orbit and was proceeding to the edge of the solar system. Once it reached that point, the ship would perform its first jump. Checking the timetable, Byron calculated the exact moment the teleporter would engage. The incredible amount of power required to jump a vessel the size of the Rennather resulted in an internal vibration unlike any other. He relished the sensation and planned his day around the event.

Most of the science personnel were missing during the morning and midday meals. Byron inquired into their absence. Senior Science Officer Seheller explained that they were working on transcribing the alien language.

"The transmission came through late last night," the man informed him. "We spent half the night processing data and started again early this morning. I don't think Mevine ever went to sleep. He's certainly dedicated."

Byron shook his head, amused by the young man's eagerness. He suspected they would find Mevine this evening draped over a workstation in a heap and unconscious from exhaustion. However, the diversion was well timed. Mevine's focus now resided on his work rather than Byron's past glories.

Before the evening meal, Byron visited the ship's grav court. He'd delayed his daily regiment to coincide with the Rennather's jump. He longed for privacy and hoped to find the court empty this time of day.

Better not be occupied, he thought. I'm in no mood for competition tonight.

Noting the green light above the press plate, he entered the court and sealed the door. A slight change in pressure signified a reduction in gravity. Byron shifted his feet, allowing his body to adjust. The alteration was minor, scarcely affecting his movement. He was still able to put a fierce spin on the ball, though.

Grasping the racket, he squared his shoulders in preparation. Clasping the ball, Byron hesitated before dropping it to the floor. Striking the surface, it sprang into the air and hovered near the release point. Before the ball could drop, he snatched it out of the air. Pivoting his body, Byron raised his racket. He tossed the ball toward the tall ceiling. With a resounding whack, his racket connected with the small object, and the ball shot toward the far wall.

Byron raced from one side of the court to the other, challenging his skills with difficult volleys. Because of the size of the court, which was hardly large enough to house a Cosbolt, he felt the temperature rise as his body generated heat from his exertions. Sweat poured from his skin, running unchecked down his arms and legs, soaking his clothes. Byron paused several times to wipe his brow, pushing the damp hair away from his face. He'd forgotten a towel, but this far into his session it wasn't worth the effort to retrieve one from his quarters. Certainly not with the ship's jump approaching.

A wild shot sent the ball out of reach. Pausing to catch his breath, a familiar hum echoed within the depths of his mind. Staggering back toward the wall, Byron slid to the floor, still clutching the racket. Resting his head against the wall, he took a deep breath and cleared his mind. The hum had increased in strength; it vibrated down his spine, causing his nerves to tingle. Closing his eyes, Byron focused on the intoxicating sensation of the ship's teleporter as it prepared for the jump.

His mental abilities had grown in strength over the years. In addition to his unique capacity to channel his own power into a ship's teleporter, he was now more aware of psychic emissions from all sources. Byron sensed the Rennather's pilot as the man tapped into the device to perform the jump. Concentrating on the teleporter, he felt the connection of man and machine as the pilot locked onto new coordinates. Even through lidded eyes, the room's lights vanished, enveloped by darkness as the ship jumped. The teleporter's power at its peak, he felt the surge of energy as the ship transferred to a new point in space.

The process complete, the device's discharge began to fade. Byron dropped his chin to his chest, his eyes still closed. Had he chosen to pilot an exploration ship, he would've performed the jump instead. On occasion, he assisted with multiple jumps, but the Rennather was not his responsibility. He preferred the mobility of the smaller ships. Certified on five different models, including the Darten, his skills were in high demand. Coupled with his unique ability to jump, not to mention accomplishments as a Cosbolt pilot, Byron had his choice of any ship in the fleet. He'd chosen to remain here.

Flexing his muscles, he pulled himself upright and reached for the ball. The door panel chirped, breaking into his thoughts. Byron scowled, annoyed by the interruption. Only a dimwit would miss the red light that signified the court was in use. Normal gravity resumed and the door slid aside. Byron assumed an authoritative pose, prepared to take the intruder to task for not observing court protocol. A young man entered the room, his head down. At once Byron recognized the gangly figure. He cleared his throat, hoping the noise would alert the intruder of the court's original occupant. The lad looked up, his eyes wide with surprise.

"Officer Byron, my apologies!" Mevine stammered, rocking hard on his heels. "In my haste, I didn't notice the court was occupied. Forgive me for interrupting your game."

By all rights, Byron should've scolded him, but Mevine's unshielded embarrassment made Byron assume a less threatening pose. "I thought you were holed up in the lab."

"Yes sir, I've been there all day," Mevine replied, shifting his weight from one foot to the other. The movement caused his unkempt hair to bob in rhythm, the curls swinging across his forehead.

"I understand you were in the lab all night, too."

Mevine ceased his nervous movements. "Yes, sir. But I was struggling to keep my eyes open. Thought some exercise would rouse me. I'd assumed the court would be empty at this hour. I'm sorry I interrupted you, sir."

The quaver in his voice tugged at the pilot's sense of compassion. Byron could not miss Mevine's red eyes or drooping posture, and the final traces of his irritation disappeared. Considering the boy's exhaustion, Byron could forgive an honest mistake. It had not interrupted his connection with the teleporter, either. Now that the moment had passed, Byron felt less reclusive. Besides, Mevine's presence provided an opportunity for a little competition.

Bouncing the ball once, Byron narrowed his eyes. "Well, as long as you're here, you may as well lose a couple games."

Straightening his back, Mevine's face broke into a smile. "Sir, I'd be honored to play a round with you."

Despite his fatigue, Mevine proved adept at grav ball. Byron relished the challenge. Pleased with the situation, he stepped up his game to match Mevine's strategic hits. Experience prevailed, leaving both men gasping for breath and exhausted.

"Not bad," Byron offered as he retrieved the ball before it rolled to the far end of the court.

"Been a few months since I played," said Mevine, rubbing his sleeve across his brow.

"We'll have to play when you're not rusty then."

The boy nodded, brushing the damp locks away from his face. Curls sticking straight out, his face reflected a youth beyond his years. Did I appear as immature and young when I entered active duty? Byron wondered.

"And sir?" Mevine asked, his brows furrowed. "I'm sorry if I offended you last night."

Byron adjusted the racket in his hand. "Don't worry about it. And we're off duty, so you can drop the sir."

"Yes..." Mevine replied, his voice trailing off before finishing the phrase. "I'm sorry, it's just such an honor to meet you. Your part in the Vindicarn War is legend."

Mevine's observation sent a ripple of regret through Byron. "I'm just a pilot," he muttered. "Besides, that was years ago."

And I'm not in the mood for adoration, he thought. Byron certainly didn't want his past accomplishments drawing attention to his current situation. Not wanting to hear more, he strode past the young man with a purpose. Mevine's next words caused him to pause.

"I almost became a fighter pilot because of you."

He turned to cast Mevine a skeptical look. "You think flying a Cosbolt is the path to glory? That facing death is what it takes to succeed?"

Mevine's shoulders drooped, matching the grimace on his face. "At least I'd have a chance to do something brave and prove myself."

A wave of dejection rolled unchecked from his thoughts. Byron sensed a desire to please and live up to expectations. Who in Mevine's life had placed such a heavy burden on the young man?

Lowering his racket to his side, Byron approached Mevine. The lad met his gaze, his eyes brimming with resignation as he awaited the older man's next words. Mustering patience he did not feel, Byron shifted the grav ball to his other hand. He touched Mevine's shoulder.

"Don't be so eager to throw yourself into the face of danger. It's a greater sacrifice than you'd ever imagine."

Mevine's thoughts remained in turmoil, but he offered a curt nod. Byron patted his shoulder.

"Besides, who says you won't do something heroic on Tgren?" Byron offered. "You might just be the one who cracks the alien code and unlocks a great discovery."

Mevine smiled. A renewed sense of purpose colored his thoughts, although not enough to hide all traces of dejection. It was enough to put Byron at ease, and his muscles unknotted. He gestured toward the door.

"Go get something to eat," he ordered. "And I'd recommend a shower or your fellow officers might refuse you entry to the lab."

"Men, I can't stress the gravity of the situation enough. I want everyone on their toes when we reach Tgren."

"Yes, sir!" all voices clamored.

Commander Korden leaned forward, his knuckles pressing hard against the surface of his desk. Byron and the other senior officers stood at attention as they received final briefing on their new assignment. Exploration carried many risks, but Byron sensed far more was at stake than just the lives of those aboard the Rennather.

"Despite the enthusiasm of our science crew," Korden drawled, his gaze passing over Officer Seheller, "I want us to take every precaution. The alien technology on Tgren could be benign in nature, but it could also be a weapon. Until we've assessed the situation and confirmed its purpose, I am treating it as a threat. Understood?"

"Yes, sir."

Glancing at his computer screen, Korden punched the keypad with force. "Complicating matters is our current relationship with the Tgrens. Their initial gratitude toward our presence has waned with our refusal to share more in the areas of communication and transportation until their own technology advances. Since their planet boasts a large supply of the chemical compounds required to manufacture our teleportation devices, we've done our best to pacify the Tgrens by offering training for their pilots. That gesture will continue while we are present."

The commander's eyes fell on his senior pilot. Byron nodded in acceptance of his expected duties while on Tgren even as he cringed inside. Training a group of primitives who'd only recently taken to the sky sounded tedious at best. He hoped they possessed at least a basic understanding of aerodynamics.

Straightening his posture, Korden glanced again at his computer screen and raised an eyebrow. "After recent testing of the citizens of Ktren, the city closest to the ruins, it was discovered that the Tgrens possess minor mental abilities as well."

Byron managed to suppress his surprise as a wave of astonishment filtered through the room. Korden frowned, his thick brows forming a grimace far more imposing than his lips.

"The Tgrens have not welcomed this discovery with enthusiasm. They view our telepathy and ability to teleport with caution, claiming it unnatural."

Officer Narunva gasped. "But they wanted advancements in communication..." he protested.

"You think they'd be grateful," another officer added.

"Well, it's up to us to convince them otherwise," Korden said. "Remember, we can only push so far. We cannot cause relations to crumble into disrepair. While on Tgren, we are all ambassadors of Cassa. Understood?"

Byron joined the others in affirmation. Korden punched another key.

"We've also had reports of rogue ships in the area," he said. "These multi-race raiders are to be treated as hostile. They have not bothered the Tgrens, but the last Cassan ship to visit this system was attacked by a small band of fighters. Officer Byron, you and Garnce are to remain on alert. These rogues recently captured one of our neighbors' ships, but the Zerrens were able to track down the raiders and retrieve their vessel. I want to avoid a similar incident. We've enough to deal with on the planet's surface."

With that, the commander dismissed the room. Before he could depart, Korden's thoughts reached his mind.

Officer Byron, remain.

Stepping aside, Byron turned to face the commander. The door closed behind the last officer and he stood at attention, expecting an even stricter warning from Korden regarding his behavior on Tgren. The men had served together for many years and Byron's tricks were no secret to the commander. The pilot doubted those ploys would be tolerated on Tgren. If relations were strained, he needed to remain on his best behavior.

"You will be pulling double duty on this assignment," Korden announced, sinking into his chair.

Puzzled by the lack of reprimand or warning, Byron stared at the commander. "Sir?"

Leaning back in the padded chair, Korden scrutinized him through narrowed eyes. Byron could sense nothing in the commander's thoughts, although he did not press past the mental shields. However, humor tugged at Korden's lips. The man liked to toy with his senior pilot.

"In addition to pilot training, which will be restricted to their best men I assure you, I want you to assist the current psychic technician on the planet. Officer Illenth has only tested a small percentage of the men thus far, but the Tgrens possess great potential."

Korden leaned forward, his frame causing the chair to creak in protest. "At all times, I want you listening for those with potential mental abilities. Report your findings to Officer Illenth. And if anyone displays exceptionally strong powers, I want to know about it. Understood?"

"Yes, sir," Byron replied. It was a step up from pilot training, but probing the minds of others didn't rate high on his list, either. This assignment would stretch the limits of his patience.

"Dismissed!"

Byron turned to leave. As he reached the door, the anticipated order rang in his head.

And try to stay out of trouble, Byron.

He flashed the commander a grin. *I don't cause trouble, sir. It just seems to find me.*

Korden cocked an eyebrow. *I've heard that before.*

Chapter Three

The dining hall buzzed with excitement during the midday meal. The Rennather was approaching Tgren, and those working on the alien encryptions were eager to reach the surface. Byron watched with amusement as Mevine inhaled his meal, shoveling food into his mouth at a frightening pace. The lad leapt to his feet the moment he finished and bounded out of the hall.

Boy's got too much energy for his own damn good.

Garnce's thought made Byron drop his chin to hide a smirk. No one could accuse Garnce of possessing ambition, and the man scoffed at the quality in others.

He's young and naïve, Byron countered. *Let him enjoy the moment.*

A guffaw from the pilot signified Garnce's opinion on the matter. Byron finished his meal and departed before the man's sour attitude sullied his day.

Byron retrieved his pack from his quarters en route to the hanger. Once the Rennather established orbit around Tgren, both shuttles were scheduled to carry personnel and supplies to the surface. Byron would return to the ship on occasion, but the bulk of the transports would fall to Garnce. The man had grumbled over this development, claiming he'd be run ragged during this assignment. Byron ignored his protests. Garnce never failed to comply with orders in the end, even if it required a verbal prompt. As the senior officer and pilot, Byron had made it clear he expected Garnce to follow commands. He preferred a lack of attitude as well, but at least Garnce's skills in the cockpit placed value on his presence.

Performing the preliminary checks, Byron prepared his shuttle. Several pieces of cargo were brought on board, the hanger crew struggling under the weight of the large crates. Once secured in the hold to his satisfaction, Byron returned to the cockpit to await his passengers.

He confirmed the landing site one more time, calculating the best approach. Their destination was a high desert city nestled in between two mountain ranges where severe cross-winds were possible. The shuttle could withstand gale force winds, but he doubted the inhabitants' ships were as sturdy. Byron wondered how many of the Tgren's first attempts at flight had ended in disaster.

Officer Byron?

Byron spun around in his chair and discovered Mevine just inside the shuttle's open hatch. Several large packs were slung across his shoulders. It was miraculous Mevine could even move under the weight, let alone enter the shuttle without making a sound. Rising to his feet, Byron gestured toward the cargo hold.

"Stow your gear in an empty hold," he ordered. "Then take a seat."

Mevine shifted his feet, his gaze traveling to the cockpit. "Sir, could I ride up front in the co-pilot's seat?"

"Why?"

"I've never seen the view from the cockpit."

Byron frowned and the shields around his mind tightened. Garnce rode with him on occasion, but the sensation of another person in the cockpit unnerved him. Byron preferred the seat to remain unoccupied and prepared to deny the young man's request.

"Please, sir, I won't get in your way," Mevine offered, his eyes wide with hope.

Beyond Mevine, the remaining passengers approached the shuttle. Judging from the size of the group, every seat would be occupied, including the co-pilot's chair. His gaze returned to the young officer who was still waiting for an answer.

Fine! Stow your gear first.

By the time he'd closed the shuttle's hatch and returned to the cockpit, Byron discovered Mevine secured in the co-pilot's seat. The lad lifted his chin and his lips broke into a grin. Still at odds with his decision, Byron offered a nod in return. He slid into his seat, eyes focused on the control panel. His thoughts remained guarded, but eagerness bubbled forth from Mevine's mind. Distracted by the unshielded thoughts, he worried his passenger might also develop an overactive tongue during their decent to the planet's surface.

You are not to interrupt me in any manner while flying, understood?

Yes, sir, Mevine replied, his hands dropping into his lap as he sat at attention. The young man's emotions ceased to broadcast, plunging the cockpit into blessed silence.

The shuttle loaded and secure, Byron commenced ignition. Engines humming on low power, Byron guided the shuttle across the hanger and through the first set of doors. There was a moment's pause as the atmosphere within the compartment adjusted. The second set of doors opened, revealing the full length of the landing bay. The moment he had clearance, Byron accelerated. Engines roaring, the shuttle shot out into the blackness of space.

As instructed, Mevine remained silent. However, his exuberance escaped the confines of his mental shields. Within moments, his excitement filled the cockpit. Annoyance flitted through Byron's mind, but was squelched by an unexpected memory. His first navigator had exhibited a similar lack of inhibition, allowing his emotions to bubble forth like a fountain. Thoughts of Trindel cheered Byron, and he allowed Mevine to enjoy the ride in full, reckless abandon.

Jumping into the planet's atmosphere, Byron led the way toward their destination. Cloud cover obscured the view, but he didn't require visual confirmation of their location. Guiding the ship in lower, he lined up their approach. The clouds began to disperse and the rusty hues of mountain desert came into view. Byron cleared a plateau and descended into a wide valley.

Mevine gasped. This time, Byron shared his sentiment. He'd expected rock and sand strewn across the desert floor and an inhospitable terrain. To his surprise, the valley boasted an array of vegetation. The ground below them was splashed with green, blue, and yellow plant life, concentrated around a river that snaked through the valley. At once Byron's opinion of Tgren raised a few notches, although he refused to share his excitement over the impressive landscape. He was here to work, not enjoy the scenery.

The small city resided on the far side of the open valley and to the right of the river. The plant life may have caught him by surprise, but the Tgren city's appearance was as expected. Short, squat buildings of white stone clustered together in an uneven pattern. From the air, it appeared as if a giant, complex maze was under construction. Byron hoped the city's amenities compensated for what it lacked in appearance. Of course, he could always spend his nights in the shuttle if the Tgren culture proved too primitive.

Inching the shuttle closer to the ground, he aimed for the flat stretch that was the designated runway. Reducing speed to a near hover, Byron landed the ship on the mark indicated by the coordinates. As he powered down the engines, his eyes were drawn to a group waiting outside the nearest hanger. Three men and two women stood at attention, their gaze upon the shuttles. Their burnt umber-colored uniforms fluttered lightly in the breeze. Another man emerged from the hanger, stepping out into the bright sun. Byron at once recognized a fellow Cassan. The man's light skin and brown hair were in sharp contrast with the others, not to mention the deep blue of his military attire marking him as an outsider. While his own skin was pale, Byron's jet-black hair would help him to blend with the natives.

Maybe after a week in the sun, I'll tan enough to pass for a Tgren, he thought.

Mevine began fumbling with his harness. Byron was still shutting down systems when the scientist bolted into the main compartment of the shuttle, an urgency to disembark emanating from his thoughts. Byron leapt from his seat, determined to reach the hatch before his overeager passenger. He didn't want Mevine to press the wrong button and cause the door to jam.

Byron waited until the shuttle was clear of passengers before exiting the craft. The dry air tickled his nose as the scent of dusty, sand and exotic plants filled his senses. It was a sharp contrast to the odorless, recycled air aboard the Rennather. The desert sun felt hot on his face. It wouldn't be long before the arid heat caused him to break out in a sweat.

A strong breeze tousled his hair as he stepped away from the shuttle, reminding Byron that he needed a trim soon. Korden was not as strict as some commanders, but Byron didn't want to press his luck. He bucked enough rules and regulations.

Once those on both ships had convened outside, the group by the hanger approached. The Cassan reached them first, pausing long enough to offer a proper salute and greetings to Second-in-Command, Anceptor. The man beckoned the newcomers into the hanger to acquire their security clearance before proceeding further.

Byron understood the need to follow protocol, but the formality obviously frustrated Mevine. The lad bounced on his heels, the heavy packs across his shoulders limiting his movement. Mevine glanced around and paused when he noticed the pilot staring at him.

Relax! You'll hurt yourself, Byron thought.

Mevine's eyes widened. He brought both heels down with great force. *Sorry, sir,* Mevine answered. *And thank you for allowing me to ride in the cockpit with you.*

You're welcome.

The security check complete, Anceptor ordered the retrieval of the cargo. Byron oversaw the operation, chastising a clumsy science technician when the man shoved a crate into the shuttle's interior wall. Tempers flared among the men and an exchange of words threatened to bring a halt to the process. Byron maintained order, asserting his authority lest they forget he was the second highest-ranking officer present. The science officers were eager to begin their work but Byron didn't want exuberance to overrule proper procedure.

The cargo was loaded onto a large, motorized cart for ground transpiration to the site. Byron eyed the oversized engine with skepticism, concerned the weight of the crates would be too much for the primitive machine. One of the Tgrens climbed into the open seat and pressed several buttons. The cart lurched forward with a roar. The engine emitted a black cloud in response. A couple more false starts and the device achieved a slow but steady speed. The science team followed on a similar cart lined with wood benches. Byron caught Mevine's worried expression as that cart's forward progress proved just as awkward.

Damn, wonder if their ships emit the same smoke when they fly? Garnce speculated in a private thought to Byron..

Byron chuckled. *Make them easy targets, wouldn't it?*

Movement near the hanger caught his eye, and Byron noticed a man with a patch of yellow on his uniform. The two Tgrens who remained turned to Anceptor.

"Sir, our prefect has arrived," the woman announced, speaking slow and with care.

The commander nodded at Garnce. *Remain here with the shuttles*, he ordered.

Gladly, Garnce thought in a private exchange with Byron.

A security officer from the Rennather accompanied Byron and Anceptor. As they approached the building, a large Tgren in a dark yellow uniform appeared in the hanger's open door, flanked on either side by guards. The man's uniform was stretched across his frame, although the fabric appeared new. He didn't bulge from the uniform, but judging from his thickness, the Tgren's years were catching up to him. Byron suspected the man didn't partake in heavy exertions either.

Their escort came to an abrupt halt and snapped to attention, saluting the man. "Prefect Orellen, I present Commander Anceptor, from the Cassan ship Rennather."

"Prefect Orellen," Anceptor stated in his most diplomatic tone.

"Commander Anceptor," the man replied, his deep, gravel voice resonating with authority. "Welcome to Tgren. I trust your team is now on its way to the ruins?"

"Yes sir, and I hope to take a look at the site before returning to the Rennather."

"Of course."

Byron sensed caution in the man. While his expression remained neutral, Orellen's eyes spoke of mistrust as he sized up the commander. The prefect was several years older than the ship's second-in-command. Orellen might use that to his advantage. However, Anceptor was tough and poised for command of his own vessel soon.

The prefect glanced at Byron before returning his gaze to the commander. "Come, let us step out of the heat," he offered.

They followed the Tgren leader as he led them toward an open door. “Our heat can be quite stifling this time of day,” said Orellen, his strides long, but slow. “It would not do for our guests to experience heat stroke their first day on Tgren.”

“We will do our best not to expire on you,” the commander replied.

The doorway led from the hanger into a small office; its stone walls providing some protection from the sun. The room was several degrees cooler than the outside air even with multiple windows open. Byron noticed maps and charts tacked across the walls. The lone shelf in the room was stacked several feet high with rolled parchments, the light breeze causing the papers to rustle. The row of gauges and computer screens to his left reminded Byron of his history lessons as a child. Cassan technology had advanced so far since those early days.

The personnel in the room stood at attention until the prefect signaled for them to resume their work. Their Tgren escort pulled two chairs together and Orellen indicated for Anceptor to take a seat. Byron stood to one side, his hands clasped behind his back. Since he was not directly involved in the conversation, he could spend time examining the room.

A woman brought them drinks, offering Byron a sweet smile. Her short hair framed a face that was wide, but proportioned for true beauty. He managed to return her smile and his gaze followed the young woman’s retreat to an alcove off the main room. Alien races weren’t high on his list of choices for female companionship; however, he might make an exception while on Tgren.

Officer Byron!

Anceptor’s commanding tone echoed through his mind. Byron returned his attention to the senior officer at once. He discovered both men staring at him and Byron realized he’d missed part of the conversation. Anceptor’s eyes displayed patience, but the prefect’s scowl threatened to burn holes in Byron’s skin.

“Yes, sir,” he responded, focusing on his commander.

“Officer Byron,” said Anceptor, turning to face the prefect, “is to assist Officer Illenth with the psychic testing. He is also available for the continued instruction of your best pilots."

The prefect rolled his eyes and assumed a disinterested pose. "Psychic testing," he grumbled, dismissing the importance of mental abilities with those words. Orellen's angry stare fell on Byron and his lips curled in a threatening manner. "And our pilots have been fully instructed by several shuttle pilots."

Byron shielded his indignation at the man's attitude. Before he could speak, Anceptor responded first.

"Prefect Orellen, I'm sure you've had several excellent shuttle pilots assist your fighters," he said. "That is why I'm sure you'll find Officer Byron's qualifications and skill level of interest. He is a fighter pilot, fully trained on two of our military's best ships. With over twenty years of experience and high recommendations from all commanding officers, Officer Byron is one of our best. He is also," added Anceptor as he glanced at Byron, "a decorated war hero."

Byron suppressed a grin and was partially successful. A loud guffaw from Orellen wiped the smile from his face.

"A war hero indeed," the prefect drawled. "Well, Officer Byron, you might possess talent, but I'll not have you filling my pilots' heads with delusions of war conquests."

"No, sir," Byron answered in a respectful tone, his muscles tense. When Orellen's attention returned to the commander, Byron downed his water in one gulp. The pilot wanted nothing more than to escape the company of the prefect.

A young Tgren approached Orellen and announced that his plane was ready. The man's expression changed at once. Byron detected smug satisfaction as the prefect ushered them out of the room.

"I've requested the service of our best pilot for our flight to the alien ruins," Orellen announced as they crossed the hanger.

A small plane rested on the runway. Byron eyed the craft with reservations. The wide wings were disproportional to the stubby body. The bulky engines dangled from the wings like overripe fruit in danger of falling in the slightest breeze. Recalling Garnce's observation, Byron wondered if they emitted the same black smoke as the cart. That the plane appeared new, its sandy colored paint glistening in the sun, was a small consolation. He doubted it was capable of proper flight.

The pilot emerged from the craft and stood beside the small hatch. Noting the slight frame within the orange flight suit, Byron wondered if their best pilot was a child. A strong crosswind moved across the runway, stirring the dust. The breeze caught the pilot's hair, sending a tangle of long, black tresses cascading into the air, pulling hard at the flight cap. Byron hesitated as he realized their pilot was a woman.

She stood at attention as they approached, one hand resting on the wing of the plane. Her smile grew as the prefect drew close, revealing natural beauty. Her mischievous grin also suggested an adventurous spirit.

"Prefect Orellen!" she cried in greeting.

The man paused, offering her a fatherly smile, before turning to the Cassans. "Commander Anceptor, let me introduce Athee, our finest pilot," he said, his chest out with pride.

Still smiling, she extending her hand to the commander. "Pleased to meet you, sir. Welcome to Tgren," said Athee, her rich voice pleasant on the ears.

Now that he was closer, Byron sensed mental ability within the woman. It wasn't subtle, either. An aura of power sprang forth from her mind, sending ripples across his thoughts. The energy produced a radiance that bordered on visual. Its strength penetrated his mental barrier, intruding on his thoughts. Athee turned to face him and Byron shielded his mind at once. Her brows came together and she appeared puzzled. Byron's body stiffened and he wondered if she'd heard his thoughts despite the shields.

"Officer Byron!"

Anceptor's reprimand jolted Byron from his thoughts. He caught the commander's frown and realized his shields had blocked the man's mental prod for a response. However, the prefect's scowl was far more menacing. Byron returned his gaze to Athee. She smiled and he noticed her extended hand.

"Forgive me, pilot Athee," he said, holding out his palm.

Her eyes reflected amusement as she grasped his hand. Her firm and confident handshake was at odds with her petite form. Byron managed a faint smile and relaxed his shields.

He did not want to miss another silent command from Anceptor.

Releasing his hand, Athee tilted her head to one side. Byron caught a wave of emotion and realized she was admiring his appearance. Embarrassed, he shifted his gaze to his commander, who still appeared annoyed by his pilot's inability to pay attention.

"Shall we board?" the prefect asked, breaking the awkward silence.

Is this assignment going to be a problem, Officer Byron? Anceptor asked as he mounted the short steps behind the prefect.

No, sir! My apologies, but the psychic strength of our pilot caught me unaware.

The commander paused in the doorway. *The woman?*

Yes, sir.

Anceptor glanced past Byron. *She'll require testing. Judging from the prefect's reaction that may prove difficult.*

The Cassan security officer was instructed to remain behind, as the plane only held four passengers. Byron took a seat on the second bench beside the prefect's personal guard. Orellen embarked on a spiel regarding the finer points of Tgren aircraft while Athee prepared the craft for takeoff. His words were designed to impress, but they did nothing to reassure Byron. He felt safer in his Darten, surrounded by enemy vessels, than in this poorly designed plane.

Athee started the engines. Byron glanced out the tiny window to his right. As expected, a plume of black smoke billowed forth as the motor came to life. The engines gained strength, causing the smoke to disperse. The plane rolled forward and started down the runway. Velocity increasing, Byron was aware of every jolt as the tires bumped across the uneven surface. The end of the track loomed closer, giving way to wild vegetation. His muscles tightened and he grasped the seat below him.

I've faced a thousand enemy ships, and now I'm going to die in this damned plane, he thought.

At the last moment, the nose pulled skyward. The wheels left the ground and the shaking ceased. Continuing to accelerate, the plane banked to the left and cleared the bushes.

Byron caught Athee's exhilaration as the craft soared higher. Relaxing his grip on the seat cushion, he sighed with relief.

They circled the surrounding area in a slow, gentle arc. The prefect pointed out various landmarks below as they passed. Byron only half listened to Orellen's words. His attention focused instead on the young woman flying the plane. Her excitement continued to project as they glided high above the ground. Despite Athee's feelings, she was focused on her flying. Confidence rippled from her mind as she guided the plane with precision. Byron doubted she realized her thoughts were overheard by anyone. Anceptor was correct–Athee required testing.

Athee brought the craft in lower and Byron could just discern a thin strip of open ground on the valley floor. The surface of the rocky mountain to their left flashed by in a blur as she prepared to land. Byron braced himself for a rough landing, determined to keep his seat. The craft touched down with a gentle bump, and while the craft jolted down the runway, it was no worse than the takeoff.

The plane taxied to the end of the path. Glancing out the window, Byron noted several makeshift buildings and tents residing at the foot of the mountain. The material of the Tgren's shelters fluttered in the breeze. Turning the vessel in a circle, Athee brought the plane to a halt and turned off the engines.

"Excellent flight, Athee," the prefect said, turning to Anceptor. "She placed first in four of our five flight competitions this year."

Athee glanced over her shoulder and grinned. "Bragging on me again, Uncle?"

Uncle? Byron thought, staring at the back of the man's head. Great!

They exited the craft and were greeted by several Tgrens. Byron noted the empty carts and wondered if Mevine's trek to the site had been as adventurous as this journey. He hoped the scientist hadn't fallen off the cart in his zeal to reach the alien ruins.

Strolling past the campsite, they entered a wide opening in the mountainside. The cave had been reinforced with metal beams and cleared of debris. The air inside was much cooler although a dusty smell permeated Byron's nose. Simple incandescent bulbs dangled from thick wires, providing light for their passage. The prefect continued to speak and his voice reverberated down the tunnel. Byron followed several paces behind Orellen and Anceptor. He concentrated on his footing as the tunnel dipped lower, winding deeper into the mountainside.

Byron looked up just in time to see the prefect turn to the left and enter a side passage. He followed behind his commander, maintaining distance from Orellen. Byron hesitated when his boots struck metal. The walls were no longer rock but of a substance which created a deep, metallic blue sheen. The passageway extended in both directions with lights strung on thick wires along the floor. The bulbs weren't the only illumination, though. The tunnel was ringed with blue lights that cast an unusual glow on the passageway.

Ruins, indeed! This place is very much alive, he thought, aware of a deep hum within the walls.

They continued down the tunnel to the right and soon came upon a large, round doorway. The others stepped inside and Byron followed. The nondescript passageway had not prepared his senses and Byron's step faltered.

A strange smell permeated the air and Byron recognized the warm aroma of plasma. A giant ball filled with a semi-transparent green liquid occupied the center of the room. Held in place by metal tendrils gripping the base, it was elevated above the main floor. As he gazed at the ball, a burst of pure, white energy arced from the metal fingers. Byron didn't flinch, but he felt the discharge on his skin. The electrical throb briefly overshadowed the deep hum, sending vibrations through his head.

Another burst filled the ball, and secondary lights caught his attention. Byron noticed small, transparent tubes running out from between the metal tendrils. While he watched, another pulse sent waves of energy rippling down the tubes. He followed one line and discovered it connected to a crescent shaped console. Raising his gaze, Byron realized there were multiple workstations in the area. It was then that he noticed dozens of Cassans and Tgrens occupying the room. The men were bent over consoles and equipment, their voices an uneven pitch of noise compared to the pulsating ball.

Noting the array of lights filling the rounded walls of the cavernous room, his gaze traveled toward the high ceiling. White light spiked from the center, traveling down the walls. Byron frowned, puzzled by the sight. The room itself appeared encased in a plasmic globe. The pulses were weaker but more frequent, and with every arc of energy, thousands of tiny dots appeared across the ceiling. In all his years of travel, Byron had never encountered technology such as this.

"Impressive, isn't it?"

Startled by the close proximity of her voice, Byron discovered Athee at his side. She had removed her flight gear and her long, wavy hair now draped over her shoulders. Her eyes were on the rounded ceiling, the soft bursts of light bathing her skin in a soft glow. He sensed curiosity in the woman.

"I'll be more impressed when we discover its purpose," Byron answered, peering at the nearest device.

"Think it's a weapon?"

Byron leaned closer to the set of pulsating lights. "Always a possibility. Whatever it is, we need to be cautious."

Amusement rippled through her mind. "So, until proven otherwise, you consider anything alien to be a threat?"

Straightening his shoulders, Byron faced the woman. With her cap removed and hair free, Athee's youth was very apparent. She couldn't be much older than Mevine. Athee's face was narrower than the woman's in the hanger office, with high cheekbones and a long, elegant nose. While her beauty was undisputable, a single train of thought ran through Byron's mind: She was the prefect's niece. That meant off limits.

"Not everything," he said, aware she still awaited his reply.

Athee stood up to her full height and lifted her chin. "So, was my flying satisfactory, Officer Byron?"

"Yes. Your approach and landing need improvement, though."

"Is that so? Would you care to show me the proper technique, Officer Byron?"

Sensing her playful challenge, he smiled. "If I can do it in my fighter."

Grinning, Athee placed her hands behind her back. "Ah, but that would be cheating," she charged, pivoting her body to gaze once more at the ceiling.

Byron was about to respond when he caught sight of the commander and prefect on the other side of the room. Athee's mischievous thoughts echoed in his mind, toying with him. Slamming his mental shields into place, Byron shut out her presence.

Damn it, what are you doing? Stop flirting with her! he thought.

Glancing around the room, Byron caught sight of Mevine. His company presented other problems, especially if the scientist began asking more questions about Byron's past, but he preferred a familiar challenge he could handle. Excusing himself from Athee's presence, he strode across the room.

Mevine was hunched over a tiny panel in a corner, his fingers flying across his personal computer pad. Byron stood to one side, afraid he would scare the young man. When it became apparent Mevine was oblivious to his surroundings, Byron touched his mind.

Mevine?

Glancing up from his work, Mevine met Byron's eyes. "Officer Byron! I'm sorry, I was engrossed with these figures."

"I could tell," said Byron, crossing his arms. "Must be fascinating."

"Oh, it's incredible!" he said, his face lighting up with joy.

"Think you can decipher it?"

"The language is old and complex," Mevine said, rubbing the side of his forehead. "It'll take time."

Byron glanced at the screen, but the symbols meant nothing to him. Offering Mevine a faint smile, he patted the lad's shoulder. "I'm sure you'll crack the code."

Mevine sat up straight in his chair. As evidenced by his unchecked emotions, Byron's words had bolstered the young man's confidence. Feeling overwhelmed, Byron nodded and moved toward the exit.

Damn, doesn't anyone know how to shield? he thought as he retreated from the alien room.

Chapter Four

The others in his party did not linger in the ruins and reconvened outside. The return flight was uneventful, save for the intense discussion between the commander and the prefect. Both expressed concerns that the alien site might be a threat.

"Prefect Orellen, with your permission, I'd like to request that more security be brought to the surface," Anceptor announced.

"Commander, I understand your concerns, but additional Cassan forces shouldn't be necessary."

"Prefect, it would only be to ensure the safety of those working on the alien site."

"I still have reservations about your men poking around the site," Orellen said. "My people are already alarmed by the discovery. If they see a troop of soldiers descending on our city, it might cause a panic."

Byron's gaze flicked to Anceptor. The commander's jaw was set and forehead wrinkled with concern.

"If the alien site is a weapon or a situation develops, we need a team in place that can handle it," Anceptor replied, his voice cold. "We want to ensure the safety of your people as well as our own."

Orellen continued to resist Anceptor's plan to bring more Cassan security to the surface The commander persisted and the prefect finally conceded.

The conflict resolved, Byron's attention shifted to the view outside. He knew their science officers were taking every precaution, but the Tgrens were neither prepared, nor experienced, for this type of work. The thought of untrained natives wandering the alien site was a great concern. He didn't want his demise to come from an explosion set off by ignorance any more than he wanted to die in this plane.

Upon their return to Ktren, Anceptor requested a guide to take Byron to Officer Illenth's facility. The prefect seemed happy to rid himself of the pilot's presence and asked a security guard to escort Byron.

"You will take your quarters there as well," Orellen said, dismissing Byron with the flick of his hand.

Annoyed, but relieved to escape the man, Byron left to retrieve his bag. The Tgren man waited outside the shuttle while Byron secured the vessel. None of these people could fly the ship, but he didn't want curious hands damaging the interior.

Byron touched Garnce's mind and discovered the pilot asleep in his cockpit. Lazy fool, Byron thought as he followed the security guard toward the hanger. Damned lucky fool, too.

They crossed the empty hanger, the wind blowing at their backs. Forceful voices reached Byron's ears as he followed the Tgren out an exit on the far side. He found the prefect and commander in the middle of a heated discussion. Anceptor's thoughts were shielded, but Byron recognized his tone. The man meant business.

Officer Byron, wait.

His escort continued to the left, but Byron was not about to disobey Anceptor's request. He paused to face his commander and noticed Athee on the other side of the prefect. Her confusion and agitation broadcast unchecked from her mind and only added to the confusion. Suspecting she was the subject of their argument, he approached the two men with care.

The security guard reappeared at his side and the sudden movement caught Orellen's attention. The prefect turned toward Byron, his face twisted with indignation.

"What's this nonsense about my niece possessing strong psychic abilities?" he demanded.

Gripping his flight bag even tighter, Byron waited for Anceptor's nod before replying. "I am sensitive to the mental emissions of others," he explained, "and her powers broadcast loud and clear."

Uttering a Tgren expletive, the prefect clenched his fists. The commander narrowed his eyes.

"Prefect Orellen, she should be tested," Anceptor stated.

"I questioned this whole business of psychic abilities from the beginning," began Orellen, raising a threatening finger. "While it may be natural for Cassans, we on Tgren use our voices to communicate."

Until this moment, Athee had remained silent. Byron sensed indignation at the prefect's words and she found her voice at last.

"Uncle!" she exclaimed, grasping his forearm. "What if I do possess mental powers? I want to be tested."

The two faced each other, locked in a battle of wills. The prefect's wrinkled forehead carried down to his chin, adding force to his square and unrelenting features. Byron doubted many challenged the man and fewer still met with success. Kin or not, a woman of Athee's age and stature stood little chance against a man possessing Orellen's disposition.

However, more than just determination flowed from Athee. A force beyond mere emotion radiated from her mind. She might be unaware of her powers, but they now cascaded like a torrential downpour. Her stance, one hand resting on her uncle's arm while the other casually grasped her gloves, revealed none of the energy pulsating in her thoughts. Only her focused expression gave evidence of Athee's mental strength.

Her uncle let out a disgruntled bark and shook his head. "You'll do what you want regardless," Orellen growled, eyes averted from his niece. "Go with Officer Byron."

Athee's thoughts matched her triumphant grin. Standing to her full height, her gaze turned to Byron as if he were her next conquest. He winced and threw up his mental shields to guard against casual encounters. She'd entered his mind once today. That was enough.

Tell Illenth to report his findings to me immediately, the commander ordered as Byron and Athee departed with the security guard.

Their escort led them to a small cart with only two benches. Byron selected the rear seat on purpose. He exhaled a deep breath when Athee slid in front of him. However, the moment the cart's rattling ceased and it achieved an even pace, she turned to face him.

"So, I have strong powers?" she asked, her arms resting on the back of the seat.

"Yes," Byron replied, his gaze traveling to another cart as it passed.

"Will this test reveal what I can do?"

Byron shrugged, his eyes averted. He was now wary of the prefect's niece. Byron kept his mental shields raised. With his attention focused on the barrier around his mind, the sights and sounds of the city were but blurs and background noise. He had to maintain distance...

"You don't talk much, do you?"

Athee's question, punctuated by a solemn tone of curiosity, caused his gaze to shift to the young woman in front of him. Byron was cautious when it came to personal disclosure and he did not feel like engaging in a lengthy conversation. The cart hit a bump, sending a jolt through his spine. His bag shifted, providing a diversion. Pressing his lips in a thin line, Byron shook his head and reached down to secure the pack.

"Officer Byron, have I offended you?"

He raised his head, his mouth open to deny the accusation. Athee's chin rested on her forearm and in his bent position, their faces were only inches apart. Jade-green eyes, wide with concern, met his. Her smile was gone, further compounding her forlorn expression. With his shields locked into place, Athee was not controlling him in any manner. A twinge of regret for his indifferent attitude toward the young woman pricked at Byron's conscience.

Byron leaned back in his seat. "You've not offended me, Athee. What would you like to talk about?"

"Can you really sense powers in others? We were told a machine was required to detect psychic ability."

"The machine is more accurate," he explained, noting they were passing a market area. Exotic colors vied for his attention and an assortment of smells attacked his nose.

"But you can still sense powers?"

"Yes."

"How?"

Byron met her gaze and shrugged. "A gift I suppose."

"What else can you do?" she asked sitting up straight in her seat.

The cart rounded a corner, jostling its passengers. The market square was left behind, replaced by the white stone of plain buildings. Without visual distraction, Byron's attention returned to Athee. He contemplated his answer, as disclosure meant he was revealing a secret known only by a select few. On an alien planet resting beyond the boundaries of Cassan space, discretion hardly seemed necessary.

"I can power our ship's teleporters."

Athee's brows came together and she shook her head. Byron licked his lips and leaned closer.

"Our teleporters allow us to jump from one point in space to another. They're fueled by a complex energy compound. One of the required elements is found here on your planet. I won't bore you with the details, but most ships drain the teleporter's energy after two jumps in close succession," he explained, tapping his fingers together. "I can funnel my own mental energy into the teleporter and perform multiple jumps."

"Oh," she said. "You mean you can create that compound with your mind?"

"My powers stimulate the elements that create the energy, providing a quick burst that is enough to fuel a jump."

"Is that an unusual power?"

Byron nodded. "Only one in 800,000 Cassans possess the ability."

"Guess that makes you really special then."

Grasping the seat as the cart lurched to the right, Byron's nerves jolted. Shields still in place, he could not sense her emotions or thoughts and wondered the true meaning behind her words. A cloud of smoke billowed from the cart's engine and the wind blew the offending soot in their direction. Byron coughed, thankful for the diversion. As if on cue, the engine also emitted a sick cough and spluttered into silence. They had reached their destination, none too soon for Byron.

Without further words, Byron ushered Athee inside. He located Officer Illenth and introduced the young woman, repeating Commander Anceptor's request for a full testing.

"My machine only covers the basics, but let's see what it detects," he said, brushing aside strands of hair that were many months past a regulation haircut.

Byron observed while Illenth performed the test. The device was small and designed only to measure overall mental strength. Athee sat motionless as Illenth attached electrodes to her temples, his long fingers moving rapidly. Once satisfied with the connection, the man returned to the machine and pressed several buttons.

The information that flashed across the screen was foreign to Byron. However, he noted Illenth's change of expression as data continued to compile. The man's eyes grew wide and threatened to burst from his sunken sockets. He stared at the readout for several minutes, one finger rubbing his chin. Byron was tempted to lower his shields, but resisted the urge. He did not want two sets of emotions overwhelming his senses.

Growing impatient, Byron shifted his feet. The sound pulled Illenth from his thoughts and he glanced at the waiting pilot. The psychic officer turned off the machine with a single flick of a switch. Exhibiting a gentle touch, Illenth removed the electrodes from Athee's head.

"If you would please wait outside," he instructed, coiling the wires in his hands.

"How'd I do?" she said, rising to her feet.

Illenth cast a quick glance at Byron. "You definitely possess strong mental abilities," he admitted. "I need to discuss the next step with Officer Byron."

Athee hesitated, her lips pressed together in defiance. Byron gestured to the door and she strode from the room, her boots striking the floor with force. Sliding the door shut, he turned to Illenth.

What's the verdict? he asked, using his mental voice to prevent Athee from overhearing their conversation.

Illenth leaned one hand on the machine, his fingers tapping the metal in unison. *Her psychic powers are the strongest I've seen thus far... by a long shot! I'm limited with this machine, though. A complete examination would be required to determine the full extent of her abilities, but I'm unable to do that here.*

Officer Narunva has the necessary equipment on board the Rennather, Byron offered.

The man nodded. *Tell Commander Korden I recommend a full evaluation. I'm sure the prefect will object, so be prepared.*

Considering Athee is his niece, I don't doubt that, Byron added, aware that it complicated the matter. Orellen was already annoyed, and suggesting Athee travel to the Rennather might send the man into a raging fit.

Hopefully the commander can convince him, thought Illenth.

I'll inform Korden.

Byron turned to leave, but a nagging question tugged at his thoughts. *Is she really that strong?*

Officer Illenth halted his nervous strumming and his eyes narrowed to mere slits. *The woman's powers registered higher than most Cassans.*

Byron stared at the man in surprise. The implications were staggering. A Tgren woman with powers greater than the average Cassan? That would alter their relationship with this race if further testing revealed Athee's abilities were even stronger...

Damn, I wonder if she's stronger than me? Byron thought as he left Illenth's office.

He arose early the next morning in preparation for a flight to the Rennather. Byron had collapsed in his temporary quarters, too tired to care about amenities. The previous day's events had weighed on him all evening, and today held the potential of yet more emotional strain. He wished he could remain in bed, but duty called.

Upon arrival at his shuttle, Byron began his preflight check. Only a couple empty cartons and two crewmembers were scheduled for the flight. Today's transport should've fallen to Garnce, as shuttle flights were his responsibility during this mission. However, it was the potential third passenger that placed this trip in Byron's hands. He doubted the prefect would allow his niece to travel to the Rennather for further testing, but nevertheless, Athee was scheduled to join them this morning.

The two men traveling to the ship arrived, along with the empty crates. Byron made sure the cartons were secure before instructing his passengers to fasten their harnesses. He wondered how long he should wait for his third passenger when the sound of voices reached his ears. Peering out the open hatch, he noticed Athee, Orellen, and a security guard approaching the ship. Neither the woman nor her uncle appeared happy. The prefect presented choppy gestures with his left hand as he spoke. Taking a deep breath, Byron stepped outside and awaited his final passenger.

"Uncle, you can't deny my right to know if I possess abilities," said Athee, her long stride resonating annoyance as her boots struck the ground.

"This whole business of mental powers is unnatural," Orellen scoffed. The prefect came to an abrupt halt and grasped her elbow. "Not to mention preposterous! Tgrens speak with their mouths, not their minds."

"It's not preposterous!" Athee retorted, pulling her arm free. "What if our people possess such abilities? Think of the implications, of what it might mean in our advancement. Imagine if we could expand our lines of communication and maintain contact with every plane, every city. This might be our answer."

"And it might be nothing at all."

Athee placed her hands on her hips and stared at her uncle. The man scowled, his lips set in a thin line. This did not seem to deter the young woman. Byron remained at the foot of the ramp, unwilling to get involved. He lowered his shields just a little, listening for stray thoughts and emotions. As expected, determination poured forth from Athee. He also sensed her influence of persuasion working on the prefect. Athee might not understand her powers, but she already knew how to manipulate. Once she gained full control and comprehension of her psychic abilities, that trait could very easily become dangerous.

"If only your father were here..." began Orellen, his voice low.

"Well, he's not! So this is my decision."

"Your leaving the surface of this planet is my decision, young woman," the prefect countered, assuming an authoritative stance. "Your safety is also my responsibility."

Athee shot Byron a desperate look. "I'm sure Officer Byron will keep me safe."

He responded, compelled to validate her statement. "Nothing will happen to Athee while she is in my care," Byron told the prefect. "You have my word."

"The word of a Cassan," Orellen replied.

Angered by the man's insult, Byron stood to his full height and clenched his fists. The prefect's words indicated he doubted Byron's promise held any merit. In a position of power or not, Orellen had no right to speak to him that way.

"Uncle!" exclaimed Athee.

Byron held his ground, fighting the impulse to strike the look of contempt off the Tgren's face. The prefect turned to face Byron, his nose wrinkled with disdain. Squaring his shoulders, he raised one finger in a threatening manner.

"If anything happens to her, there will be severe repercussions," he asserted. "You started this nonsense and I'll hold you personally responsible for any harm that befalls my niece."

Turning to Athee, he threw his hands in the air. "Go!" Orellen cried. Before she could respond, he stormed away from the shuttle.

Athee shook her head. She met Byron's eyes in passing as she strode up the ramp and into the shuttle. Byron made certain the man was on his way to the hanger before closing the hatch. When the panel indicated a perfect seal, his shoulders sagged in relief.

Aware he needed to assist Athee with her harness, Byron stepped away from the door. Unable to locate her, he frowned. The other two passengers were secure in their seats and gave no indication as to her whereabouts. Alarmed, Byron peered into the cockpit. Athee now sat in the co-pilot's seat, her harness in place and eyes scanning the control panel. Concerned, he entered the cockpit. She looked up and smiled.

"Your controls still amaze me," she said, her eyes reflecting childish wonder. "So much information to process."

Hesitating, Byron grasped the back of her seat. "You've been in a shuttle before?"

"Of course. The previous shuttle pilot even gave me a ride over the valley."

I bet he did! Byron thought, staring at the attractive young woman. "Well, you need to go take a seat with the other passengers."

Athee tossed her hair aside and eyed him expectantly. "I thought I'd ride in the cockpit with you."

"That's probably not a good idea."

"Why not?"

"That's the co-pilot's seat."

"Do you have a co-pilot?"

"Well, no..."

"Then this seat is open."

Byron sighed in exasperation. Releasing her seat, he ran his fingers through his hair. This woman is too stubborn for her own good, he thought. He didn't want her in the cockpit. She was an inexperienced passenger who'd never ventured into space. The jump alone could cause her to panic or get sick. Of greater concern were the emotions she would project during the flight. He'd endured Mevine's inhibition, but didn't care to repeat the experience.

A hand grasped his arm. Startled, he glanced down.

"Officer Byron, this might be my only flight into space," said Athee. "Please allow me to enjoy this experience from the cockpit."

Byron regarded the young woman with caution. He sensed no trace of mental manipulation as she gazed at him. Only her words and expression could persuade him. Byron considered her inquiry and decided Athee could ride in the cockpit. Besides, if he denied her request, she might complain to her uncle. The man despised him enough already.

"You can sit in the co-pilot's seat, but if you touch so much as one control or utter a single word, I'll secure you in the cargo hold on the return trip. Understand?"

Athee grinned, apparently undeterred by his threat. "Yes, sir."

To her credit, the young woman neither spoke nor moved as the shuttle took flight. Athee's hands remained clasped around the armrests, her gaze on the scene unfolding outside the cockpit. However, while her voice was still, that did not prevent her excitement from emanating like a beacon from her mind as the ship ascended further into the sky.

Byron was tempted to perform a rapid accent and give the Tgren woman a good scare. Perhaps she wouldn't be so quick to request the co-pilot's seat if the opportunity arose again. However, her elation reminded him of Mevine. Byron decided it would be wrong to douse her enthusiasm and kept the vessel steady. When he'd gained the proper altitude, he informed Athee of their impending jump into space.

Athee gasped. "You're going to teleport the ship?" she said, breaking her vow of silence.

"Yes," he said, noting her fingers as they grasped the seat even tighter. "So don't be alarmed when the view outside changes."

Byron selected his coordinates. Reaching out to the teleporter, his mind tapped into the device and merged with its power. Envisioning his destination, he jumped to the new location. A split second of darkness outside the cockpit was followed by a view filled with stars.

With his mind open from connecting with the teleporter, Athee's thoughts filled his head. His passenger's reaction revealed no fear, and only her elation and delight flooded his mind. Byron began to shield out of habit, but he hesitated, reluctant to quiet the thoughts stirring in his head. Mevine's elation had reminded him of Trindel, but Athee's feelings plunged deeper. Her joy was like a pleasant ripple across his thoughts, mimicking his own forgotten, ecstatic sensations during teleportation. Caught up in her amazement, Byron allowed himself a smile.

As if she sensed their shared connection of joy, Athee turned to look at him. Byron reigned in his pleasure and assumed a more controlled expression.

"That was incredible," she said in a hushed voice.

Byron guided the shuttle on a tight arc. "Let's see if I can top that then," he said as the Rennather came into view.

He glanced at Athee and caught her smile as she viewed her first spacecraft. The Rennather wasn't a large ship, but she was still impressive. He'd assumed the sight of the exploration vessel would terrify someone who'd never viewed a ship of such size. Athee's lack of fear or intimidation was unexpected and refreshing. Byron enjoyed her enthusiastic response.

Once in the hanger, he instructed Athee to wait while he assisted the other passengers. The flight crew removed the empty cartons and Byron performed a final check before ushering the Tgren out of the shuttle. She followed, taking in the scenery as they crossed the hanger. Byron noticed several men observing their passage, eyes wide with curiosity. No woman currently served on the Rennather. Most of the crew had never seen a Tgren in person, either. Athee's presence drew a great deal of attention. Byron moved with haste toward the exit.

Informing the commander of Athee's arrival, Byron was instructed to escort her to Officer Narunva's facility. Anceptor was on his way and Korden would join them when he had a free moment.

Byron located Officer Narunva's office. He introduced Athee to the Rennather's senior psych scientist. The older man offered her a gentle handshake in greeting, his deep-set eyes twinkling. Narunva gestured to a secluded observation room and followed Athee as she entered. He instructed the woman to have a seat in the lone chair.

"It won't hurt," he said, hooking electrodes to her temples, "but the probing of your mind may seem unnerving at first. This machine will delve deeper than Officer Illenth's device. Just relax and it will feel like a faint tickle in your head."

A faint tickle? Yeah, right!

Byron shook his head and retreated from the room. That wasn't how he remembered the numerous invasions he'd endured as a child. Prying adults had pierced his mental shields on many an occasion, all in the name of psychological analysis. Those instances were more akin to a blazing fire tearing through the mind. Granted psychic testing was less invasive and painful than forceful entry, but Byron preferred to avoid mental probing altogether.

Anceptor joined them as the senior psyche officer emerged from the room. Narunva ran through the basic tests first. The observation screen revealed a calm woman seated in the tiny room, neither flinching nor tense as her brain waves were recorded. Narunva checked individual levels of psychic strength, his fingers racing across the keypad.

Completing the first series, the man began the final round of tests, which involved his mental presence in her mind. Anceptor's eyes followed the readout, but Byron focused on Narunva. Until now, no other man had sensed her psychic powers or felt her emotions race through their thoughts. Would the man discover the true depth of her abilities? Impatient for the procedure to end, Byron shifted from one foot to the other. It was a relief when he sensed the separation of their minds.

Narunva had just informed Athee they were finished when Byron became aware of Korden's presence in the room. The commander nodded at Anceptor and his senior pilot before turning to Narunva, his brow pulled together.

"What are your findings?" Anceptor asked, clasping his hands behind his back.

Narunva pressed his keypad, bringing up a new display on the screen. "She scored high in several quadrants," he announced, his eyes scanning the figures. "As expected, Athee is capable of telepathy and bonding. However, her abilities go beyond that of the average Cassan female."

"Oh?"

Korden's inquiry was loaded with more than mere curiosity. Byron edged closer to Narunva and held his breath.

"She scored high in shield penetration, higher than most Cassan women. Judging from these figures, there's a potential for mental persuasion and manipulation as well."

That doesn't surprise me, Byron thought. He'd experienced her controlling powers firsthand.

The commander's frown deepened. "We'll need to treat that ability with respect and care."

Narunva met the commander's gaze and nodded. "That's not all, sir. She scored high in the area of teleportation."

Byron's mouth dropped open in bewilderment. How is that possible? Cassan women lacked the ability to fold space. How could this Tgren woman possess such powers?

"Are you certain?" the commander demanded.

"Yes sir. I performed that analysis three times, just to be certain. Athee has the ability to teleport."

Regaining his composure, Byron glanced first at Anceptor and then at Korden. Shock colored the second-in-command's thoughts. The commander appeared to be processing the information, his lips pressed together and expression neutral. Byron shielded his mind, although he was sure everyone had sensed his disbelief of Narunva's assessment. Holding his breath, he awaited Korden's response.

"Officer Byron," the commander said, his eyes never leaving the computer screen. "Please provide our guest with a tour of the Rennather while I contact the proper authorities on this matter."

Byron's muscles tightened further. "Yes, sir."

The prospect of escorting Athee throughout the ship didn't excite him. It wasn't that Byron disliked the Tgren woman. He simply didn't want Athee in his head again. Byron followed Korden's orders without protest, though. Athee bubbled with excitement as Byron guided her along the passageways. She asked many questions and awaited a satisfactory answer before posing her next query.

At first, Byron played the reluctant host. However, as they proceeded on the tour, he began to enjoy the opportunity to display his familiarity with the Rennather's functions. He didn't get to flaunt his knowledge outside of the cockpit very often. His captive and attentive audience fueled the desire further, and Byron provided detailed descriptions that were likely beyond Athee's comprehension. That didn't seem to stop the flow of questions though.

After a lengthy monologue regarding the ship's propulsion system, Athee grew quiet. They had reached the bridge and selected a position on the upper deck, away from working personnel. The Tgren woman grasped the edge of the railing and stared with wide eyes at the view screen. Byron crossed his arms and waited.

"How long have your people been exploring space?" she said without turning her head.

"Over seven hundred years."

A spark of envy escaped her thoughts. "Our history barely goes back a thousand years. We only achieved flight thirty years ago."

Byron dropped his chin. "I'm sure you'll achieve space flight in your lifetime."

"I hope so." Athee leaned away from the railing, her hands still clenched around the top bar. "Ever since your people made contact with us, venturing into space has occupied my thoughts. This trip is like a dream come true."

Her feelings of appreciation were genuine. Athee's child-like innocence and candid disposition were in sharp contrast to Byron's thoughts of cocky superiority. Hadn't Bassa always preached humility? The stab of guilt caused him to drop his air of supremacy few notches.

Athee straightened her posture and cast him a warm smile. "Thank you for bringing me here."

"You're welcome."

By adopting a more unassuming position, Byron found he enjoyed his duty as tour guide even more. He continued the tour, his attitude more positive. When the commander requested their presence in his office, Byron's disappointment mirrored hers.

They were instructed to take a seat. Athee and Byron dropped into adjoining chairs. The commander assumed a relaxed position, his spine pressed against the back of the chair, but his brows were pulled together in consternation. He did not waste time with frivolous words. Korden got right down to the meeting's purpose.

"I spoke with Chancellor Dentex," he announced, "and with Prefect Orellen. After much deliberation, we've agreed your abilities should be further developed. We are also to widen our search for mental powers of your strength. It's unlikely this is an isolated incident. We need to locate other Tgrens who exhibit similar capabilities and bring the most promising on board for testing."

Athee did not speak, but Byron sensed her amazement. He shifted in his seat, still processing this development.

"Officer Byron, I am altering your duties on Tgren."

"Sir?" he questioned, sitting straighter in his chair.

"In addition to training the Tgren pilots and assisting Officer Illenth, I am placing you in charge of instructing Athee on the use of her psychic powers," replied Korden.

"Me, sir?"

"Illenth's duties are about to double and he will be pressed for time," the commander explained, leaning forward to reach his keypad. "Our primary objective, the alien ruins, is still our focus. I can't pull anyone from their current assignment. At any rate, you are the only qualified officer in the area of psychic development."

Byron glanced at Athee. Her brow furrowed and he shielded his thoughts. *Sir, I'm hardly qualified to train…*

Korden's finger came down hard on his computer's keypad. "Your records indicate you have experience drawing out mental abilities. Granted it was twenty years ago and during the Vindicarn War, but you're the best I have right now."

Fighting to control his expression, a surge of emotions gripped Byron. The commander was referring to an incident involving his navigator and a disrupter blast. At the time, Byron had relented and assisted Bassa in his recovery by allowing the man access to his mind. However, that hardly qualified him as a psychic trainer. Moreover, the last thing Byron wanted was this Tgren woman's thoughts invading his mind.

Sir…

It's not a request, Byron.

The commander's firm tone was loud and clear in his mind. Byron rolled his eyes and sank further in his seat.

If the Tgrens possess telepathic abilities, then we need to develop that skill. Considering we've been unable to meet their demands for better communications thus far, it would greatly improve our relations with the Tgrens.

Pressing his lips into a fine line, Byron nodded. Beside him, Athee shifted in her seat.

"Byron's to teach me how to use my powers?" she asked, breaking the silence.

The commander's attention shifted to the young woman. "Yes, he will instruct you how to properly use all of your abilities."

All of her powers? "Even teleporting?" Byron exclaimed. An excited jolt from Athee caused him to regret his words.

"I can teleport?" she cried, sitting up straight in her chair.

Korden's eyes narrowed. "Tgrens do not possess the technology just yet. However, with our continued presence on this planet, it might be prudent for Athee to understand the concept. Tgren resources do contribute to our teleportation devices.

"Officer Byron, you are to focus on pilot training in the mornings," the commander said, leaning back in his seat. "Afternoons you will assist Officer Illenth, with a minimum of two hours devoted to Athee's training. More if necessary. Understood?"

Korden's authoritative voice left no room for discussion. "Yes, sir," Byron answered, his thoughts slipping further into gloom.

The commander's eyes narrowed. *Keep her manipulative powers in mind. I will instruct our crew to remain mentally alert while on Tgren. I'm sure she's not the only one, and I don't want any of our people caught unaware. And she may only possess a trace, but you should exhibit caution when training Athee.*

Yes, sir.

"You are dismissed!"

Athee burst from her seat and thanked the commander. Byron rose slowly, his body just as reluctant as his brain to comply with his new assignment. The act of entering another's mind and sharing his own thoughts was such an invasion of his privacy. He'd only let down his guard for one person, and that had taken a tremendous amount of trust. Byron didn't even know Athee, let alone trust her. Every afternoon promised two hours of torture.

"Can we begin today?" Athee asked when they reached the corridor. She straightened her shoulders, eyes sparkling with enthusiasm.

Byron hesitated. His mind searched for a plausible excuse to delay until tomorrow. To his chagrin, he could not think of one.

"Might as well," he replied, his churning stomach protesting that answer.

Excitement exploded from Athee's mind. Byron winced as an overload of emotions shot through him.

And the first thing I'm teaching you is how to shield, he added, ignoring her startled look as his thoughts rang in her head for the first time.

Chapter Five

Byron returned Athee to the planet's surface, lost deep in thought. When the shuttle landed, he noted the time. The trip to the Rennather had devoured most of the morning. Pilot training would have to wait until tomorrow. Athee promised to meet Byron later that afternoon for her first session. She bounded across the runway, her mood as high as her steps.

Glad you're excited, Byron thought, still dreading the experience.

Garnce's shuttle sat near the main hanger. There were several crates beside the hatch waiting to be loaded. Byron emerged from his ship the same moment as Garnce. The man approached him and talked Byron into an early lunch. Listening to the pilot grumble over poorly loaded cargo did nothing to settle his mind. When they returned to the shuttles, two Tgrens approached carrying a small carton between them. They requested transport to the alien site.

"It's very fragile," one of the men explained, glancing at the container.

"Damn, I was just there an hour ago!" Garnce exclaimed, gesturing toward the mountains.

The pilot's reaction brought the Tgrens to an abrupt halt, the carton swinging between them. Byron quickly intervened.

"I can take you," he offered.

Garnce shook his head. *These people are so damned disorganized*, he thought as the men followed Byron to his ship.

Once at the site, the Tgrens thanked Byron for a smooth flight and carried their cargo into the cave. However, Byron was in no hurry to return to Ktren. Determined to kill some time, he followed the men to the control center.

The scene was just as chaotic as the previous day. The hum of machinery and numerous voices assaulted Byron's ears. He sidestepped two scientists and brushed against a panel. Several new pieces of equipment were in evidence, creating an obstacle course. Locating Mevine at his station, Byron decided to have a word with him.

An untouched plate of food sat nearby. Hunched over his computer screen, Mevine seemed oblivious to his surroundings.

"You're not eating?" Byron asked.

Mevine jumped, his body lifting from the stool. He looked up at Byron, then glanced at his waiting meal.

"I will," he promised. "Sir."

"You'll function better with some food in your stomach," Byron said. He'd missed many meals over the years, but few were by choice.

Mevine's chin dropped and he reached for his bread. "You're right, sir. I just lost track of time."

Leaning closer, Byron peered at Mevine's computer screen. "Any progress?"

Chomping down on the roll's crust, the lad touched his keypad with his free hand. The display changed, revealing a large portion of alien text.

"The problem is it's a mixture of symbols, numerals, and a written language. Or so we believe," said Mevine through a mouthful of food. "We've isolated the numbers and a team is working on them now. We're still trying to separate the letters from the symbols, though. If indeed they are two different entities."

"You're not sure?"

Mevine shook his head, his shoulders slumping. "I can show you some of the encryptions if you like," he offered, glancing up at Byron and poising his fingers over the keypad in anticipation.

Byron shook his head. "Afraid I can't stay. I was given a new assignment to occupy my afternoons."

"Oh?"

"One of the Tgrens shows remarkable psychic talent and I'm to train her on the use of those powers."

"Her?" Mevine's face broke into a smile.

"Yes, a young woman. One of the pilots."

The lad swiveled on his stool to face Byron. "Is she pretty?" he asked.

Byron chuckled, amused by the boy's interest in such a minor detail. "Yeah, I guess so," he admitted, trying not to dwell on Athee's appearance. He didn't need further distractions; her powers of manipulation were enough.

"Sounds like a good assignment to me, sir."

"If you say so. Well, I need to return," he said, taking a step away from the young man. "And you need to eat."

"Yes, sir," the young man answered, blindly reaching for another handful of food. In his haste, he almost knocked the plate to the floor.

Byron shook his head as he retreated from the room. At least he'd maintained more poise when he was Mevine's age. Coordination was not a skill the young officer possessed, outside of the grav court. The lad was all right, though. Without question, he was far better company than Garnce.

When he arrived at Illenth's office, Byron found Athee waiting. She was chatting with the senior officer, but ceased the moment her instructor entered the room. Pivoting her body to face him, she flashed a triumphant smile.

"I'm ready," she declared, straightening her shoulders.

Byron glanced at Illenth, hoping the man would come to his rescue and offer assistance. The officer presented a smile and gestured toward the door.

"I've two men to test this afternoon," he explained. "But there's an empty room across the hall that should suit your needs."

Athee's eagerness rang loud in Byron's mind. She strode past the pilot with a bounce in her step. He flinched, but the psyche officer gave no indication that her mental transmissions bothered him. Puzzled, Byron shot Illenth an inquisitive look.

You can't hear her?

I sense the stir of emotions in her presence, just not to the extent that you do. Your perception is far stronger than mine, he replied with a shrug. *Let me know if you need anything.*

I need my head examined for agreeing to this, Byron thought, following Athee into the hall.

The room was small. It boasted only one elongated window from which sunshine streamed. A desk, a table and three chairs occupied the office, creating a sterile and lifeless environment. It suited Byron's needs, though. At least the room's temperature felt cool on his face.

"Take a seat, please," he said, gesturing to the chairs around the table.

Athee sat in a chair. Adjusting her position, she pulled it closer to the table. Byron secured the door and selected the chair opposite the young woman. She wiggled even closer, a grin on her face. Athee placed her elbows and hands on the table.

"You're teaching me how to shield first?" she asked, repeating Byron's words from earlier that morning.

Leaning one arm on the table, he took a deep breath. "Not just yet."

"What does it mean to shield?"

"Shielding is to prevent your thoughts from broadcasting and also to prevent others from entering your mind."

"Oh. Why did you claim you'd teach me to shield first?"

Under the table, Byron's hand grasped his knee in an effort to remain patient with the woman. "Because you are broadcasting your emotions for all to hear."

Athee's eyes widened and she leaned away from the table. "You know what I'm feeling? What I'm thinking?" she gasped in a horrified voice.

"I can't hear specific thoughts, just general feelings," he assured Athee, hoping to quiet the panic that pulsated from her mind. "I'll teach you how to control that, but first, I need to teach you how to access it."

She eyed him with caution and leaned forward again. "How do I do that?"

Byron reached deep into his memory. A disrupter blast had numbed Bassa's senses. Athee's abilities weren't inactive, just out of control. Helping her to find the proper channels would be easier than coaxing mental powers from the ashes of a disrupter-fried mind. At least, he hoped that was the case.

"First, I need you to stop talking," Byron instructed, "and relax."

Athee's mind settled into a gentle stir of excitement tinged with anxiety. "Now what?"

"You're still talking."

"Sorry."

Byron shook his head. This was going to be difficult. Why couldn't Narunva train her on the Rennather? Surely, the man had more experience with new psychic powers. Was there a reason Korden wanted Byron to work with Athee?

Pressing both elbows on the table, he fixed the Tgren woman with a firm stare. She returned his gaze without the slightest trace of intimidation, her green eyes unusually bright in the low light. He'd meant to turn on the light, but didn't want to get up now. The window provided enough illumination for his purpose.

Hear my voice?

Her lips parted in surprise. "Yes."

No, I need you to respond with your mind. Hear my voice and answer me with your thoughts.

Byron sensed her attempt to reply. Her thoughts stirred, but formed no clear words. He enticed her to respond several times, desperate for Athee to answer without assistance. After a few moments, she leaned away in frustration.

"What am I doing wrong?" she said, clenching her fists.

Dropping his chin, Byron pulled his arms tighter across his chest. Entering another's mind was not an experience he relished. Since she appeared unable to connect with the correct brain waves, he needed to go in and pull her thoughts along the path. Like it or not, he had to encroach upon her thoughts.

Let me show you how.

Entering Athee's mind, he felt for the portion that controlled telepathy. Most Cassans resisted probing to a degree, as it violated one's privacy. Byron detested the sensation. To his surprise, Athee offered no resistance. Her mind was open and willing, like that of a child. Unprepared for such trust, Byron fumbled for a moment before locating the telepathic center of her mind. Now he had only to connect and provide a path for Athee to follow.

You need to stretch those mental muscles. Follow my voice. Focus on nothing else but the strength of my voice. You pos-

sess the same ability. Talk to me as if you were speaking out loud, only use your mind instead.

How?

Just like that.

Athee's eyes grew wide. Byron nodded and gestured with his fingers for her to continue. *Again. Follow my voice and tell me your name.*

Determination arose deep within her mind. *Athee,* her thoughts whispered.

Louder! Project that voice and talk to me.

Her brows came together. *Athee,* she thought, her mental voice stronger but still faint.

Project louder. Give it some effort. Damn, woman–I know you like to talk!

I do not!

Byron grinned. He'd struck a nerve. *Yes, you do. Now prove it.*

Athee frowned, indignation flowing through her mind. *Now you're mocking me.*

No, I am trying to get you to use your mental voice by any means possible.

She continued to banter with him. Every time Athee used her telepathy, her voice grew stronger. Much to his relief, it began to overshadow her emotional projections. Under normal circumstances, constant chatter irritated Byron. Something in the innocence of Athee discovering her mental voice for the first time prevented the experience from grating on his nerves. Her genuine delight and eager questions regarding her telepathy reminded him of a babbling stream; a constant noise that soothed the senses.

Noticing the passage of time through the open window, Byron leaned away from the table. He realized his legs and back were stiff from sitting. He'd dreaded this experience, but survived several hours of intense mental training. His obligations were satisfied, at least for today.

Now remember, if you use your mental voice around other Cassans, they will hear you, he cautioned as they exited the room. *I'll show you how to shield tomorrow, but for the time being, don't project.*

And don't make any smart remarks?

A smirk tugged at her lips. Byron sensed mischief and returned her grin.

Don't pick a fight with someone who can kick your ass, he thought before retreating to the stairwell that led to the sleeping quarters. *Because I won't save you.*

"You wanted to see me, Uncle?"

Orellen glanced up from his work. His desk was strewn with papers, but the ones in his hand caught Athee's eye. The prefect liked to check flight patterns on occasion and held the week's patrol schedule.

"Yes, I did," he said, laying aside the papers.

"All of the patrols have been covered," she asserted, concerned her uncle might think she'd slacked in her duties as lead pilot. Athee had designated other pilots to fill the void in the schedule due to her training with Byron.

"Yes, and to my satisfaction." The prefect leaned back in his chair, his thick fingers strumming the desk. "Istaner informed me of your flying instructions today with the Cassan officer."

I bet he did! Athee thought, shifting her weight. Istaner had vocalized his dissatisfaction with Byron's training style more than once in her presence. She tended to ignore her cousin's grumblings. Istaner complained about everything.

"But you've failed to report your progress with the psychic aspect of that man's training," he said, fixing her with a fierce stare. His expression did not intimidate Athee.

"I'm sorry, Uncle. We've had two sessions thus far. I learned how to focus on my powers yesterday. Today Byron taught me how to project and shield my thoughts. By the time we finished, he stated I was quite proficient."

Orellen's expression grew less harsh, but he didn't appear convinced. Her uncle remained skeptical even after the report from Narunva. He continued to assert that mental powers were unnatural and impractical. And he didn't believe Tgrens possessed the same ability as the Cassans. Athee decided there was only one way to prove her abilities.

Uncle, I can now speak with my mind.

Her words had the desired effect. Orellen's eyebrows rose and his mouth opened, stretching his face. This removed some of the baggy wrinkles that marred his skin. Feeling triumphant, Athee laughed.

"You heard me!" she stated, slapping his desk with her palm. "And it's not a freakish ability. Uncle, think of the possibilities. If we could all communicate with our minds, we could stay in contact with our pilots, even if our radios fail. Emergency calls could go out immediately. Transmissions to other cities could be instantaneous."

The prefect's hands dropped to his lap. He offered no protest, but continued to stare at his niece. Athee sensed this was her one opportunity to reach him and bury all disbelief.

Uncle, if you needed me, needed anyone, all you'd have to do is speak with your mind. You'd never lose contact.

Athee presented her most disarming smile, hoping to soften the implication of her statement. Her aunt had died in a rockslide that claimed many lives, most of which were lost due to the inability to locate those buried under the rubble. Had they possessed mental abilities at the time, her aunt might've lived. She sensed that same thought now echoed in her uncle's mind.

While his emotions were caught up in the memory, Athee focused her thoughts on persuading her uncle to see the advantages of telepathy. Orellen could be stubborn. However, she knew how to sway his opinion. She held a special place in his heart as his only niece, and after the death of her father, they'd grown even closer. Athee now relied on that bond to convince her uncle to see reason.

"My dear, that is incredible," he murmured.

"It is, and we all share this trait. The Cassans can help us find and use our psychic powers to their full capacity, too."

Orellen offered a curt nod and leaned forward. "It appears I need to reconsider my position on the matter," he said, enunciating each word with care.

Athee smiled even as she suppressed her delight. Now that she understood her abilities, she could use her power of persuasion to greater effect. Byron could teach her telepathy and teleportation, but there was one skill she'd already mastered. It pleased Athee to know her instructor did not share the strength of her talent, either.

"I wouldn't flaunt that trick just yet," the prefect cautioned. "You might frighten someone who's not prepared to hear the voice of a fellow Tgren in his head."

Athee crossed her arms and chuckled. "I caught Erenta by surprise this morning," she confessed, still amused by her fellow pilot's stunned reaction. "And Istaner's next."

"Athee!"

"Uncle!" she countered. "I get so few opportunities to best my only cousin. Grant me this one indulgence."

Orellen shook his head and reached for a fresh stack of papers. "You're already a better pilot than Istaner," he grumbled.

Allowing a laugh to escape her lips, Athee circled the desk and gave her uncle a hug. He resisted at first, affecting cold indifference. She continued to cling to his shoulders, determined to break down all resistance. Soon, Orellen grasped her arm, patting it with affection.

"Just don't repeat that in his presence," he ordered. "You'll give my son an inferiority complex."

She planted a kiss on his cheek and released his neck. "I wouldn't dream of it."

Athee patted his shoulder and turned to depart. She felt triumphant in her ability to manipulate her uncle's line of thinking and sway it to the betterment of her people. It also assured continued sessions with Byron, which was a personal victory. Athee wanted to discover her full potential. She also wanted to spend more time in the company of the Cassan officer. He presented a mystery she was determined to unravel.

"One more item I wanted to discuss," Orellen said in a firm voice.

Athee paused at the door and eyed her uncle with curiosity.

"I want you to exercise caution around this Officer Byron. I know his type all too well. Unattached and lacking inhibition or restraint. I don't trust the man. You be careful, Athee."

"I can handle the Cassan," she stated with confidence, offering her sweetest smile. "After all, I handle you, don't I?"

Her uncle scowled and shook his head. "Be gone!" he ordered, his attention returning to his work.

Athee retreated from her uncle's office and grinned as she strode down the hallway. I've mastered you, my dear uncle, she thought. Now I just need to figure out what makes Byron tick.

The seven Tgren planes landed, and Byron waited until all were on the ground before setting down the shuttle. Cutting off the engines, he leaned his head against the seat and exhaled slowly.

The seven pilots under his tutelage were the best the city of Ktren had to offer, but they still lacked many skills. Athee topped the list, and another Tgren by the name of Erenta showed promise, but the remaining five made too many errors. Byron reminded himself their planes were incapable of tight maneuvers, which compounded issues. That still did not excuse poor execution of basic training exercises. After six days flying with the Tgren pilots, he wondered how any of them were still alive.

He rubbed his temples, grateful for the cool air in the cockpit. I don't know how they fly in this heat, he thought, releasing his harness. Byron leaned forward and checked the ship's systems. He needed to return to the Rennather soon for fuel. Perhaps he'd schedule a flight for this evening.

Glancing up, he noticed several of the Tgren pilots had gathered in the shade beside a hanger. He recognized Athee among those assembled, her long hair blowing across her shoulders. She and the others were listening to the tallest man in the group, a pilot named Istaner. Judging from his rapid gestures, the man was agitated.

Byron grimaced. Athee's older cousin was difficult. The man voiced his opinion without hesitation. Istaner's demeanor matched that of his father's and he questioned every instruction. The man considered himself a superior pilot, but since his skills did not match his boasts, Istaner's attitude annoyed Byron. His patience with the Tgren pilot was growing thin.

I should fly my Darten tomorrow instead, he thought. Get in some target practice.

Hungry and ready for a decent meal, Byron released the hatch. A small cart rolled up as he descended the ramp. The engine emitted a plume of smoke as it came to a jarring stop.

Coughing, he pivoted away and noticed Athee approaching the shuttle. Byron glanced back at the cart as the lone passenger leapt to the ground. The two reached him at the same time.

"Officer Byron, can you take me to the Rennather?" Seheller asked. "I need to retrieve a piece of equipment from my lab."

His stomach rumbled in protest, but Byron could hardly refuse the senior science officer passage. At any rate, a meal aboard the ship sounded more appetizing. He might even have time to take his Darten out before returning to the surface.

"Of course."

The man nodded and returned to the cart. Glancing at Athee, he noticed a smirk on her face. She had mastered shielding, but Byron didn't need to hear the woman's thoughts to know she was scheming.

"Can I come along?" she said.

Byron stared at her in surprise. "We'd need clearance first," he explained.

"So ask."

"Commander Korden's not going to grant permission just because you want to see the ship again."

Athee cocked her head and fixed him with a firm stare. "No, but he'll grant permission so you can begin training me to teleport."

Exasperated, Byron shook his head and grasped the frame of the hatch. He wanted a peaceful ride to the Rennather and an opportunity to relax before returning to Tgren. Instructing Athee on how to tap into the ship's teleportation device did not factor into that equation.

Officer Seheller approached, a pack over his shoulder and a large computer tablet in his arms. Byron stepped aside and allowed the man entry to the ship. Athee placed one foot on the ramp and a hand on her hip, still awaiting his answer. He felt the pressure of her mind, prompting him to comply with her request. Her powers of persuasion were too strong for his tastes.

You don't always get what you want, you know, Byron told her, crossing his arms in defiance.

She raised one eyebrow. *No, but I was promised training, and that included learning how to teleport.*

Byron scowled at her, annoyed by her reasoning, not to mention dogged persistence. Athee was the most stubborn person he'd ever met. However, if he didn't acquiesce to her request, she would badger him all afternoon during their session.

"Fine, I'll contact the commander."

He returned to the cockpit. Pressing the com button with force, Byron requested a word with Korden. While he waited, he seethed quietly. Byron couldn't decide which annoyed him more–Athee's obstinate demand or his inability to stand his ground. After facing countless battles and hostile environments, Byron had allowed a petite, unarmed girl to get the best of him.

Officer Byron?

He sat up straight, unprepared for a mental response. Byron didn't like to bother the commander without good reason. Korden's tone bore no trace of irritation, though.

Sorry to interrupt you, sir. I'm returning to the ship with Officer Seheller and a second passenger who requires clearance.

One of the Tgrens?

Yes, Athee. She wants to experience the teleporter and begin training on the device.

There was a pause. *Has she achieved an acceptable level of proficiency in other areas?*

Yes, sir. Byron grasped the edge of the console, fighting with his next thought. *Achieved and surpassed.*

Permission granted, but proceed with caution, Korden instructed. *Remember, Byron, you are responsible for that young woman. She represents far more than just a Tgren with unusual powers.*

Yes, sir.

Byron's shoulders sagged in defeat. Running fingers through his hair, he stared at a patch of sand on the floor. Damn desert planet, he thought. Invading my life on every level.

Gaining control of his frustration, he arose from his chair. *If you're coming, get in,* Byron informed Athee.

She entered the cockpit within seconds. He refrained from meeting her gaze, unwilling to witness her triumphant expression. Once the hatch was secure, he returned and dropped into his seat. Grateful she'd mastered shielding, as he didn't want to feel her smug thoughts, Byron started the engines. He wasn't about to allow her victory on every level, though. Athee's second trip into space would not be as smooth as the first.

"Byron?"

Gritting his teeth, he cast a sideways glance at his passenger. Athee stared at him, her head listing to one side. She offered a gentle smile.

"Thank you," she said.

He sensed her thoughts of gratitude and realized Athee's words were genuine. Byron managed a curt nod before lifting the shuttle off the ground. Despite his original intentions, the ship's accent was gradual. In any case, Seheller might've voiced displeasure with a rough flight.

First, you need to understand the process, he told Athee. *When I jump the ship into space, focus on the powers I use to tap into the teleporter.*

Check.

Achieving the proper altitude, Byron leveled the shuttle. *Now, concentrate on me.*

Athee's presence filled his mind. Shielding all other thoughts, he allowed her to feel his connection with the teleporter. During normal jumps, Byron used his own powers rather than drain the unit. Athee needed to experience a standard jump, though. Linking with the teleporter's energy, he visualized the coordinates. The hum of the device loud in his head, Byron jumped the shuttle.

The Rennather became visible outside the cockpit, its surface reflecting the system's sun. The burst of excitement from his passenger was simultaneous.

"I felt it!" she cried.

Byron's chest filled with pride, pleased with her response. He angled the shuttle for the landing bay, bringing the runners down without so much as a jolt. The vessel came to gradual halt and he shut down the engines.

"You really enjoy teleporting, don't you?"

Byron glanced at Athee, startled by her comment. He'd kept his feelings hidden during the jump. Had she heard his thoughts or was the woman just that perceptive?

"Yes, I enjoy it," he admitted, his gaze returning to the view outside the cockpit.

"I guess some things can't be shielded."

Unnerved by that thought, Byron said nothing more.

Seheller thanked him for the transport and requested a return flight after the midday meal. Grateful for an opportunity to eat familiar food, Byron promised he would wait for the science officer. He asked the hanger crew to refuel the shuttle as well. Satisfied his ship resided in capable hands, he led Athee from the hanger.

She asked many questions as they traveled to the dining hall, eager to know more about teleportation. Once they arrived however, her attention was diverted by several crew members anxious to discover more about Tgren's natives. Byron suspected their curiosity stemmed more from the fact Athee was a woman. He monitored their comments during the meal, prepared to intervene with a stiff reprimand if necessary. For the most part, he was able to eat without interruption.

Eventually he pried Athee away from her new admirers. Amidst protests, they returned to the hanger. The shuttle was fueled and ready to go, but Seheller was not yet present. Byron glanced at his Darten, sitting off to one side. With Athee in tow, he couldn't take out his fighter as planned. He pressed his lips together, suppressing the disappointment that arose in his chest.

"Is that yours?" she said, breaking into his thoughts.

Byron nodded and Athee grasped his arm.

"Can I see it up close?"

Altering his course, he led Athee to the tiny fighter. Designed for maneuverability, it was not much smaller than the Tgren's single pilot planes. However, that was where the similarities ended. Byron heard the woman's gasps of amazement as she circled the craft. Waiting by the narrow, rounded nose, he let her explore the exterior.

"I bet it's fast," she called.

"Damned fast," Byron boasted.

Athee came around the front of the Darten, one hand resting on the nose. She met his cautious stare and cocked her eyebrows. "Care to show me sometime?"

That question elicited a smirk from Byron. "You'll see it in action tomorrow. Thought I'd fly it during our training session."

"Well, that hardly seems fair," Athee said, placing her hands on her hips.

"You'll just have to keep up with me."

Her indignant expression was priceless. However, he sensed she was prepared for the challenge.

Officer Seheller arrived a moment later with a small carton in tow. Byron ushered his passengers back into the shuttle and prepared the ship for takeoff.

This time when we jump, I want you to join my connection with the teleporter, he informed Athee as they entered space. *You are to observe only, understood?*

Yes, sir.

He felt her presence as he touched the device. Tapping into its power, he performed the jump. Byron was impressed with her aptitude and the ease at which she connected. Athee was indeed a fast learner.

Descending over the valley, Byron asked Seheller if he would prefer to land at the site.

Officer Byron, I'd appreciate that, the science officer thought.

The detour only consumed a few minutes. After he'd delivered his passenger, Byron launched the shuttle skyward once again. Achieving a suitable cruising altitude, he set course for the Tgren city.

"You said you could funnel your own power into the teleporter, correct?" Athee suddenly asked.

"Yes," he answered, altering the shuttle's course as the city came into sight.

"Show me how you do it."

"Now? We're almost there."

Her disappointment rang loud in his mind. Out of the corner of his eye, Byron noticed Athee's body sink in her seat. The afternoon's excursion had resulted in a pleasant experience, much to his surprise. He decided to accede to her request.

"Let's achieve some distance first," he said, turning the shuttle away from the Tgren city.

Circling over the plateau, he scanned for Tgren planes. No aircraft occupied the sky and he selected a point of reentry.

Focus on my bond, he instructed.

Channeling his own power into the teleporter, Byron connected with the device. Athee's strong presence filled his mind as he prepared to jump. The teleporter hummed with added intensity as he locked on his coordinates.

Jump!

A surge of power flowed through his mind. The valley vanished, replaced by a view of the city. Byron's grasp on the controls tightened as the extra energy continued to pulsate in his thoughts. Athee's delight reverberated in his head and Byron struggled to hold his shields in place. With trembling hands, he brought the shuttle in for a less-than-perfect landing. The ship shuddered and came to an abrupt halt.

"That was incredible," Athee exclaimed.

Byron shut off the engines, his heart racing. He couldn't let her detect his discontent. Locking his shields in place, he focused on the ship's systems. To his relief, Athee did not notice.

"Shall we count that as today's lesson?' he asked, eyes focused on the control panel.

Athee swiveled in her chair. "I think that's fair."

She wished him a good day and exited the craft. Byron remained in his seat, his mind reeling.

Her power joined mine, he thought. Athee can perform multiple jumps as well.

Byron slumped in his chair. Through the cockpit window, he watched as the Tgren woman entered the hanger and vanished from sight. His mind continued to mull over the implications.

Damn, what else is she capable of doing?

Chapter Six

Soaring over the plateau, Byron banked left. This sent his ship into a gentle dive. He glanced at his radar and counted seven planes on his tail. Following in a single, ragged line, the vessels mimicked his maneuver to the best of their ability. He'd lost a couple of them during the course of the morning, but none of the pilots straggled now.

Skimming the craggy side of the plateau, Byron pulled away and leveled his flight. It felt good to fly his Darten again. The ship protested the tame flight patterns, but he couldn't outfly the Tgren planes or place the pilots in danger. He'd let the tiny fighter enjoy her freedom when they returned to space.

Any problems back there? he asked Athee.

We're good, she responded.

The plane directly behind him rolled back and forth. Byron grinned at the movement, which did not alter the aircraft's course or cause it to lose momentum. Athee's control and precision flying were admirable qualities in a pilot her age. The woman possessed an excellent sense of placement. She was daring, but not stupid. If Athee stayed the course, no pilot on this planet would match her abilities.

Imagine what she could've done in a Cassan fighter, he thought.

Byron checked the formation while contemplating the next maneuver. The third plane dipped lower and began to weave from side to side.

I think Istaner is bored, Athee informed him.

Gritting his teeth, Byron gripped the throttle tighter. *I think your cousin is a pain in the ass,* he replied, unable to conceal his distaste for the arrogant pilot.

Athee chuckled. Her amusement eased Byron's concerns. He'd taken a chance insulting the prefect's son. Fortunately, his protégée was sensible. She was not impressed with Istaner's abilities in the cockpit, regardless of his social and family status.

Well, he began, *feel up to a challenge?*

You bet. What do you have in mind?

Byron glanced at the radar. They were approaching a mountainous area, filled with numerous peaks and valleys. It was perfect for what he had in mind.

Tell the others to keep up if they can. But no stupid moves. Your uncle would call for my head if any of you died on my watch.

He waited while she relayed the information. The Darten's cockpit lacked room for the clumsy portable radio he'd used in the shuttle, for which he felt grateful. The primitive device was a poor excuse for a communication module. Besides, he possessed a far more reliable means for conveying his instructions.

We're ready, Athee called.

Altering his course, Byron increased his speed. The planes lagged for a moment before catching up to the fighter. Smiling as they approached the first narrow valley, he prepared to enjoy himself. Istaner wouldn't be bored now!

Banking to his left, Byron slipped into the valley. The mountains flashed by in a blur of red and gold. The walls drew closer and the canyon began to twist and turn. Byron reduced his speed, aware the planes were incapable of performing such tight maneuvers at their current pace. However, he didn't want to make it too easy for the Tgren pilots. If they were to improve, they had to stretch.

Pulling up on the throttle, he altered course. The Darten shot out of the narrow valley. Glancing at the radar, Byron saw one plane totter and drop behind. Altering the ship's trajectory, he sent the Darten into a nosedive. Another plane missed the mark and fell behind, but the others managed to stay with the Cassan fighter.

Selecting a deep valley, he reduced speed. The Darten slipped in between the sandy cliffs. One airplane came in too fast and dropped close to the canyon's surface. Byron breathed a sigh of relief as the pilot corrected his course. Flying near the valley's peaks, he continued following the erratic pattern as it sliced across the plains. Several planes faltered, pulling above the mountainous ridges to avoid impact before returning to formation, and one aircraft gave up entirely.

Byron was enjoying the chase, but he needed to push the Tgren pilots harder. Pulling out of the valley, he gained altitude. The open air beckoned like the vast expanse of space. Now he could demonstrate the maneuverability of the Darten without the risk of sending a plane into the side of a mountain.

Reining in his speed, Byron ran through his standard drill. He led the planes on a wild chase across the sky, always remaining several lengths in front of his pupils. One by one, the Tgren vessels dropped behind, unable to keep pace with his tight turns. He grinned when the third plane missed a turn and was forced to give up the chase. Istaner wasn't so skilled after all.

Swinging wide, he visually confirmed that only two planes remained. Athee still clung to his tail and he believed the second ship belonged to Erenta. The most capable of the seven pilots, he was not surprised they were the only ones to match his maneuvers.

Athee's triumphant cry echoed in his mind. *You couldn't shake me!*

Byron smiled. He had one remaining trick. *Oh yeah?*

Touching the teleporter, he jumped the ship. Reappearing behind the second plane, Byron chuckled as both aircraft's flights wavered.

Gotcha! he announced.

You teleported. That's not fair.

Laughing at her angry retort, Byron accelerated and shot over both planes. Within seconds, they were but specks in the sky.

Byron!

Performing a tight roll, he circled around. *You wanted to see what the Darten could do,* he offered. Displaying the power and agility of his fighter wasn't the only reason for his antics, but it provided an excuse. The Tgren pilots needed to be reminded of the superior technology of the Cassan fleet.

He flew past the planes and they pivoted to follow. *That concludes today's lesson,* he told Athee, leading the Tgrens toward Ktren. *I'll see you this afternoon.*

You bet you will, Athee replied, annoyance evident in her mental voice.

Byron chuckled. He rose higher while the Tgren planes continued on to the city. His eyes strayed to the lead plane. Athee would be difficult this afternoon if he didn't pacify her now.

You flew well, he thought as he tapped into the teleporter. She didn't respond, but his compliment had the desired effect of curtailing her irritation.

He returned to the Rennather in high spirits. As he was leaving the hanger, Byron almost ran into Mevine. The young man tried unsuccessfully to prevent his pack from falling yet somehow managed to hang on to the box in his hands.

"Officer Byron, I'm sorry," he cried, struggling to maintain hold of the box.

Byron scooped the bag from the floor and held it out for Mevine. "That's all right. I didn't expect to see you on the Rennather again so soon."

Mevine nodded and took the pack from Byron, slinging the bag across his shoulders. "I had to return for some clean clothes and new equipment. I'm sorry, I was trying to catch the shuttle before it departed."

Frowning, Byron glanced over his shoulder. The second shuttle was nowhere in sight. "I think you missed it."

Mevine stepped forward and scanned the hanger, his mouth open in horror. "I tried to hurry," he said, adjusting the pack when it threatened to fall off his shoulders. "I need to get back to the site this afternoon."

"Garnce will take you to the planet's surface when he returns."

The young man's face fell. "He'll be so mad," he murmured.

Byron had no doubt Garnce would offer a few choice words on the matter. His fellow pilot possessed little patience. The lad's expression suggested he'd already tangled once with the pilot and didn't care to repeat the experience. Byron realized he felt sorry for the science officer. The least he could do was save Mevine from Garnce's wrath.

"You're welcome to catch a ride with me after the midday meal," he offered.

Mevine's eyes widened. "Really, sir?"

"Sure, it's not a problem. Have you eaten?"

When Mevine shook his head, Byron held out his hand. "Let's store your gear first and then grab a bite to eat," he said, relieving Mevine of his bag before it tumbled again from his bony shoulder.

The boy attacked his food with relish. Byron wondered if Mevine had eaten at all today. No wonder he's so scrawny, he thought as the plate emptied. Someone needs to monitor his food consumption.

Eventually Mevine's food no longer vanished at an alarming rate. Byron asked the science officer of his progress with the alien language. The lad's expression brightened and he launched into a detailed account. His enthusiasm bubbled forth as he explained a recent breakthrough and potential deciphering of the language. Mevine appeared happiest when discussing his work. While Byron was unable to comprehend the particulars of language interpretation, he understood Mevine's passion. Flying was Byron's primary infatuation, and the only thing that caused his pulse to quicken.

"I need to retrieve another flight suit from my quarters," Byron announced as they exited the dining hall. "Should only take a minute."

Taking the nearest telepod, he led Mevine to the officers' level. Byron entered his quarters and moved toward his long locker. He glanced at his computer screen. No messages awaited his attention. Over the years, he'd lost contact with most of his comrades, but on occasion he received messages from Ernx and Nintal. The last time he'd seen his former squad members, Nintal had achieved the position of squadron leader. The navigator and his pilot were starting a new assignment on another flagship. Byron couldn't help but speculate about his own rank had he remained a Cosbolt pilot. Without his navigator, that would forever remain a mystery.

He noticed Mevine hovering outside the door. "You may enter," said Byron, opening his locker.

The thin door clattered against the wall and Byron reached for a flight suit. Only one suit remained, a testament to his lack of clean clothes. I need to bring my dirty laundry next trip, he thought, folding the suit over his arm.

Closing the door, Byron discovered Mevine peering at the photo by his computer. He'd forgotten the framed picture resided in plain sight. Byron hesitated, unsure how to respond to the situation. Mevine straightened his shoulders and glanced around the room. The young man's eyes fell on Byron and he snapped to attention.

"I'm sorry, sir, I was only looking," he said, his words tumbling across his tongue. "Is that, I mean, was that your navigator?"

Byron nodded. "Yes."

Mevine glanced again at the photo. "You were really young."

"That was taken on the Sorenthia, so I was probably a year or two younger than you are now."

Turning to face him, Mevine raised his chin. "He must've meant a lot to you."

Spoken in earnest, those words stirred Byron's emotions. His gaze traveled to the photo as he recalled the man who'd changed his life. His former navigator had believed in him until the end. He'd never find a friend like Bassa again.

"He was closer than a brother," he admitted.

"I'm sorry, sir," offered Mevine.

Sensing sympathy from the scientist, Byron cut off his thoughts and raised his personal shields. "Shall we go?" he said, gesturing toward the door.

The other shuttle returned as Byron was preparing to depart. He exchanged greetings with Garnce, but refrained from mentioning the passenger aboard his ship. The pilot complained that demanding science officers were cutting into his meals and Byron chuckled. Garnce deserved the aggravation.

In the co-pilot's seat, Mevine sighed. "Thank you again, sir," he said, brushing aside his unkempt hair.

"No problem," Byron replied, increasing speed as the ship left the hanger.

The lad sank further into his seat. "I wish I was closer to my brother," he said, fidgeting with his harness. "We don't have anything in common though."

"Is your brother military?"

"Oh no! He's a resident councilor, following in our father's footsteps."

Byron frowned. "Who's your father?"

"Chancellor Dentex."

Startled, he glanced at Mevine. "I didn't know you came from such a prestigious family," he said, surprised by Mevine's background. The boy didn't act like the son of a chancellor.

The young man shrugged. "I'm pretty much an outcast, so it doesn't do me a lot of good."

Byron pondered that thought as he tapped into the teleporter. A moment later, the blue skies of Tgren filled their view.

"Do you have any family?" Mevine asked, his eyes on Byron.

"Older sister. Haven't spoken to her in years," he answered curtly.

"No mate?'

"No time."

Mevine's head dropped against the seat. "I want a mate someday. Be nice to share my experiences with someone who cared."

Unable to respond to Mevine's candid admission, Byron guided the ship to the alien site in silence. Mevine thanked him for the ride before bounding out of the shuttle. Byron secured the hatch and returned to his seat. He stared at the controls, his mind replaying their exchange.

He'd never shared his experiences with anyone. Only his former navigator knew any of his inner thoughts. For six short months, Byron had enjoyed friendship with a man who believed in him to the very end. Like everyone else in his life who mattered, that person had vanished from his world.

Shaking his head, Byron reached for his harness. Annoyance rose in his chest for allowing Mevine's words to trigger such thoughts.

This is why I'm better off without friends, he thought as the shuttle left the ground.

One more jump.

Athee nodded, her hands curling around the armrests. She aligned her powers with Byron as they connected with the teleporter. Locking on to their destination, she waited for his signal.

Jump!

The stars vanished. Outside of the cockpit, clouds obscured their view. A moment later, the shuttle dropped and the ground became visible. Athee flashed him a triumphant grin.

"Yeah, you're getting good at this," Byron admitted.

Compliments from the Cassan pilot were rare and she beamed with pride. "Bet I could fly this thing, too."

Byron emitted a bark of laughter. "You think so?" he taunted.

"Yes, I do," she declared. "I've watched your actions every time we've flown. I can master the controls."

"Takes more than that to fly a shuttle."

Annoyed by his lack of confidence, Athee grabbed the throttle in front of her. "Let me try."

Glancing in her direction, Byron shook his head. "If you think I'm turning over my shuttle to an inexperienced pilot..."

"The master controls are right there in front of you."

"Yes, but..."

"And you can jump us out of trouble in the blink of an eye," she countered. "Unless you doubt your own abilities."

She perceived indignation in his thoughts and knew she'd struck a nerve. Confident to a fault, Byron resented any implication that he lacked skill as a pilot. He cast an irritated scowl Athee's direction.

"Damn you're annoying sometimes."

"Are you going to let me try?"

"And stubborn!" he added, shifting in his seat. "Fine, I'll let you fly the ship, but only for a moment."

Flying high above the mountains, Byron drilled her on control functions. She answered without hesitation, recalling the purpose of each gauge and button with accuracy. However, her precision frustrated him further. Athee couldn't understand why he was so irritated. Did he want his protégé to fail? Or was there another reason?

Before she could question his attitude, Byron instructed her to take the throttle. "Remember, it responds faster than your planes. Use a gentle touch and don't overcorrect."

Athee wrapped her fingers around the control, her hand barely large enough to grasp it in a proper manner. Feeling her adrenaline rise, she waited for his signal.

"We're level and steady," he announced. "Turning it over…now."

Byron tapped a button. The shuttle wobbled for a moment before Athee found her center. She leaned forward, eager to see the view outside the cockpit now that she controlled their direction.

"No, stay in your seat," he ordered. "A sharp bank and you'll be tossed, even with the harness on."

Nodding, she relaxed her posture. Athee grinned, delighting in the feel of the craft. Smooth as glass, the shuttle was the gentlest ship she'd ever flown. There was no rushing wind or rattling of bolts. The vessel glided with ease through the sky.

"Is it all right if I alter our course?" she asked.

"Remember, gentle touch."

Pulling the throttle a hair to the right, Athee felt the difference at once. The shuttle began banking to the right in a slow arc.

"She's so responsive!" Athee cried.

"This thing is sluggish compared to my Darten," Byron said, his tone no longer severe.

"I'd love to fly in one of your fighters," she mused, straightening the shuttle.

"One step at a time."

He allowed her several minutes of indulgence. Athee wanted to send the vessel into a tailspin, just to see how she'd respond, but refrained from such a reckless maneuver. Byron would never grant her permission to fly the shuttle again. As much as she enjoyed the experience, Athee wanted to repeat it again in the very near future.

The Cassan resumed full control, landing the shuttle with precision. His reaction to her desire to fly and her accurate recall of cockpit functions still puzzled Athee. She wanted to know why it seemed to annoy him. In truth, there were many questions she wanted to ask, both about the Cassans in general and about Byron in particular.

"So was my performance satisfactory?" she asked as he powered down the engines.

"For someone who's never flown a Cassan vessel?" he exclaimed, pressing a few more buttons before leaning back in his seat. "Yeah, you did all right."

Athee unfastened her harness and stretched her arms. It felt good to be free of the restrictive straps. Turning to Byron, she decided to seek the answers to her questions.

"Why did it bother you I knew the controls so well?" she demanded.

His gaze flicked her direction for a moment before his attention returned to the control panel. "It didn't bother me."

"Yes it did. I sensed your irritation loud and clear."

Her words elicited a concerned glance from the Cassan. "You shouldn't be able to pick up on this so quickly," he offered, checking the readout on the ship's screen.

"Because I'm a woman?"

"No, because you're a..."

"A Tgren? You really think so little of us?" she demanded.

Byron leaned back in his seat. "No, I just..." his voice trailed off, and the pilot raised a hand to his forehead. "I didn't expect to find anyone with your capabilities on this planet."

His last admission rang true in Athee's mind. Byron had answered honestly, and his reply made Athee feel better.

Something else had nagged at her thoughts ever since her first encounter with the Cassans, though. She decided now was a good time to ask.

"Why aren't there more women in your fleet?" she inquired, pivoting her chair to face Byron.

"Because Cassan women can't fold space."

His direct answer caught her off guard. "That's it?"

"Men possess the ability to teleport, women the ability to bond," he explained, unfastening his harness. "Space travel is hindered when one can't teleport, as many ships only use telepods for internal movement."

"Oh." The explanation was anticlimactic, but he'd offered a new snippet of information that intrigued her. "So, what does it mean to bond?"

Swiveling in his chair, Byron leaned forward. "When a man and woman make the decision to become mates, it is the woman who binds their minds together. Once bonded, they are mentally connected forever."

Athee's chest tightened with excitement. The idea of connecting with someone for life appealed to her. Now that she could communicate with her mind, the thought of a permanent link with another person was enchanting beyond words. What was it like? Was it as fulfilling as she imagined?

Did her instructor have the answers?

"Do you have a mate?" she said.

Despite his shielded mind, she interpreted surprise. "No, I don't," he answered, his eyes dropping to the floor.

"Is bonding one of my abilities?"

Byron raised his head at once, his mouth slightly ajar. She found it was moments like this, when he lacked restraint or control, that were the most revealing with regard to his personality. Athee liked Byron, but his cold indifference was a difficult obstacle to surmount.

"Yes, it is," he answered, his tone wary.

"So I possess both male and female abilities?" she said, her question more of a statement. "Is that what annoys you about me?"

Her question caught his attention. Byron locked his shields into place. "The strength of your powers doesn't bother me," he asserted.

Athee suspected that wasn't entirely true, but doubted she could force Byron to admit it. She decided on a new approach.

"Something makes you uncomfortable in my presence, though," she asserted. "I know I intimidate a lot of men, but someone of your status and ability shouldn't feel threatened."

Byron leaned back in his chair, his brows pulled together. "You ask too many questions."

"How can I learn if I don't ask?"

Rising to his feet, Byron stared down at Athee. "I like my privacy," he announced before retreating from the cockpit.

His statement left an icy chill in the air. Confounded by his refusal to talk, Athee rose to her feet. She stepped into the main hold, pausing to listen. Sound emanated from the rear of the ship. Aware she would get no further answers today from her Cassan trainer, she opened the hatch and exited the craft.

Numerous aircraft dotted the runway. Athee knew every plane by sight, and these were not familiar. Curious about their visitors, she entered the hanger. One of her uncle's guards approached and greeted Athee.

"The prefect has requested your presence," the man announced.

Athee followed the guard to his cart. She rode in silence, her mind mulling over her conversation with Byron. His final words still rang in her ears. At first she'd believed he was avoiding her question, but the more she pondered, Athee realized that was indeed his answer. It had nothing to do with her on a personal level. He just didn't enjoy sharing his time and personal space with another person.

He resents opening his mind more than anything, she thought, adjusting her position in the seat.

Arriving at the state building, the guard ushered her inside. He led Athee to the largest meeting room and several voices assaulted her senses. Stepping into the open doorway, she scanned those present. A dozen men, most dressed in fine clothing, stood around the oval table. Each deep in conversation with his closest neighbor, the men failed to notice her entrance. Peering around the nearest man, Athee caught sight of the prefect speaking with Commander Korden.

Uncle Orellen, you sent for me?

His head snapped around, causing his chin to jiggle. The prefect's eyes fell on Athee. His surprise gave way to a more serious expression and he called for order.

"Gentlemen! Before you depart, you must witness a demonstration of our potential future communications."

The prefect gestured toward Athee. Her muscles tightened as every head turned in her direction. Recognizing one of the men, she realized the prefects from the surrounding cities had gathered here today. The small crowd drew still and the dignitaries eyed her with expectancy. Feeling self-conscious, she placed her hands behind her back. Holding her breath, Athee waited for further instruction.

"My niece tested high for psychic ability and has been training with one of the Cassan officers," Orellen stated. "I want you all to bear witness to what may very well solve our communications dilemma."

Athee hesitated. Her uncle wanted her to speak using her mind, but she had no idea what to say, or if her words would be heard by untrained minds.

Start with your name and rank, Korden suggested.

Meeting the commander's gaze, she nodded. *I am Athee, daughter of Abemnent, and First Pilot of Ktren.*

There were gasps of astonishment across the room. Athee sensed a mixture of curiosity and fear among the visiting dignitaries. Several men began talking at once, demanding a full explanation. The prefect to her right expressed indignation, pointing at her in a threatening manner. Athee edged closer to the exit, the guard at her side. It was a moment before Orellen brought order to the room.

She was asked to speak several more times. Commander Korden's voice joined hers as he explained the advantages of telepathy, which silenced some of the protests. Listening to the exchange of words, Athee realized it was a continuation of an earlier discussion. As the conversation drew to a close, she hoped the other prefects had a better understanding of mental abilities after witnessing one of their own use the power. It would take more than one pilot's mental voice to convince them, though.

Orellen asked his niece to wait in his office. Relieved for an excuse to escape the negative energy permeating the room, Athee retreated to the other side of the building. Commander Korden's parting thoughts of encouragement raised her spirits a notch.

Her uncle's office sat in a rare state of organization. Even his desk was free of papers. She often busied herself with straightening Orellen's workspace; however, today that was not an option, as the task had already been completed.

Feeling restless, Athee wandered to the window, which offered a splendid view of the valley. She stared at the city and the landscape beyond the river. To her left, the mountain curved out of sight, eventually leading to the alien ruins. Ktren resided in a beautiful location, but Athee realized she'd outgrown the scenery and the narrow views of those inhabiting the city. After witnessing the reactions of those in the main council chamber, it was obvious those views were even more restricted outside of Ktren's boundaries.

"Fools," she muttered, crossing her arms.

With a loud creak, the door opened. Athee spun to face her uncle. He strode to his desk and dropped a large stack of papers on its surface. Resting one hand on his chair, Orellen rubbed his forehead. Straightening his shoulders, he turned to face his niece, his expression grim. Athee's fury renewed.

"Those men are idiots!" she declared, her arms dropping to her sides.

"They are also prefects," he reminded Athee.

"Why can't they see the value of telepathy?"

Orellen sighed and leaned against the desk, his hands gripping the edge with force. "Because telepathy is only one of many issues. The appearance of the Cassans has presented numerous difficulties. Add the potential threat of this alien technology and our own psychic ability, and it's simply too much for those men to handle."

"But it's the answer to communication problems," Athee cried, stepping closer.

Shaking his head, the prefect pulled aside his chair and sank to his seat. He pulled the stack of papers closer, his fingers pulling on the corner. "If only more of our people possessed your ability," Orellen stated, looking up at his niece.

"Officer Illenth continues to find others with traces of psychic ability," she offered, feeling hopeful. "He's working to entice telepathy from at least three men, and I'm sure there are more who possess that trait."

Her uncle leaned back in his chair. "Unfortunately, I can't pin all of our hopes on a possibility. Not when I am caught in the middle of a power struggle."

Concerned by the weight of those words, Athee approached her uncle. She rested a hand on his shoulder in an attempt to comfort the man. Orellen patted her hand and offered a weak smile.

"I still harbor doubts regarding these psychic abilities," he began, holding up a finger when Athee opened her mouth to protest. "They threaten to tear us apart even as the potential for unification appears."

Athee rested her hip on his desk as she swung around to face her uncle. "What do you mean?"

"The Cassans are superior to us in every fashion, no matter how hard we deny it. We've craved catching up to their technology even as they've denied us the opportunity. Tgren may possess compounds for their teleportation machines, but they do not consider us equal partners in any sense of the word.

"Until now," he declared, squeezing her hand. "You've proven that we can function on the same level as the Cassans, at least in terms of mental abilities. You are vital to the improvement of our alliance with their race. And, I get the impression from Commander Korden that you are important to the Cassans as well."

She cocked her head. "Because I can teleport?"

"Yes. You are valuable to both sides. If we can improve relations with the Cassans–which means all Tgren territories must be in agreement–I think there is great potential in such an alliance.

"In the meantime, I'm caught in the crossfire, with a potentially dangerous piece of alien technology residing in our mountain..."

"Then we need to try harder on all accounts," Athee declared, cutting off his digression.

Orellen smiled and pulled Athee's hands into his own. "You never give up, do you my dear?" he asked, a twinkle in his eye.

She grinned, aware of the source of her determination. Her uncle never admitted defeat under any circumstance. When he was alive, Athee's father never gave up either.

"Now, if you'll excuse me, I've a lot of work to do before dinner," the prefect announced, releasing her hands.

Athee leaned forward and gave her uncle a kiss on the cheek. Strolling toward the exit, she paused in the doorframe.

"You're not canceling the Hlerre Festival tomorrow night, are you?" she asked. The semi-annual event, held to give thanks for another season of prosperity, was one of her favorites.

"No," Orellen announced. "In fact, I've invited Commander Korden and his crew to join us for the celebration. Relations always seem to improve over food and spirits."

"And dancing!"

Her uncle's expression exhibited astonishment and Orellen set down the papers in his hand. "You don't intend to dance with the Cassan officers, do you?"

Athee winked. "Just one," she said, closing the door before her uncle could voice a protest.

The Hlerre Festival wasn't the largest of their celebrations, but it presented the most relaxed atmosphere. The formalities were brief, which meant more time for revelry. With good food and a variety of local spirits, inhibitions would lower as the evening progressed. Athee intended to take advantage of the situation and seek Byron's company. Surely, he couldn't maintain an air of professional detachment all night.

Maybe I'll finally see past that confounded shield of his, she thought.

Chapter Seven

Jump!

Outside, the stars vanished. Athee maintained her lock on the teleporter and their destination. The device hummed in her mind, charged by psychic energy of her own creation. On cue, the sky over Tgren appeared. Clutching the throttle tighter, Athee confirmed the shuttle's steady flight before glancing at Byron.

"Did I do it all?" she gasped, doubting what she'd just experienced.

"Yes, that was all you."

Athee let loose a jubilant cry. She confirmed their flight pattern before her gaze returned to her instructor. To her surprise, Byron grinned. His genuine pride in Athee's successful solo jump displayed not only in his eyes, but in his thoughts as well. It was a rare moment the reserved Cassan allowed any emotion to escape his mind. Athee felt privileged.

I felt your presence though, she thought, turning the shuttle on a gradual arc.

Just as a precaution. I am still responsible for your safety, Byron reminded her. *You had control of the ship and the teleporter, though.*

Was that the correct amount of power?

Yes.

She smiled, pleased with his assessment. Byron was the expert on the transference of mental energy into the teleporter; she was fortunate she shared his unique ability.

Who trained you? Athee thought, curious if his teacher also shared that trait.

My Cosbolt instructor and navigator.

A stray thought flickered through his mind, one Athee had caught during previous exchanges. *Bassa?* she asked, hoping she'd interpreted the name correctly. As if on cue, Byron's mind closed.

"Yes," he answered, shifting in his seat. "Now, let me guide you in landing this ship. It requires a smooth touch."

Together, they brought the ship down on the runway. Concentrating hard, Athee mimicked his moves. She observed with interest as he shut off the engines and essential system controls. Her plane boasted only a handful of gauges and switches, while the shuttle's entire control panel glowed with buttons, dials, and screens. It was a complex vessel, but Athee thought she could fly it in a pinch. Perhaps next time he would allow her to take off as well.

Byron released his harness, but made no move to rise from his seat. Athee realized his energy was waning and knew this was her window of opportunity.

"You're not missing the festival tonight, are you?" she asked, removing her harness and turning to face him.

He ran his fingers through his hair, frowning with annoyance as he pulled at the strands. "I'll be there," Byron answered, shaking his head. "Damn, one of these days I need to make time for a haircut."

The locks fell back into place. Parted in the middle, the tips touched the top of his cheekbones. In Athee's opinion, the thick strands framed his face well.

"I think you look fine for the festival," she assured Byron, rising to her feet. "Better get some rest, though."

"Why?"

"You'll need energy for dancing."

Leaning forward, Byron slowly rose to his feet. "Sorry, I've no experience with Tgren dance moves."

"I'll teach you."

He met her eyes, his expression reluctant. Athee funneled her energy into persuading Byron to dance with her tonight. He was aware of her manipulative powers and was likely to balk at her efforts. Athee had learned subtlety, though. She could mask her mental persuasions and move the wills of others without detection. In his exhausted state, Byron's mind was no match for hers.

"All right, one dance," he declared, his eyes narrowing. "I refuse to make a fool of myself, though."

"Would I allow you to look foolish?"

Athee exited the craft with an extra spring in her step. Persuading him to dance with her was a small victory. Tonight, she planned to accomplish even more.

Byron made a trip to the Rennather before the evening's festivities commenced. Several scientists accompanied him, including Mevine. Commander Korden had ordered everyone on Tgren to take a night off from their duties. The science officers had worked nonstop since their arrival, and the men were due for a break. Proper casual attire was required, as the men were to blend with the natives while still maintaining a certain level of professionalism. Judging from the prevailing odor in the shuttle's main cabin, Byron hoped that included a shower. No one would approach the science officers in their current condition.

Upon his return to the surface, Byron retreated to his quarters to change. Dressed in his finest tunic and pants, he emerged from the Cassan facility. The night air felt comfortable; devoid of the customary stifling heat. He took several deep breaths to clear his head. He had to remain in control tonight.

Following two junior officers to the festival, Byron entered Ktren's primary courtyard. The Tgrens had gone to great lengths decorating for the event. Flowers were strung on wires across the court, the thin cords twining around the light poles that dotted the main square. Vendors occupied the edges of the yard, taking advantage of the gathering crowd. Tables filled with local cuisine occupied the inner row of booths, free and available for consumption. Byron hoped the accompanying spirits were also free of charge. He wondered if he possessed anything of value to trade should he find payment was required.

Music filled the air and he noticed a group of musicians near the center of the square. At the moment, no dancers moved in rhythm to the beat. Hearing the complexity of the piece, Byron cringed. Why had he promised Athee a dance? He couldn't keep pace with the music, let alone manage unknown dance steps. His mind began to scheme ways in which to break their agreement.

The smell of food diverted Byron's attention. He approached the nearest table, laden with exotic fruit and vegetable dishes. An older woman beckoned him to try a bite. He sampled the dish with hesitation. The vegetables were sweet and he licked the spoon clean. Nodding to the woman, he waited while she filled a bowl. Thanking her for the food, he scanned the square for refreshments. Catching sight of Officer Illenth with a drink in his hand, he approached the man.

"Byron!" the psych officer called in greeting. "Glad you decided to join the festivities."

"I could hardly refuse Korden's order," Byron answered with a wry grin.

"And why would you want to?" Illenth demanded, holding up an overladen plate of food. "No one throws a party like the Tgrens."

"Well, all I need right now is a drink."

The man led Byron to another booth and he secured a glass of dark purple spirits. The fruity taste was more subtle than the smell, which threatened to overpower his senses. He decided it would suffice. Illenth moved through the gathering crowds and toward a string of tables. Over the commotion, Byron heard his name called. He caught sight of Mevine at one of the long tables. Indicating his choice to Illenth, they joined Mevine and another science officer.

"Have you tried the berry wine?" Mevine asked, holding up his glass. A small trace of red liquid remained. Judging from the lad's relaxed expression, it was not his first drink of the evening.

"I'll try it next," Byron answered, peering into his glass. "Not sure what I have now."

"It's made from rtrax," Illenth announced, holding up his drink. "A small, round fruit that grows near the river. It's a Tgren staple."

"You've been here a while," Byron observed, scooping a spoonful of vegetables into his mouth.

Illenth grinned. "I arrived here a week before the last Hlerre Festival. Tgren's the best assignment I've had in years."

Mevine finished his drink and rose from the table. "I need to try rtrax wine," he announced before scurrying away from the table. His rapid movement did little to hide his uneven gait.

Byron shook his head. Guess I better keep an eye on the boy, he thought.

He sampled two more dishes and a yellow bread that crumbled sweetly in his mouth. Byron located the source of Mevine's berry wine and sampled that brew as well. The young man's penchant for nervous chatter increased with each sip of his drink. The alcohol revealed a bolder side to Mevine. His antics amused rather than annoyed Byron. At least Mevine was a happy drunk. Garnce's negative and belligerent attitude grew even more unpleasant when he drank. Byron preferred to avoid the sour pilot tonight at all costs.

The music came to an abrupt halt. A voice over the crackling intercom system announced the arrival of the prefect. Byron glanced over his shoulder, mildly curious. He caught sight of the man as he entered the main square. Attired in elegant and regal clothing, Orellen was not alone. His son accompanied him, dressed in similar attire and strutting with his chin held high.

Unimpressed, Byron's attention shifted to the woman on the prefect's arm. His mouth fell open when he noticed a familiar trail of long hair. He pivoted in his seat to get a better view.

Clad in a bright red, sleeveless shirt and long, multi-colored skirt, he hardly recognized his protégé. Athee's hair was pulled away from her face and tied with red ribbons, the length of her tresses brought forward across one shoulder. Her gait was graceful as her uncle led her to the center of the square. Orellen faced his niece and the music began again in earnest. Istaner extended his hand to a young woman waiting at the edge of the square. The two couples began to dance while everyone else watched. Mesmerized by the change in the woman's appearance, Byron's eyes were on Athee as she danced with her uncle. She couldn't be the same person.

"It's tradition," said Illenth, breaking into his thoughts.

"What is?" Byron asked, glancing briefly at the man before his attention returned to the main square.

"The prefect and his family enjoy the first dance of the evening," the man explained, leaning closer. "The prefect normally dances with his wife. I guess Orellen began dancing with his niece after the death of his wife."

"From her thoughts, I perceive they are close."

"The prefect considers her part of the immediate family. Athee lost her father shortly after the prefect's wife died. I understand her mother died some years ago."

Byron shot Illenth a startled look. "I didn't realize both her parents were dead."

Illenth's brows came together. "You've been working with her for weeks now," the man stated, implying Byron should've known.

"I haven't delved that far into her mind."

If you're not connecting on all levels, then how do you know the full capacity of her abilities? Illenth thought, not bothering to conceal his stunned disbelief.

Remember, I can hear what others can't. I don't need to go deep to access her powers.

The man's brows remained furrowed. However, his answer apparently pacified the psychic officer. Illenth turned his attention to his glass, downing the last of his drink. Byron returned to observing the center court. He continued to follow the Tgren woman as she moved across the dance floor. He knew the extent of her abilities. Illenth might object to his lack of full connection, but Byron didn't need to dig deeper to know Athee's powers rivaled his own.

The music ended, eliciting a round of applause from those gathered. The prefect escorted Athee from the dance floor. Byron lost sight of them in the swirling crowd. He glanced at his companions and realized only Mevine remained at the table. The lad tipped back his glass and emptied its contents.

Better slow down, Byron thought, taking another sip of his wine.

Why? Am I drunk? Mevine thought, his eyes wide as disbelief resounded in Byron's head.

No, but you will be soon, and you're not sleeping it off in my quarters.

The dance square filled as the music began once more. Commander Korden stopped by their table, pleased to see the men enjoying their evening. Byron held his breath, worried Mevine's deteriorating condition would reveal itself in the boy's words or uninhibited mental transmissions. Somehow Mevine managed to shield his thoughts long enough to fool the commander, and Korden continued on to the next table. Byron permitted the young man to refill his drink with the promise that this glass would last more than ten minutes.

He'd just finished his wine and risen to his feet when Byron noticed Athee approaching. Their eyes met and her face lit up with joy. Feeling trapped, Byron set his empty glass on the table and waited. Athee stopped in front of him, a full glass of spirits in her hand.

"Enjoying the festival?" she asked.

"Yes, I am," he told her, his fingers on his empty glass. "Good food and good drink."

"Have you tried Jtal?" Athee said, holding up her glass.

"No, I haven't."

She held it out for him to sample and Byron hesitated. "I've not even had a sip yet," Athee promised. *And I assure you it's not poisoned.*

Byron took the glass from her hands and raised it to his lips. The difference in quality struck him immediately. This was the good stuff.

"Knew you'd like it," she said, retrieving her glass and setting it on the table. "Now, I believe you promised me a dance."

"One! And you better make me look good."

Athee's expression was one of amusement. Before she could respond, Mevine's voice broke into their conversation.

"Damn, have you tried the Jtal?" he gasped, coming to an abrupt halt at Byron's side. His eyes widened as Byron and Athee turned to face the young man.

"Officer Byron, I'm sorry," he stammered, his speech further impeded by his state of intoxication.

"That's all right, Mevine," Byron answered. "Can you watch Athee's drink while we dance?"

Mevine stood at attention, the movement causing the liquid in his glass to slop over the edge. "Yes, sir."

Byron let Athee lead him onto the dance floor. She positioned his hands and instructed him to follow her movements.

You taught me how to fly a shuttle, now I'll teach you how to dance.

Her comment elicited a smile from Byron. *Fair enough.*

The music began and she stepped to the left. He followed her movement, feeling self-conscious. Athee projected her next move, visualizing the steps in his mind. With that assistance, he mirrored her actions with more accuracy. Allowing her to guide him with her thoughts, Byron's confidence grew with each step. Smiling at his partner, he realized that she was grinning in return.

You don't feel foolish, do you? Athee thought.

Straightening his back to his full height, Byron eyed her with suspicion. *Not unless you intend to embarrass me.*

Not tonight anyway.

The tempo picked up and Byron was again forced to concentrate on her mental guidance. He followed Athee as they glided across the dance square, weaving around the other couples with ease. By the time the music stopped, he'd mastered the steps.

Offering a round of applause for the musician's skillful playing, they returned to the table. Mevine flashed Byron a foolish grin. Feeling strangely self-conscious, Byron avoided meeting his eyes. Athee retrieved her drink and cocked her head at Byron.

"Would you like a glass of Jtal?" she said.

Byron nodded and she pressed her drink into his hands. "Take mine. I'll get a fresh glass."

Before he could protest, she whirled away and vanished into the crowd. Sinking onto the bench, Byron took another sip. It was by far the best spirit of the evening, smooth and not too sweet. He wished he'd discovered it first.

Setting his glass on the table, he noticed Mevine staring at him. The young man grinned, mischievous thoughts dominating his mind.

"Is that the pilot you've been training?" he said, enunciating his words with care.

"Yes, that's Athee."

"You like her, don't you?"

Byron leaned his arm on the table. "Mevine, she's a Tgren."

"She's really pretty," the lad offered.

"She's also the prefect's niece," he said with exasperation.

"And she obviously likes you," Mevine countered, gesturing with a wide sweep of his arm.

Byron leaned away and grasped his glass. There was no arguing with the lad in his present condition, though he did ponder Mevine's observation. He'd not considered Athee's interest anything but a desire to satisfy her own curiosity regarding flying and her psychic abilities. If the intrigue extended beyond their professional relationship, Byron didn't want to encourage the situation.

Athee returned, a fresh drink in her hand. "Have you explored the booths around the courtyard?" When Byron shook his head, she extended her hand. "Let me point out the finer delights of Ktren then."

With reluctance, he accepted her hand and rose to his feet. Byron glanced at Mevine, reluctant to leave the young man alone. If he was to explore the grounds with Athee, he preferred an escort as well.

"Can you walk?" Byron asked, suppressing his skepticism.

Mevine arose, grasping the edge of the table to steady his actions. "I can walk," he declared, his fingers curling around what remained of his drink.

The men followed Athee as she led them around the courtyard. Byron had little use for possessions, but he feigned interest so as not to insult his Tgren hostess. Mevine's fascination seemed genuine and he asked questions at every booth. They stopped often to speak with others attending the festival. Many reflected intrigue at his choice of company, but no one questioned the pilot or Athee. Byron hoped to avoid an encounter with the prefect. The man would not approve of the Cassan occupying his niece's time.

They were drawing closer to the musicians when Erenta approached Athee. He exchanged pleasantries with Byron and Mevine before asking Athee to dance. She glanced at Byron and he gestured toward the center court.

"By all means, don't let me stop you," he said. Recalling Athee's previous comments concerning the young man, Byron doubted Erenta would hold her attention for long. She regarded her fellow pilot as a friend, nothing more. Judging from Erenta's eager expression, he still entertained hopes of changing her mind.

Byron and Mevine located a table and grabbed the remaining two seats. Scanning the revelers, Byron surmised the majority of Ktren's population was in attendance. A few Cassans were in evidence, clustered in small, segregated groups. He caught sight of Illenth, deep in conversation with a Tgren man, and admired the officer's ability to blend with the natives. After many months in the Tgren sunshine, he even looked like one of the locals.

"You're going to dance with Athee again, aren't you?" Mevine inquired.

Byron's attention shifted to the boy. "I only promised her one dance," he said, finishing his drink.

"Just one?"

Mevine's tone bordered on disrespect and Byron frowned, allowing his displeasure to project. At once he sensed regret in the lad's thoughts.

"Sir, I mean, you shouldn't waste the opportunity," Mevine stammered, sinking in his seat. "She's pretty. I'm sure many others are vying for her attention."

"I wish them luck then," Byron stated, choosing to let the young man's remark slide.

Athee returned without Erenta. She paused at Byron's side, as if expecting him to rise. He held his ground, staring at the Tgren woman in defiance. He desired another dance with her, but didn't want to give Athee the satisfaction.

Mevine suddenly rose to his feet. "Athee, I'm not very good, but I'd be honored to dance with you."

Flashing a smug grin at Byron, she nodded in acceptance. Showing amazing agility for one so full of spirits, Mevine grasped her hand and walked Athee onto the court.

Byron watched the couple with an interest that bordered on concern. Mevine was awkward with his steps and clung to Athee for balance. Irritation rose in his chest as he watched the Tgren woman dance with his young friend. Mevine's actions did not please Byron. He might not be willing to acknowledge her intrigue, but that didn't mean he wanted Mevine to show interest, either.

Uttering a bark of laughter, Byron reached for his empty glass. You fool, you're jealous, he thought, rising to seek a refill of his drink.

His mood was settled when the couple returned. *Point taken,* he thought in a private exchange with Mevine. *And dance with her again at your own risk.*

The young man heeded his warning and went in search of another drink. Athee continued to guide Byron around the vendor's booths, securing refills of their glasses after the second stall. Unlike the other beverages, Jtal was not free. The man serving drinks did not charge Athee or even ask for consideration. Byron decided there were advantages to her company.

The thought of enjoying more than free drinks also crossed his mind. If Mevine's assessment proved accurate, Byron could end the evening with some physical pleasure. His earlier misgivings were muted by the amount of wine now flowing through his system.

"Tell me more about your world," she said before taking a sip of her wine.

"What would you like to know?" Byron asked.

"Which of the two home worlds is yours?"

Her question surprised Byron. He didn't realize Tgrens had access to such information. Considering the amount of Tgren history contained in the databanks, it was only fair these people knew a little about the race now occupying their land.

"I grew up on Cassa."

Athee's puzzled expression caught his eye. Lips pressed together, she tilted her head.

"But is it home?"

Byron kept his gaze facing forward. "Not really. I've been back a few times, whenever the Rennather is on leave. Even spent some time on Harenna, Cassa's sister planet. But my home is on the Rennather."

"You feel at ease on a spaceship?"

"I've spent almost twenty-one years on a spaceship. It's comfortable."

Byron pressed closer to Athee as he allowed a group of Tgrens to pass. He sensed her enjoyment as their bodies touched. Byron realized that if he wanted anything to come of this evening, he needed to instigate some of the conversation.

"So, tell me about you," he said, clearing his throat. "What are your goals?"

Athee's smile encompassed her entire face. "I've always pushed myself to the limit, but after meeting your people, I realized those limits were very restrictive. Now that I know I have mental abilities, I want more. I want the opportunity to discover my potential... my real limits."

Flashing a wry grin, she winked.

I want to do what you do!

You want to explore the universe?

I do, but, she thought with hesitation, *more than that, I want to fly a fighter plane like yours.*

And I bet you'd make a damned fine pilot, Byron thought, shielding his assessment from Athee.

Her comment further solidified Byron's opinion of the female pilot and drew him closer. He remained with Athee all evening, and even allowed her to entice him onto the dance square on two more occasions.

The crowds had begun to disperse when Byron decided to call it a night. He realized he'd enjoyed himself this evening. Athee was interesting and knowledgeable. Byron had learned a great deal about Tgren and its customs during the course of the evening. Athee liked to talk, but it was not idle chatter or inane observations. Her words held purpose; a quality Byron appreciated.

The exchange with Mevine had run through his head the remainder of the evening. He'd hoped for some female companionship while on Tgren. Byron had not considered the prefect's niece a viable source–there were too many variables. He was there to train Athee, not court the woman. Korden would not approve and Orellen's reaction might involve a slow death. Despite his attraction to the young woman, the consequences were too great to risk involvement.

However, after a relaxing evening in her company, Byron's resolve to maintain distance began to slip. He felt comfortable in her presence. Adorned in feminine attire, Athee's curves certainly held his attention. As Mevine had observed, she liked him. Byron wanted nothing more than to take advantage of a desirable and willing partner.

"Were you staying?" he asked, shielding the true purpose of his question from Athee.

She glanced at the square, still bustling with people. "I would, but I imagine my flight instructor will want to start at our normal hour tomorrow."

"With a little effort, he might be persuaded to begin later than usual," Byron offered in a casual manner.

"Oh really? I thought he was a rock when it came to schedules and flying."

"He's not as strict as you think." Byron cocked his head and grinned. "Can I escort you home?"

Athee laughed and wrapped her hand around his arm. "Yes, you may."

They exited the square. Athee led him down a narrow street. Light posts dotted the roadways and hung over doorframes, but Byron could see without their assistance. Moonlight streamed down from above, casting its glow on the white surface of the stone buildings. With a few drinks in his system, the scene morphed into something surreal.

"Sure you'll be able to find your quarters again?"

"I've a good sense of direction."

Athee made conversation as they walked. Byron tried his best to focus on her words and form intelligent responses, but his thoughts drifted. His physical receptors were filled with her feminine presence. The fingers wrapped around his arm sent jolts of desire down his spine. Her scent, mixed with a trace of sweat, enticed him further. Byron's hopes for a satisfying end to the evening rose with each step as they drew near Athee's dwelling. If the flying lesson began late tomorrow morning, so be it.

They reached a row of single-level buildings. Athee paused at one of the many doors that dotted the walls. She turned to him and smiled.

"I enjoyed your company tonight," she said. Byron stepped closer.

"I've enjoyed yours."

He sensed her open thoughts of desire, which fueled his own. Athee rested a hand on his chest, her posture relaxed, but expectant. He grasped her elbow and she edged forward, chin held high. Her eyes sparkled with intensity as he leaned closer. Byron no longer cared about protocol or restraint. He wanted Athee.

A loud bark of laughter, followed by giggles, interrupted their moment. Byron glanced at the two revelers as they passed. The girl was a Tgren, but the young man was Cassan. The lad met his eyes, and Byron recognized the ensign at once.

"Officer Byron," the boy said in passing, ogling Athee. The girl on his arm grinned foolishly and giggled again.

The couple continued on their path. Byron's attention returned to Athee, and she moved closer. However, the sight of the ensign had dampened his spirits. How many men from the Rennather had witnessed their involvement tonight? He had monopolized Athee's time and left the festival in her company. If word got back to Commander Korden...

You idiot! You can't do this, he thought, releasing Athee's arm.

"I need to get back to the compound," he explained, placing some distance between them. "I'll see you in the morning."

Byron heard her disappointment and confusion pounding at his thoughts. Before she could voice a protest or question his actions, he retreated from the awkward scene. He did not slow his pace until he was within sight of the building that housed the Cassans. Byron felt relieved he'd escaped even as his male instincts protested his decision.

No, he thought, clenching his fists in frustration. Athee is off limits.

Entering the compound, Byron bounded up the stairs two at a time. He opened the first door on the left and entered his room. A single light burned from a tiny lamp by the bed. He surveyed the meager accommodations with disgust. He'd had the opportunity to sleep elsewhere and backed out due to fear.

Annoyed with the situation, Byron sank onto the small bed and rubbed his forehead. His entire body ached, and it wasn't from an overindulgence of wine. The pain irritated him, like a suit chaffing his skin. And it was more than a lack of physical satisfaction that bothered him. It was the feelings that now stirred in his chest.

Damn it, you can't get close to her, he thought. You can't get close to anyone!

Chapter Eight

"How do you feel today?"

Mevine glanced up from his work. His red eyes and pained expression indicated the Tgren wines had taken their toll on his body. Byron suspected his friend had indulged more than he was accustomed to at last night's festival, especially if he was still feeling the effects this late in the afternoon.

Mevine moaned and leaned back in his chair. "Awful," he admitted, his shoulders sagging. "Felt like I was going to die this morning."

Byron chuckled. "Maybe you should take it easy on the spirits next time."

Closing his eyes, Mevine nodded in acceptance. "I know. Last night I was just so nervous though. I'm really not good in social situations. Thought it would help me relax."

"You were relaxed all right. And bold!"

Mevine's face fell. "Sir, I'm sorry if I said or did anything inappropriate," he offered, his thoughts colored with genuine regret.

Moved by Mevine's forlorn expression, Byron patted his shoulder. "Don't worry about it." He glanced at the computer screen. "Making any progress?"

His question brightened the young man's mood. "Yes. I guess a night away from our research did some good. We've confirmed these ruins are the remains of an alien ship."

"Oh?"

"Whether it was originally housed in a cave or buried in a landslide, we don't know. But analysis of a full scan this morning revealed all the components of a spacecraft."

A functioning alien craft, Byron thought.

"And a breakthrough was made this morning with the language. Take a look."

Mevine pulled up a new screen. The Cassan alphabet was displayed on the left and the alien letters on the right. Several items were highlighted on each side of the equation.

"We've matched a dozen letters to our own, including four that Officer Seheller believes are vowels. Once we've matched a few more, we can begin deciphering the text."

"Looks like we're a few letters short," Byron observed, noting the abundance of letters on the right hand side of the screen.

"A few." Mevine glanced at Byron and his shoulders sagged. "All right, the alien text outnumbers our symbols three to one. But, we believe they're a variation in sound. Most of the symbols resemble nothing in our language, but the first batch we deciphered bore a strong resemblance. Hopefully, we can start transcribing the text by tomorrow. That is, if my head ever stops hurting," Mevine added, rubbing his forehead.

Byron suppressed his amusement. The boy was miserable enough. "Was it worth it, though?" he said.

"I guess," Mevine said with a shrug. He pivoted in his chair to face his visitor. "Did you have a good time?"

Leaning against the computer console, Byron crossed his arms. "I suppose I did," he admitted, his thoughts returning the evening's events. Could've been better, he thought, recalling the night's final moments.

Mevine managed a weak smile. "That Tgren woman really likes you."

"Oh, you think so?"

"You really should pursue her."

Byron shifted his position, uncomfortable with Mevine's suggestion. "Why are you so concerned with my personal life?" he inquired, trying to avoid a threatening tone.

"I think you'd benefit from some companionship," Mevine explained. "I mean, I wish someone was interested in me. I don't want to go through life alone."

Byron didn't need to sense the boy's dejection. He could see it in his eyes. Mevine's longing ran deep. A lack of family acceptance further compounded the issue. Taking into account Mevine's gangly appearance and absorption with his work,

Byron suspected no girl had ever given him a second glance. He felt sorry for the boy. A person could do far worse than befriend Mevine.

Shifting in his seat, Mevine shrugged. "I just figured someone should be happy," he mumbled, his eyes dropping to the floor.

Mustering strength he didn't feel, Byron moved closer. He placed a hand on the boy's shoulder. Mevine looked up and Byron offered a smile.

"Don't give up yet," he said, hoping to restore confidence in the young officer before he sank to an unreachable depth. Mevine sat up straighter and nodded. His thoughts still swirled with doubt, but desperation receded to the back of his mind.

"Mevine!"

The men turned toward the speaker. Officer Seheller gestured for Mevine to join him on the other side of the room. Byron's hand dropped and Mevine rose to his feet, his movement slow and deliberate. He opened his mouth, but Byron spoke first.

"I'll see you tomorrow," Byron announced, offering a brief nod.

Before he exited the room, Mevine's voice echoed in his head. *Thank you, sir.*

He paused in the wide doorway, but the young officer's attention was focused on Seheller. Glancing around, he noted a difference in the atmosphere since their arrival on Tgren. Filled to capacity with equipment and bodies, the room vibrated with energy. If they were as close to deciphering the alien text as Mevine boasted, those present had every reason to be excited. They were on the verge of a great discovery.

Byron continued on his way, his footsteps reverberating down the empty corridor. Few men remained outside in the heat. No one noticed his passage as he returned to the shuttle. He contemplated a trip to the Rennather. Options for entertainment on this planet were limited and his evening was devoid of a scheduled activity. An hour or two on the grav ball court sounded more appealing than wandering the city alone or sitting in his drab quarters at the Cassan facility.

Am I happy? Byron thought, staring at the shuttle's lifeless controls. He shook his head to clear his mind and started the ship's engines. Of course I am. Who wouldn't be happy in my situation?

Byron pushed the exchange with Mevine from his thoughts and lifted the shuttle into the sky.

"And then I turned around, and this damned fool was gone!"

Garnce pointed a thick finger at Byron. His tale amused the small group gathered in the Rennather's dining hall, but it was obvious the man still carried a grudge. Athee laughed, her attention shifting to the pilot. Byron's wicked grin indicated he had no regrets having left Garnce.

"I wasn't sticking around. Those Quintanaz felines were in heat."

Garnce scowled at Byron. "Well you didn't need to run off and leave me standing there defenseless," the man said with exasperation. "And you knew those plant samples we'd collected attracted them, too. Damned creatures followed me all the way back to camp, rubbing their foul stench on my legs."

Byron propped his elbow on the back of the chair beside him, his expression smug. "At least I didn't spend the next two days rubbing citric salt on my body to eradicate the smell."

"Stuff burned like fire, too," Garnce grumbled as he reached for his drink.

Athee cocked an eyebrow at Byron. "You're terrible."

"But at least I smelled good," he added, leaning away as Garnce raised a threatening hand.

The shuttle pilot declared he needed to return to the planet's surface. Garnce strode from the dining hall, his rapid movement mirroring his annoyed thoughts. Byron met Athee's gaze and offered a playful smirk.

"Guess I need to watch out for that mean streak of yours," she stated, leaning her elbows on the table.

"What he failed to describe was the three hours preceding our encounter with the felines. Garnce complained the whole time we were gathering those samples. I wanted to kill him at that point."

"And you never complain?"

"Not when it won't change anything."

She couldn't argue with that logic. Complaining grated on her nerves as well. Istaner voiced his negative opinion on a regular basis, finding fault with everyone but himself. Only their blood relationship had prevented Athee from retaliating with a tirade of her own.

When the dining hall emptied of occupants, Byron suggested they return to the shuttle and continue her lesson for the day. Athee had enjoyed the opportunity to eat a meal on the Rennather and listen to her tablemate's accounts of their travels. The world beyond Tgren seemed vast. She envied the Cassans their freedom to explore. Perhaps one day soon her people would take to the stars. She intended to lead the way, too.

Athee had enjoyed an hour with Byron in a relaxed atmosphere as well. It still hurt that he'd walked off the night of the festival, especially after showing such clear interest. Enticing him to talk about it was out of the question. Byron's shields had remained in place. He only lowered his mental barrier enough for minimal contact during jumps. Athee had buried her frustration and focused on her flights and psychic training with the Cassan. He remained friendly toward her, but Athee doubted she could coax him to such a level of intimacy again.

"Can I take the shuttle out of the hanger?" she asked, fastening her harness.

He eyed her with suspicion. Athee presented what she hoped was her most disarming smile. It often worked on her uncle even without mental persuasion. Byron hesitated and she thought she'd lost the battle until he offered a grin.

"Once we reach the outer landing bay, I'll turn the controls over to you. Sound fair?"

"Sounds fair to me."

The blast of a siren jolted Athee out of her seat. Red lights began to flash across the hanger, pulsating in sync with the siren. Byron cursed and unfastened his harness.

"Stay here," he ordered.

"What's happening?"

"Byron!" the commander's voice resonated from the shuttle's com unit. "We've got company. Five rogue ships just appeared on the starboard side."

The pilot leapt to his feet. "I'm heading for my Darten right now," he answered, dashing from the cockpit.

"Byron!" Athee called. He was already gone. *Rogue ships? Are we under attack?*

A distant rumble was followed at once by another. *That would be an affirmative. Stay put!*

Through the cockpit window, she watched him run across the hanger to his fighter. Two crewmembers were already attending his ship. Byron leapt into his Darten. The canopy slid into place and Byron secured his helmet. Yanking the steps out of the way, one of the men flashed the pilot a signal. The tiny ship rolled forward, moving toward the bay doors.

The siren continued to blare its warning and the noise pounded at Athee's chest. She had experienced an attack on Ktren several years ago, and fear had fueled her adrenaline. Once airborne, Athee had focused on the invading planes and maintained her composure even as her fellow pilots were shot from the sky. She'd controlled her fear by taking action. Unfortunately, she had no such recourse here.

Her pulse raced as Byron's ship vanished. The inner hanger doors closed, adding finality to the moment. Frustrated to lose sight of him, she unfastened her harness and reached for the com. Pressing buttons, she searched for the universal link. Athee had to know what was occurring beyond these walls.

Come on, come on! Where is it? she thought, growing frantic.

"We've confirmed hostile," a voice cried over the com and Athee jumped at the sound.

"Preparing to launch now," Byron replied, his voice unusually calm.

"Garnce has been notified and will join you shortly."

Biting her lip, Athee sank into the pilot seat to wait. She strummed her foot on the floor, anxious for a snippet of information. Several other voices came over the com, confirming the attack. Upon hearing a man state the shields were holding, she wondered what would happen if they failed. Would the Rennather explode?

"Engaging," said Byron, his voice clear over the com.

She listened as Anceptor announced the ship's guns had clipped the wings of one of the hostiles. Her palms began to sweat as she strained for Byron's voice. Could he handle four ships on his own?

"Two down," he announced.

Athee's stomach muscles relaxed. The odds were shifting in Byron's favor. Now if he could eliminate the last three ships...

"Damn it!"

Byron's exclamation jolted Athee out of her seat.

"Four more rogue ships, port side," Anceptor announced.

A rumble rolled over her head, punctuated by a second, louder sound. Athee grasped the edge of the console and peered up at the hanger's ceiling.

"Shields holding."

Athee caught her breath. She stared at the com unit, her heartbeat pounding in her ears.

"I'm hit!"

Those words poured like ice over Athee. Memories of her father's final flight raced through her mind.

"Status report."

There was a pause before Byron answered. "Another ship down. I can still fly, but I'm leaking fuel."

Athee leapt from her seat. Frustrated with her inability to see, as she didn't dare link with Byron while he was flying, she began to pace the cockpit. If we were on the ground, I could help, she thought, digging her nails into her palms.

Another voice confirmed the remaining five rogue ships were still attacking the Rennather. Rumbles echoed from the far side of the hanger, the sound penetrating the persistent siren. Athee paused and waited, her body shaking. If Byron died...

"Damn it, where is Garnce?" his angry voice blared over the com. "I need help!"

Athee couldn't remain idle any longer. Snapping into action, she closed the shuttle's hatch and slid into the pilot's seat. Punching several buttons, she fumbled to secure her harness as the ship's systems came online. She'd observed Byron dozens of times. While she didn't understand all of the controls, Athee knew how to power the shuttle. The vessel wasn't defenseless, either. She located the switch that activated the weapons, making a mental note for later. Taking a deep breath, she ignited the engines.

Glancing up from the controls, she caught sight of a crewmember waving his arms over her head. Athee chose to ignore the man and grasped the throttle. She had to help Byron.

"Who's piloting that shuttle?" a new voice demanded over the com. "Identify yourself."

"This is Athee," she answered. "Open the hanger doors."

"You are not authorized to fly that ship."

"Open the doors!" she screamed, pulling back on the throttle. The shuttle lifted from the hanger floor and she edged the craft in the direction of the exit.

"Athee, you are to power down immediately."

The sheer volume of the commander's voice caused her to jump. She stared at the com link, her hands trembling as she grasped the throttle. Athee was not bound by Cassan military law, but if she disobeyed the commander's orders, it might jeopardize their races' relationship. Did she dare risk destroying that fragile bond for one man?

"Damn it, I'm in trouble!" Byron cried in a desperate voice.

"Commander, I'm going out there to help him whether you like it or not," she responded, lifting the ship higher in the air. And if you won't open the doors, I'll find my own way off this ship.

"Athee, power down!"

Closing her eyes, she reached out to the shuttle's teleporter. The unit's hum vibrated in her chest. Athee latched on to its power. Edging the shuttle forward, she opened her eyes and visualized a spot outside the landing bay.

You can do this, Athee thought, the teleporter's energy crackling in her mind. *Jump!*

The hanger and flashing lights vanished. She found herself staring at stars. Throttling forward, she gained some speed and glanced at the radar. Several ships occupied the space over her head.

A jolt startled her and Athee grasped the console with her left hand. A ship shot overhead, its grey underside all but a blur. She pressed forward, determined to pursue the vessel.

Byron's presence filled her mind. *What are you doing?* he screamed.

I'm here to help you. Athee increased her speed to catch the rogue ship.

Damn it, get back to the Rennather now.

No!

Without warning, another ship came into view, headed straight for the shuttle. Athee thrust the throttle forward and dove, gasping as laser blasts flew over the ship.

Shields! Activate the shields.

Athee scanned the controls, terrified another ship would appear while her attention was diverted. She located the switch and engaged the shuttle's shields. Another blast jolted her from above. Uttering a gasp, she wrapped both hands around the throttle. She'd activated the shields just in time.

Head for the surface, ordered Byron. *Don't risk a jump though.*

Athee was about to protest when she interpreted his intentions. Glancing at the radar, she realized a ship was on her tail and closing the distance. Pressing downward, Athee wove the shuttle from side to side, hoping to confuse her attacker. A laser flashed past her ship and her heart missed a beat. She was losing ground...

The ship suddenly vanished from the radar. Athee noticed a second ship behind her and realized it was Byron.

Damn it, you're going to get yourself killed!

Athee pulled up on the throttle and changed direction. Her nerves tingled so hard that the hair on her arms stood erect. She was scared, but not about to give up on Byron.

You can't outrun them, he thought, his tone severe.

Then what can I do? Athee cried as she noticed two ships approaching.

The Darten shot across her field of view. *Distract them. Head into deep space.*

Obeying his command, she pushed the engines to maximum capacity. The rogue ships pursued the shuttle, drawing closer with each passing second. Byron stayed with her and she kept him in her sights on the radar. The Darten increased speed and shot across her canopy. Before Athee could react, the fighter vanished.

Her attention shifted to the radar. Byron's ship materialized behind the two ships. Athee yanked on the throttle and veered to the left to provide him a clean shot. When she looked at the radar again, both ships were gone.

Stay here, Byron thought.

Still shaking, Athee agreed. She rotated the shuttle to face the Rennather, determined to be ready if needed. Byron's Darten accelerated as it raced toward the ship. She could see the remaining three rogue ships firing at the craft, their laser blasts bright against the blackness of space.

Another ship became visible near the Darten. She gasped. Athee pressed on the throttle, propelling the ship forward. The vessel changed direction and Athee recognized the other shuttle.

About time! she thought, slowing her ship to gentle drift.

"Who's flying the other damn shuttle?" Garnce exclaimed over the com.

There was no verbal response, but Athee sensed Byron had relayed the identity of the occupant using his mental voice. Considering the fury that had consumed in his earlier thoughts, she was grateful to have missed that exchange.

Byron destroyed one more rogue before the remaining two ships beat a hasty retreat. He pursued them for a moment, his tiny fighter moving at top speed. The enemy vanished from view before he could catch them. Exhaling the breath she'd held for what seemed like hours, Athee slumped in her seat.

"What are you doing in that shuttle?" cried Garnce, his voice indignant over the com.

Athee straightened her posture and grasped the throttle. "Someone had to help Byron!" she charged, accelerating toward the Rennather.

The other shuttle circled closer. "You idiot! Do you even know what you're doing?" the man demanded.

"Garnce!"

Byron's angry retort silenced the man. Athee glanced at the radar and realized the Darten now flew below her.

"All ships, return to the Rennather at once!" bellowed Korden, his voice filled with fury.

"Garnce, help me guide her in," Byron said. The Darten swung out beside the shuttle. *Athee, can you land?*

Licking her lips, she focused on the approaching hanger entrance. *Yes, I can land the shuttle.*

Let Garnce guide you. Match his speed and trajectory.

The second shuttle moved into position on the other side. Keeping pace with the vessel, Athee guided the ship into the hanger. Their speed decreased and Byron's ship shot ahead of the shuttles. She felt a moment of panic as he raced toward the far wall. The Darten's runners touched the surface, reducing the headlong flight of the fighter. Athee had no time to contemplate his sudden stop as Garnce's ship dropped closer to the floor. Emulating his actions, she brought the shuttle to a hover in front of the first set of hanger doors. Once through both sets of doors, Athee returned the shuttle to its previous location and set the craft down with a gentle thump.

Athee attended to the systems, shutting down each one with care. The moment the cockpit fell silent, she slumped in her seat. Forcing her fingers to release the throttle, Athee stared at her trembling hand in disbelief. Jumping into the battle to help Byron had seemed like a good idea at the time. Now she realized the recklessness of her decision. She was lucky to be alive.

Open the door, Byron instructed.

The chill in his voice scared her worse than the rogue fighters. Fumbling with the harness, Athee rose to her feet. She stumbled to the hatch on shaky legs and pressed the button. Byron stood a few paces from the shuttle, body rigid and fists clenched by his sides. Eyes narrowed to mere slits, his scowled threatened to tear through her soul. Athee couldn't recall a time when he appeared more furious. And despite his habit of shielding, anger poured from his thoughts.

The commander wants to see us right now.

Without waiting for her answer, Byron strode toward the exit. Athee had to move fast to keep up with his long gait. She felt the presence of the crew as they walked across the hanger, but she kept her eyes averted. She refrained from speaking and shielded her thoughts.

Once they stepped into the telepod, Athee felt the need to say something. *Byron...*

Don't!

She glanced at him. His eyes remained forward and posture closed. Fury no longer emanated from his thoughts. In fact, she couldn't sense anything coming from the pilot. His mental shields were locked into place, sealing her from his mind. Feeling helpless, Athee shifted her gaze. She clenched her teeth in frustration.

They entered the commander's office and his disapproval slammed into her body like a physical blow. Korden rose from his chair, his dark eyes locked on Athee as she approached. She paused at a respectable distance and prepared for an uncomfortable scene.

"You were given orders to power down the shuttle," the commander stated in a voice that implied she was not to speak. "You do not possess the training or clearance to fly a Cassan ship. And yet you risked your life, and the lives of others, by teleporting the shuttle out of the hanger bay and engaging enemy fighters. You further risked my only fighter pilot in the process, not to mention the shuttle."

Athee held her own, but his tone sent chills down her spine. She wondered what her uncle would say when he heard about the incident.

The commander sat down. "I'd like to know how you learned to fly that shuttle in the first place," said Korden, his accusing eyes falling on Byron.

"Sir, I watched Officer Byron's actions every time we were in the shuttle," she offered in a quivering voice. Byron was already furious with her behavior. Athee didn't want to aggravate her instructor further by implicating his involvement.

The commander's attention returned to Athee and he hesitated, contemplating his next words with care. "Well, as of this moment, I am grounding you. No more training in our shuttle. You are not to set foot on a Cassan ship again. Do I make myself clear?"

Athee's heart sank as he spoke those words. "Yes, sir."

"You may possess unique skills, but that does not give you unlimited freedom on this ship. I don't care if you can teleport to the other side of Cassan space. I will not have you endangering my crew. Understood?"

"Yes, sir," she answered, her thoughts returning to her uncle. "Sir, will the prefect be notified of my actions?"

Korden leaned forward and scowled. "If your uncle knew what had transpired here today, it would jeopardize our races' relationship. I can't let the actions of one brash Tgren destroy everything we've worked so hard to build. The prefect will not be notified."

"Thank you, sir."

"Officer Byron, you will escort Athee to the surface at once. Any further psychic training will be performed on the ground, understood?"

"Yes, sir."

"Dismissed!"

Byron was silent as they returned to the shuttle. Athee tried to keep her emotions shielded, but the turbulence in her mind made it difficult. The commander's words still pressed against her chest. He'd called her to task for her rash behavior and revoked all privileges. The scolding was expected and the punishment just, but the loss of flights aboard the Cassan ship tore at her heart. She relished the hum of the teleporter in her mind. Now she'd never feel it again.

Several hanger personnel surrounded Byron's shuttle. He asked if there was any damage preventing a flight to the planet's surface.

"Cosmetic only, sir," the crewmember replied, patting the shuttle. "Just a score mark on the roof. All systems check out, though. She's good to fly."

Byron entered the ship and Athee followed. She almost ran into him when he stopped, his body blocking entrance to the cockpit.

"You're riding back here," he said, indicating the two rows of passenger seats.

Stung by his refusal to allow her in the cockpit, Athee dropped into the seat closest to the open hatch. Byron waited until her harness was secure before exiting the craft. Puzzled by his behavior, Athee leaned to her left and peered out the hatch. The pilot strode across the hanger to his Darten. Several crewmembers were examining the craft's exterior. A man with a computer pad approached Byron. They circled the ship and paused near the tail section. She recalled Byron's comment during battle that he was losing fuel. Even at that distance, Athee noted damage on the Darten's surface. His little fighter had taken a beating.

Byron took his time and Athee started to fidget. Her nerves had settled, but the confines of the harness caused her to grow restless. Leaning over to peer out again, she noticed Byron crossing the hanger. The pilot's long stride revealed his aggravation even more than the scowl on his face. Sitting straight in her seat, she waited quietly while he boarded and closed the hatch. Without even so much as a glance in her direction, Byron entered the cockpit. He prepared the shuttle for flight in silence.

Athee sensed the teleporter as they jumped. Her heart ached to share the experience; however, she didn't dare tap into the device. As the hum faded from her mind, she wondered if that wouldn't be the only thing now silent in her thoughts. What if Byron never spoke to her again? The commander forbade training on the shuttle, but what if the Cassan pilot ceased all psychic instruction? The loss of access to the teleporter now paled in comparison to the absence of Byron's voice in her head.

The shuttle came to a gentle rest and Byron shut off the engines. The absence of sound sent a shockwave through Athee's body. Fighting to control the emotions that swelled within, she unfastened the harness with trembling fingers. Free from the restraints, she leaned forward and stared at her shaking hands. Byron entered the main cabin and light flooded the shuttle as he opened the hatch. The finality of the moment was the crushing blow. Unable to hold back the tide, Athee covered her eyes and let out a sob.

She kept her tears brief. Aware that Byron continued to wait by the door, she lifted her head. His arms were crossed as he leaned against the wall of the shuttle, affecting an air of closed indifference. The pilot stared out the hatch and did not meet her eyes as Athee rose to her feet. Troubled by his lack of response, she made one last effort to reach out to the man.

"Byron..." she began, her voice cracking from the effort.

"We'll discuss it tomorrow," he answered, not bothering to turn his head.

Shoulders slumped in defeat, she moved toward the open hatch. Pausing at the open ramp, Athee glanced at Byron, but his eyes remained fixed on the open desert beyond the runway. Grasping the frame of the hatch, she lowered her chin in shame.

"I couldn't just sit there and listen to you die," she whispered.

Athee didn't wait for a response. There wouldn't be one anyway. Bolting down the ramp, she trotted across the runway and into the closest hanger. Athee ignored those she passed, too caught up in her own agonizing thoughts. She'd lost an incredible opportunity, although it paled next to the possible outcome of today's battle.

I didn't want to lose you as well, Athee thought, muffling a sob as she ducked out of the hanger.

Chapter Nine

Feeling better after an hour on the grav court, Byron retreated to his quarters. He wanted to enjoy a meal on board the Rennather before returning to Tgren. After yesterday's incident, he was in no hurry to depart either. What awaited him on the planet only represented more stress.

He was finishing his meal when Korden requested his presence. Byron wondered if the commander wanted to discuss Athee's reckless shuttle flight in detail. He prepared his thoughts for such a conversation. After a good night's sleep, he felt rational and able to converse on the subject.

Korden was on his feet when he arrived, and Byron remained standing. "You wanted to see me, sir?"

"Yes," the commander answered, setting his computer pad on the desk. "The crew chief informed me that he may not be able to repair your Darten."

Byron nodded. "I spent several hours with him this morning, assisting with the repairs. The real issue is the fuel tank and our lack of proper replacement parts on board."

Korden's eyebrows rose. "That type of damage usually results in a large explosion and a short memorial," he offered in a fatherly tone. "You were damned lucky yesterday, Byron."

Garnce should've moved his ass faster, Byron thought, shielding his accusation from the commander. Shifting the blame to his fellow pilot would not fix his ship.

"And you weren't the only one," the commander added.

"Sir, I apologize for leaving her in the cockpit when those ships attacked," Byron announced, prepared to accept full responsibility. At least Athee had hidden the source of her extensive flying knowledge. "I had no idea she'd do something so stupid."

"The problem is that we've allowed her too many liberties," said Korden, sinking into his chair. "Damn, she teleported right out of the hanger bay. Not sure if I'd credit that to exceptional talent or blind luck."

"It won't happen again, sir."

"No, it won't." Folding his hands in his lap, Korden regarded Byron with curiosity. "Have you discussed this incident with her?"

"No sir, I was too angry yesterday," he answered, recalling the fury that gripped him when the shuttle materialized outside the open bay. "I didn't say a word to her."

"I suggest you find time to discuss it today. She needs to understand the dangers involved. Athee's still too valuable to risk, even for someone like yourself."

The commander's choice of words puzzled him. "I'm not sure I follow, sir."

"Chancellor Dentex has taken a special interest in Athee. Our instructions are to keep this woman safe. If we can persuade her to return with us to Cassa, along with any others who show strong psychic aptitude, then it would provide proof that not only do Tgrens possess equal powers, but that dormant abilities might lie within our people as well."

Byron shifted his stance. "Her uncle would never agree to that," he said in a low voice.

Korden's eyes narrowed. "You let me worry about Orellen. You maintain communication with that Tgren woman, understood? Keep her close and involved."

Byron struggled to keep from laughing. "Sir, are you suggesting I build a relationship with the woman?"

"No, I'm suggesting you maintain that relationship, Byron. Right now, she'd follow you anywhere. Don't blow it!"

The commander's orders gnawed at his thoughts all the way to the planet's surface. He'd held Athee at a distance under the guise of maintaining a professional relationship. Now the commander wanted him to pursue further involvement. What excuse could he use now to prevent mental contact? And what did the commander mean when he said Athee would follow him anywhere?

Damn it, you don't need this in your life right now, Byron thought as he landed the shuttle.

He entered the hanger at a rapid pace. Out of the corner of his eye, he spotted a familiar figure standing in the shadows to his left. Surprised to find Athee waiting, he moved closer and grasped the edge of the hanger door. Now that he was in her presence, Byron had no idea what to say.

Athee crossed her arms and shifted her weight. "I didn't know if we were cancelling this afternoon's session, too," she explained, her voice low.

"No, just this morning's flight training. I had work to do aboard the Rennather."

She nodded. "What else can you teach me?"

"We can continue fine-tuning the skills you possess," Byron offered.

He spied several crates stacked against the wall. Indicating his preference, Byron waited until Athee was seated before selecting a crate opposite the woman. He told Athee they would continue practicing the relay of information through images. Considering her lack of words this afternoon, Byron felt it a wise choice.

After fifteen minutes of fumbling, he realized her heart was not in the exercise. Her shields were locked so tight that it was difficult to connect on any level. Leaning back, he propped an arm up on a tall crate and stared at her in exasperation. Athee met his gaze for a moment and then glanced away, her head down. Byron decided it was futile to persist with the session while she remained in this state of mind.

"You want to talk about yesterday?" he said, a hint of reluctance in his voice. "All right, you start."

Her mouth opened and she stared at him. Eyes dropping, Athee crossed her arms across her chest.

"Byron, I'm sorry," she whispered. "I just wanted to help you."

"By jumping the shuttle into battle when you barely know how to fly?"

"I know it was foolish. But I couldn't simply sit there and do nothing. Not while you were in danger. I felt helpless and it was tearing me up!"

Athee's short verbal burst caused her shields to falter. He perceived her agony and fear. Fueling those feelings was something even stronger. It was the deeper emotional current that caused him to pause. He couldn't ignore the real reason for her rash actions. Rubbing his forehead, he lowered his head and closed his eyes. Byron considered his next words with care.

"And do you have any idea what it felt like to see your shuttle appear? And to see two rogue ships pursue it at once?" Byron dropped his hand, the sight still fresh in his thoughts. "I thought for sure you were dead."

She shifted on her crate. He opened his eyes and she leaned a little closer. Athee's fearful thoughts began to settle.

"Damn it, you're important to a lot of people. Your powers are vital to the development of your people, not to mention your relationship with us. Losing you now would be detrimental."

He sensed only emptiness within Athee. His words brought no comfort. Reaching deep for the strength to disclose his feelings, Byron cleared his throat.

"And you're important to me."

A spike of emotions shot from Athee before she suppressed the energy. Byron lifted his chin and noted the look of surprise on her face. However, more than astonishment radiated from her thoughts; he sensed relief and validation.

"You're important to me, too," Athee said in a hushed tone.

She stretched out her arm, and her fingers grasped his hand. He allowed their fingers to intertwine, aware Athee needed physical contact. The glow returned to her eyes and a smile crept across her face. Feeling the genuine affection in her touch and thoughts, Byron permitted a grin to tug at his lips. Their exchange subdued his remaining traces of anger regarding the incident with the shuttle, and it receded to the depths of his mind.

Feeling vulnerable from their brief moment of candor, he patted her hand and released it. Leaning back, he noticed two engineers milling around the far hanger entrance. Their current location provided little privacy. Byron sighed and redirected his attention back to Athee.

"Sorry we can't use my shuttle," he said.

Athee pressed her lips into a thin line and nodded. "I'm not supposed to step aboard a Cassan vessel."

"Yes, and for good reason."

Her chin dropped. Guilt radiated from her thoughts, and he regretted his harsh words.

"I'm going to miss flying with you, too," Byron admitted, his eyes on his hands as he rubbed them together.

"We can still fly together."

"How?"

Athee's smile returned. "You forget I'm a pilot with a ship, too."

Byron laughed. "I wouldn't call it a ship."

Her palm came down with force on his thigh. Byron exclaimed aloud at the vigorous snap. He stared at her in surprise. Athee's eyes narrowed and she pointed a finger at her instructor.

"You've never flown with me in my fighter."

"No, I haven't."

"You got to show off your Darten. It's time I got to demonstrate my abilities in a Tgren fighter."

Byron stared at her in disbelief. Athee grasped his hand and leapt to her feet. Dragging Byron behind her, she led him from the main hanger to a smaller one further down the flight strip. He eyed the small planes that filled the hanger with trepidation. Athee rummaged through a row of beaten lockers. She pulled out a leather flight cap similar to her own. Twirling it once on her finger, she tossed it to Byron.

"I don't think this will really help if we crash," he teased, pulling the flimsy cap over his head.

Athee ignored his comment. She strode to a plane in the first row, running her hand across the nose. She opened the door and gestured toward the space behind the pilot's seat. "Get in."

Byron approached the plane and glanced at the small space. "It's not even a real seat," he protested, flashing a look of defiance.

"It'll do," she snapped. "Besides, I've carried passengers before."

"Did they live?"

Athee placed her hand on his shoulder and gave Byron a shove. Feeling apprehensive, he pulled his body into the cramped quarters behind the pilot's seat. His torso fit, but he was at a loss when it came to his long legs. Athee pulled herself into the seat, facing Byron, and grabbed one of his feet from the side. Forcing him to extend his legs, she pulled each foot forward and rested it on the edge of her seat. Turning to face the nose of the plane, she settled in her seat. With great force, she slammed the door.

Byron wiggled his body, adjusting his position. He could either lean all the way back, which cramped his neck, or lean forward and grasp Athee's seat. Choosing the latter, he braced himself as she started the engine.

"I'm going to die back here, aren't I?"

"Keep asking me that and I might consider it," she said as the plane rolled out of the hanger.

Recalling his first experience in a Tgren plane, Byron braced himself for a bumpy ride. Athee kept the jostling to a minimum as the craft raced down the runway. The nose edged skyward and he dug his fingers into the seat cushion as the tiny plane surged into the sky. The sound of wind whistling under the wings began to drown out the noise from the engines, but neither covered Athee's mental cry of joy as the plane soared over the valley.

Any planes in the air this afternoon? Byron thought, scanning the skies.

Two are patrolling south of our position, so we'll head north. The plane tilted to their right as she changed heading. *Maybe I can show you a portion of our world you've not seen yet.*

The craft continued to rise in altitude. Athee leveled the plane and Byron felt the difference in wind pressure at once. She'd risen above the stronger currents that buffeted the afternoon air every day. Her equipment might lack in quality, but Athee was a skilled pilot.

How long have you been flying? Byron asked, easing his hold on her seat.

Solo? Since I was sixteen. My father taught me the basics. He took me out every day, just the two of us, Athee thought, a hint of melancholy in her mental voice

An earlier comment from Illenth resurfaced in his mind. *Your father's gone, isn't he?*

Yes. He was killed during the Bshen War, she thought, glancing back at her passenger. Byron's position behind her seat placed his head to the side of hers, and he caught Athee's controlled expression. *The Bshens reside across the great lake. They attacked several of our neighbors before invading our land. We beat them back, but many lost their lives, including my father.*

I'm sorry.

Me too. I miss my father. However, he did inspire me to become a pilot. I joined the air regiment shortly after his death and was flying solo within a few months. It's all I've ever wanted to do.

All I ever wanted to do as well, Byron thought, peering out the window.

Athee shifted in her seat. He sensed her mood alter as well. Byron noticed several rows of low mountains in the distance and realized that was her destination. On cue, the plane began to descend. She lined their approach with the first narrow valley.

Time for some fun! she cried, increasing the plane's speed.

The uneven mountaintops rose at an alarming speed and Byron gripped her seat even tighter. The engines screamed as she darted into the valley, the left wing tip reaching out to touch the red rock. Tilting the plane, Athee raced through the narrow passage at an angle. Feeling his body slide, Byron's right arm braced against the craft's interior. He held his breath as the scenery raced by at frightening pace.

The plane edged skyward. It shot out of the canyon at great speed. Athee leveled their flight and continued to glide over the jagged cliffs. Byron altered his position in the makeshift seat. He realized his heart now pounded in his ears.

Scared? Athee thought, her tone smug.

He was not about to give her the satisfaction and shook his head. *Now I know why I'm not a navigator. I prefer to be in control of my destiny.*

She laughed and guided the plane's course for another run through the mountains. Peering over Athee's shoulder, Byron noted the narrow valley approaching. A second blind run did not sound appealing. Clutching her seat, he reached out and touched his pilot's mind. Athee permitted Byron access to her thoughts without inhibition. Projecting her intentions, she pressed the throttle forward and dove.

Tilting on a sharp axis, the tiny plane slipped between the rocks. Curving to the right, Athee followed the course of the valley. The rough outcroppings raced overhead in a flash of dusty red as the vessel angled on its side. Byron caught a twist to the left in her mind before the curve of the mountain and prepared himself. The passageway narrowed and Athee dropped even closer to the ground. The sky vanished as the plane hugged the contour of the landscape. Caught up in the thrill, Byron's adrenaline levels accelerated to match hers, fueling the excitement further. For a brief moment, their minds locked in the ecstasy of flight.

Rounding a final curve, the tiny plane began to rise. The cloudless sky came into view once more as the craft climbed. It burst from the confines of the mountains and the cockpit filled with rays of sunshine. Athee released an exclamation of joy that was seconded by Byron.

Now that was some fine flying! he thought, impressed by Athee's adept handling of the craft. Viewing their tight run through her eyes was far more enjoyable than flying blind.

Thank you. She may not compare to your Darten, but this little plane is capable of more than you realize.

Byron's thoughts returned to his damaged fighter. *Well, right now my Darten isn't capable of flying anywhere.*

She's out of commission?

I'm afraid so. I'll have to use the shuttle for tomorrow's lesson.

I'm sorry.

Byron leaned back and peered out the side window. *I still have a few tricks. Don't think you're getting off easy tomorrow.*

Oh yeah? Athee retorted. *Well, don't think you're getting off easy, either. Hang on!*

His stomach lurched as the plane rolled to the left. Byron's fingers dug into Athee's seat again as the plane continued to spiral. With great force, his center of gravity shifted. Before he could voice a protest, the craft completed its rotation and resumed a level flight. Athee laughed at his disorientation.

You think that was funny? Byron demanded, reaching around the seat. He wrapped his arm about her waist. She laughed again, undeterred by his threatening tone. Realizing she could still hear his thoughts, which were anything but hostile. Byron gave her midsection a quick squeeze.

Just wait until tomorrow! I'm giving you my worst.

Athee's laughter indicated his threat didn't scare her. Byron shook his head, but did not remove his arm. Judging from her pleased thoughts, she didn't object to the physical contact.

Like you couldn't handle my worst anyway, he thought. In or out of the cockpit!

Chapter Ten

Athee strode toward the hanger, her eyes on the two pilots several steps ahead of her. Istaner might think his hushed tones would avoid detection, but she sensed the man's indignation with today's lesson. A wicked grin crossed her lips. Byron had warned Athee he still possessed a few tricks. Implementing several new maneuvers this week, he'd revealed weaknesses in more than one pilot. To her credit, she was not one of them.

Pausing at the hanger entrance, she waited for Byron. He approached with his shoulders back and a smirk on his face. Athee placed a hand on her hip and fixed him with an accusatory stare.

"Feel better now?"

Byron stopped and glanced past Athee. His thoughts now matched his triumphant grin. The combination amused her.

"Your cousin needed to be taken down a couple notches," he answered.

She shook her head. A strong breeze pulled the hair away from her face. She gazed at the gathering clouds and frowned.

"Glad we flew this morning," she observed. "Thunderstorms are rolling in. Always makes for dangerous flying."

Byron peered at the horizon. "Maybe it'll settle some the damned dust. I swear I'm going to take half of Tgren's sand home with me in the shuttle. Why couldn't your people settle in a temperate climate instead?"

Indignant, Athee twisted around to face her instructor and prepared to counter his remark. A distant rumble caught her attention. They turned toward the mountain.

"That wasn't thunder," she said, puzzled by the sound.

They stared in silence, waiting for the source of the noise to reveal itself. Movement caught Athee's eye and a thin cloud of dark smoke twisted into the sky.

"No, that came from the alien ruins!" Byron gasped.

He began to run for his shuttle. Without hesitation, Athee followed. Their boots pounded the pavement in rhythm and fear rose in her chest. Had the cave collapsed? Dozens of people were working inside.

They reached the ship and Byron grabbed her arm. "You shouldn't come with me," he said as the hatch opened.

"We're just flying to the ruins," she protested, recalling Korden's orders. "Damn it, those are my people up there, too!"

"Come on then."

She scrambled aboard and Byron secured the hatch with haste. He offered no protest when she strapped herself into the co-pilot's seat. He ran through the systems at record speed and lifted the shuttle into the air. Athee heard the internal hum of the teleporter. On cue, the view outside the cockpit changed. She gasped at the sight of black smoke pouring out of the cave. A collapsed tunnel did not form that dense of a cloud.

"Medical kit and masks," Byron instructed, flashing a visual of their location. He punched the com button on the console. "Rennather, we have an explosion at the alien site."

Athee unfastened her harness and raced to the back of the shuttle. She staggered off balance as Byron set the ship on the ground in a hasty landing. Grasping the wall, she reached for the button. A small compartment opened. Extracting the medical bag first, she set it on the floor. Athee reached for the masks in the back. Byron joined her and grabbed the medical kit.

Masks on before entering the cave, he instructed, taking one of the masks. *And let me go first.*

Athee nodded and followed him out of the shuttle. They ran up the short incline and were met by a Tgren man.

"There was an explosion," he cried, running alongside Byron and Athee. "The others went in to help."

"How many are inside?" asked Byron, slowing his pace as he adjusted the mask.

"At least twenty."

Byron cursed and pulled the mask over his face. Athee fumbled with hers for a moment, yanking on the wide straps. Byron snatched it from her hands. He placed it on her face, tugging to secure it to her head. He nodded and moved toward the cave's entrance.

I'd tell you to wait, but I know you'd refuse. Just stay behind me.

Stepping into the smoke, Athee found her vision impaired by the swirling black soot. The lights strung down the tunnel offered little illumination. She reached out with her fingertips, fearful of running into a wall. A hand grasped hers and a soft glow appeared. Athee realized Byron held a small, portable light. The beam cut through the gloom and he moved forward, his hand holding hers fast.

They moved with care, but the floor was clear of debris. *Explosion must've occurred within the main chamber,* Byron thought. *Damn it, we've got to reach them.*

Athee picked up on his fear as an image of a young man flashed in his mind. *Your friend?* she asked, increasing her pace to keep up with his long strides.

Yes, Mevine!

Athee heard a noise ahead, followed by a hoarse voice offering encouragement. Byron paused as several men approached and held the light above his head. Two of the men were injured and one dangled from the shoulders of another, his clothes splashed with blood.

"There's more injured," one man announced, his voice muffled under the mask.

The moment they had passed, Byron yanked on Athee's hand, pulling her forward. At the entrance to the alien ruins, they met two more men carrying the lifeless body of a third. His hand tightened around hers as Byron paused again, holding the light on the procession as it passed. The man's injuries prevented identification, especially in the swirling black smoke, but the dark skin and hair revealed his Tgren origin. Athee gasped and stepped forward.

They can tend to him, Byron thought, tugging on her hand. *We've got to get everyone outside before another explosion collapses the tunnel.*

Two more groups passed as they made their way to the main chamber, and Byron hesitated each time. His friend was not among the injured. Athee sensed Byron's growing urgency and stuck close to him. She was troubled by the uncharacteristic display of emotion from the otherwise stoic Cassan. Athee had begun to doubt his ability to care, but his concern for Mevine's safety broadcast urgently from his thoughts.

They reached the entrance to the control center. The thick smoke poured from the room and it was difficult to see more than few feet ahead. She clung to Byron lest they became separated in the darkness. Athee could just make out the orb in the center of the room. The bursts of light were gone and it now lay shrouded in darkness. The hum of machinery no longer vibrated the air. All of the alien equipment appeared dark, the multitude of lights gone. Athee shuddered at the lifeless scene.

Several lights flashed around the chamber. Loud, urgent voices reached her ears. Athee's fingers gripped Byron's tighter as the smell of death reached her nose even through her mask. Someone to her left moaned and coughed. Byron kept moving forward, his mind focused on one thing.

Mevine, he cried, his thoughts unshielded in an attempt to locate the man. *Mevine!*

A cry of pain distracted her. Athee almost tripped over a piece of equipment when Byron released her hand. Desperate not to lose him, she followed the bobbing light with outstretched hands. Grasping a solid structure, she propelled herself forward and discovered Byron bent over the slight frame of a young man. Athee dropped to her knees at his side.

Mevine! he thought, his hands grasping the inert figure. Blood poured from a gash in the man's head and another on his arm.

A moan followed by a shuffling behind them caught Athee's attention. Glancing toward the sound, she discovered a Cassan sporting a similar facemask endeavoring to lift a figure covered in blood. She reached out to assist as he pushed the man into a sitting position. The Cassan attempted to wrap his arm around the figure, struggling to maintain his grasp.

Byron? she thought, unsure whom to help first.

I can carry Mevine, he announced. *Assist that man and stay close to me.*

Athee slipped her arm around the injured man and nodded at the Cassan. Together, they rose to their feet.

"Grab his leg. It'll be easier to carry rather than drag him," the man instructed, his voice loud despite the mask.

She struggled a moment before securing a hold. Glancing up, she noticed Byron awaited them, the thick smoke curling around his tall frame. Mevine's motionless body hung from his arms.

Come on.

She sensed the pilot's impatience as they stumbled down the corridor, but Byron remained only a few steps ahead. They followed his bobbing light into the tunnel, passing several men on their way into the structure. Athee grasped the man's legs even tighter, fearful she'd drop him. Byron's urgent thoughts kept her moving, and at last they emerged from the cave.

Out in the open, Byron moved with rapid steps down the embankment. He deposited Mevine's body on the soft sand. Athee guided the man in the same direction and they all but dropped their burden beside Byron's friend. In the light, the gaping hole in the man's chest became apparent at the same time Athee realized he was a Tgren. She turned at once to Byron and found him digging through the medical kit. He ripped the mask from his face in frustration. Scowling, Byron extracted several pieces of gauze and a water bottle.

"Here," he said, pushing the bag her direction.

Athee found a large strip of gauze among the items. She pressed it over the man's wound. The other man pulled aside his mask and reached for the bag. He produced a small compress and handed it to Athee, gesturing toward the man's bleeding shoulder. She covered that wound and he took over applying pressure to the man's chest. Feeling the man's neck for a pulse, Athee realized he was indeed still alive. If he didn't receive medical attention soon, though, the man would die from his injuries.

Realizing her mask was still in place, she wrestled it from her head. Tossing it aside, she glanced at Byron. One hand wrapped gauze around his friend's arm while the other pressed a damp compress on the man's head.

Come on, Mevine. Wake up! he pleaded, his mental voice urgent.

Athee observed with fearful fascination, moved by the genuine concern on Byron's face. He continued to plead with his friend, prompting Mevine to respond. Staring hard at his dirty face, Athee detected movement under the young man's eyelids.

He's coming to, she thought.

Mevine, answer me! Byron begged.

The young man moaned. He tried to raise his injured arm. Byron restrained him and Mevine opened his eyes. He blinked several times, puzzled to see the pilot.

"Officer Byron?" he murmured.

"Don't try to talk," ordered Byron, dabbing at the gash on his head. "You're safe now."

Mevine coughed and raised his free hand to his face. He gasped once and then fell into a coughing fit.

"Come on, can you sit up?" Byron said, placing a hand behind his neck.

Athee reached over and helped push Mevine into a sitting position. The young man coughed a few more times before his breathing settled into a raspy rhythm. He rubbed his forehead, smearing the black smudges on his face.

"Here, try a drink of water," Byron suggested, holding up the bottle.

A loud voice caught Athee's attention and she tried to locate the speaker. The scene was total chaos. The area outside the cave entrance lay littered with injured men. With her mask removed, she could smell the acrid smoke as it continued to drift from the cave. Those with fewer or no injuries attended to the men in dire need of medical assistance. In the confusion, it was impossible to tell how many remained inside.

Her gaze returned to the Tgren. His chest wound had soaked several layers of bandages. Athee didn't know him, but her heart went out to the man. She adjusted her hold on his shoulder, determined to stop at least one source of his blood loss. Beside her, Byron coaxed Mevine to lie down again.

"Just relax," he ordered.

Byron placed the young man's good hand over the gauze on his arm. He poured a little water over Mevine's head wound and applied pressure again.

"There was a high-pitched sound," the young man gasped, "and then the central control panel exploded."

"Shh," said Byron, resting a hand on Mevine's good shoulder. "You'll have plenty of time to explain what happened later."

"Before that there was a beam of light..."

"Mevine, stop talking!"

Byron's authoritative tone silenced the young man. He stared wide-eyed at the pilot, his mouth open in surprise. Byron offered a patient smile that seemed to put Mevine at ease.

A voice at Athee's elbow startled her. Shifting her attention, she noticed a medic examining the Tgren, pulling back his eyelids. He glanced up and peered around her.

"Officer Byron, we've four men who need immediate transport to the Rennather, or they're not going to make it," he stated. "including this Tgren."

"Let's get them loaded."

The man nodded and rose to his feet. Athee grabbed Byron's arm before he could move.

"Let me go with this man," she pleaded.

Byron shook his head. "No, the commander would kill us both if you arrived on the ship right now."

"Someone needs to go with him. He'll be terrified when he awakens and discovers he's on a spaceship."

"Athee!" Byron grasped her shoulder. His intensity forced her to look him in the eye. *Please, I need you to stay with Mevine. Promise me you will.*

His desperate tone caused Athee to catch her breath. She nodded, too stunned by the emotional charge in his words to argue. She felt movement behind her and realized men were lifting the injured Tgren onto a makeshift gurney. Byron grabbed her hand and pressed the damp gauze against her palm before placing it on Mevine's head. He gazed at his friend and touched the young man's hand.

"Athee will stay with you. I'll return soon."

Mevine nodded and Byron rose to his feet. Athee gasped, afraid to let him go.

Thank you. Stay with him.

He trotted to his shuttle, the men carrying the injured Tgren in tow. A rumble overhead caused Athee to jump, but a flash that signified lightning followed the sound. The storm couldn't happen at a worse time with injured men outside and exposed to the elements.

Swallowing hard, she shifted her attention to Mevine. The young man stared at her in confusion, his breath still ragged. She offered a smile that Athee hoped conveyed assurance and moved to his injured side.

I remember you from the festival, she thought, using her mental voice to encourage Mevine to respond in kind. He didn't need to speak right now.

You danced with Byron, Mevine thought, blinking his eyes.

Athee nodded. *Yes, I did.*

You like him.

His comment was a statement rather than a question. Athee grinned at his bold observation. *I do.*

Mevine's lips curved into a faint smile and he closed his eyes. *Good.*

Byron's shuttle lifted into the air a few minutes later. From the shouts of those around her, Athee gathered that no one remained in the cave. Her shoulders drooped, releasing some of her tension, just as another rumble echoed overhead. On the heels of the thunder, the second shuttle appeared in the sky. A moment later, a large transport plane also arrived and those outside the cave began to move.

The medic sent three more men to the Rennather. The remaining injured were to travel by plane to the Ktren medical facility. Athee assisted Mevine to the Tgren transport, guiding his unsteady gait across the uneven surface. A large raindrop landed on her cheek, striking with considerable force. She helped Mevine inside just as the downpour began.

Athee's heart raced as the plane left the ground and soared toward the dark clouds. The plane's pilot boasted many years of experience, but that didn't ease her mind as they were buffeted during the flight by wind and rain. Athee's worried thoughts remained shielded until they were on the ground once again.

Ktren's medical facility was small. Eight injured men stretched the staff to the limit. Athee stayed with Mevine as promised and even helped with his bandages. He was placed in a tiny corner room on the second floor. The medic gave him a glass of water, adjusting the sling around his arm. Athee seized the opportunity to slip out of the room.

She located a washbasin down the hall. Turning on the spigot, Athee waited while the water's temperature rose. She couldn't do anything about the blood on her flight suit, but she wanted to wash the grime and blood off her hands. The smell continued to cling to her clothes and hair. It would require several washings to remove the stench. No amount of water would wipe away the memory of today's tragedy, though.

Mevine was alone and still sitting up when she returned. His eyes revealed anxiety as she approached his bedside.

"Feel better now?" Athee asked, noting his empty glass. "Would you like more water?"

"I'm all right," he murmured. "My head hurts, though."

She patted his arm. "I'm sure your people have better pain relievers than we do. Hopefully they'll send some down from your ship."

A loud clap of thunder jolted her senses, causing her to jump. Athee's gaze traveled to the room's lone window. Rain beat hard against its surface, streaming down the pane in turrets. The building creaked from the wind and she shuddered. She hoped no shuttles would attempt to fly in such weather.

She glanced around the room and noticed a small metal stool in the corner. Moving it closer to the bed, Athee sat down. Feeling drained, she allowed her body to sag. Now that the initial fervor had receded and adrenaline no longer pounded through her system, Athee was exhausted.

Mevine opened his mouth to speak and began to cough. Athee waited until he settled before suggesting he use telepathy instead.

You need to concentrate on breathing, not talking, she chastised.

I'm sorry.

Athee suppressed her amusement. The medic had cleaned his face, but Mevine's sooty hair curled in every direction. Coupled with his thin face and large eyes, the young man's forlorn expression bordered on comical. She decided not to injure the man's pride as well and chose to focus on the Cassan pilot's feelings toward his friend.

Byron really cares about you, she offered, clasping her hands around one knee.

Mevine's head dropped against the pillow. *I'm not sure why. Sometimes I think I annoy him.*

He can be distant. I think that's how he deals with people. I'm sure you don't annoy him.

The young man plucked at his blanket with nervous fingers. *The first time I met him, I was in awe. I mean, after what he did in the Vindicarn War? Officer Byron was my hero when I was young. I know I annoyed him with my questions and comments. I couldn't even remember the name of his navigator, and I know that made him mad.*

Athee stared at Mevine in surprise. *Bassa?*

Yes. He's told you about Bassa?

No, I caught his name once when Byron was thinking about him, she admitted, stretching her legs. *When I asked, he changed the subject.*

He doesn't like to talk about him, Mevine thought, furrowing his brows. *I guess they were as close as brothers.*

He died?

Yes, during the Vindicarn War.

Athee pursed her lips. *Is that why he no longer flies a combat fighter?*

Seheller told me Byron had promised his navigator they would pursue exploration after the war, which is why he gave up his position as Cosbolt pilot. Mevine paused and adjusted his arm. *He said Byron would never fly with another navigator, either. Not after losing Bassa.*

Lowering her head, Athee contemplated Mevine's revealing statement. Byron quit flying Cosbolts because of Bassa's death? While she respected the promise to his deceased friend, why would someone with Byron's skills choose to fly a shuttle? It was a lackluster duty at best. Athee was sure training inexperienced pilots in primitive machines didn't rate high on the excitement scale either. Judging from the passionate zeal he exhibited when he flew his Darten, she surmised Byron still longed for the thrill.

"He's too good to give it all up," she murmured.

"I think so, too."

Mevine's words ignited another coughing fit. His head fell back against the pillow, and Athee retrieved his empty glass.

"Let me get you some water."

When she returned, Byron stood at Mevine's bedside. Athee paused in the doorway, loath to interrupt their exchange. The pilot's hand was wrapped around Mevine's arm. A rare, genuine smile appeared on his face. The young man returned the gesture, his thoughts of gratitude and adoration impossible to ignore. Mevine shifted his position, his eyes falling on Athee. Reflecting curiosity, Byron turned to follow his gaze.

"I was getting him another glass of water," she explained as she approached the bed and handed the drink to Mevine. Athee frowned as she viewed Byron up close. "You're soaked."

Byron brushed aside his damp locks. "It's raining hard out there." His words were punctuated by another clap of thunder.

"It's dangerous flying in this weather," Athee admonished.

He shrugged with indifference. "I carried a crew to the site before coming here with two medical officers from the Rennather. I wanted to check on Mevine first before returning to the ship to gather some equipment. The commander wants to secure the site and evaluate the situation before they begin clearing out the control center."

A gasp from Mevine caught their attention. "My computer pad! With all my work..." His words were cut off by another cough.

"As soon as the crews start clearing the room, I'll find it, Mevine," Byron announced, patting his shoulder. "Now get some rest."

Byron strode toward the door. Athee followed, concerned for his safety. He might be an excellent pilot, but the storm continued to pelt the building with wind and rain. *Byron?*

He paused in the doorframe, his attention flicking to the figure in the bed. *Thank you for staying with Mevine. He really needs someone to watch out for him.*

Someone needs to look out for you, too.

Byron managed a faint smile. The exchange with Mevine resurfaced in her mind and Athee placed a hand on his chest. She didn't want to reveal her knowledge of his past, but Athee could not contain her concern for the Cassan pilot. Byron stared at her, his eyes dark and unrevealing. To her surprise, he lifted his hand. He placed it alongside her cheek, his touch gentle. Brushing her skin once with his thumb, he nodded before turning toward the stairs. Athee watched his rapid descent, feeling torn and confused. Byron vanished from sight, leaving her alone in the hallway.

Remembering her duty, Athee returned to Mevine's side.

Chapter Eleven

"What I want to know is exactly what happened yesterday!"

Korden scowled at those present in the Rennather's conference room. All of the senior officers were gathered, along with Ktren's prefect. Byron had retrieved the man before the meeting and Orellen was not happy with the situation. The prefect sat at the commander's side and across from Byron, his expression livid. Adjusting his feet, Byron tried to focus on Korden.

The commander tapped the computer pad in front of him, his finger strokes forceful. "According to the damage report, we lost half of our equipment and three lives, including two Tgrens, in the blast. Officer Seheller, your men were only supposed to be processing data. What happened?"

"Sir, we've spent the past few days translating the data as ordered," Seheller replied, leaning forward. "One of my men was working on the main control panel with the assistance of a Tgren scientist. They were scanning the unit's systems, trying to access the mainframe. For whatever reason, a probe was activated. It scanned Officer Detrena first before falling on the Tgren, Ullen. The man's face twisted with pain and Detrena moved to intervene. The light from the probe vanished and Ullen dropped to the ground. The device beeped three times in warning. Before I could reach Detrena, it exploded. He didn't survive."

Korden leaned back and rubbed his forehead. "Was Detrena's computer pad recovered?"

"Yes sir, but it was damaged. One of my men is trying to retrieve the information."

Byron shifted his feet again. After escorting the commander to the site and viewing the damage firsthand, he wondered if any of the equipment in the room could be salvaged. He'd located Mevine's computer pad and delivered it to his friend, but it had sustained damage as well. Still confined to his bed, Mevine had probably stayed up half the night trying to save his data.

"I want to know what you intend to do next," Orellen demanded, his fist coming down on the table. "Everyone in Ktren is terrified of another explosion that might very well take out half our population in a rockslide."

"Sir, I don't think that's a possibility," Seheller countered, his gaze shifting to the commander. "This was an isolated incident..."

"Isolated incident?" bellowed the prefect, his face flushing red. "Two of my men are dead!"

"Prefect Orellen," said Korden, his voice ringing with authority. "We are equally distressed over this incident. I don't want a repeat of yesterday's explosion either. I am going to maintain a full security team on site while we search for answers. Officer Seheller, your men are to exercise extreme caution. Understood?"

"Yes, sir."

"The High Command expects a full report by tomorrow morning," the commander announced, glancing at his computer pad. "They are contemplating sending a flagship as well, to secure the area."

That news surprised Byron. He wondered which flagship would grace the skies of Tgren and for how long. Perhaps he could secure replacement parts for his Darten.

"Officer Progar, what is the status of the injured?" Korden asked, turning to the senior medical officer.

"Two men are critical, including Ullen, whose mind is still unresponsive. The other four are recovering. On the surface, five of the men have already been released from the Ktren facility, and the other three should be discharged by tomorrow morning." The man paused and shook his head. "Considering the condition of those we received here on the Rennather, it's a miracle we didn't lose more men."

Korden glanced at Byron. "We have the response time of our senior pilot to thank for that small mercy. Not to mention the safe transport of the injured by several pilots, including one of your own, Prefect Orellen."

The Tgren man nodded, although the praise appeared to do little to ease his aggravation. Byron did not look forward to the return trip to the surface.

The commander requested further information on the items recovered from the site. Another officer filled him in on the details, giving a list of the salvaged equipment. Korden stressed again that those working the site were to proceed with caution before he dismissed the men.

"Commander, I would like to see the remaining Tgren in your medical facility before I return to the surface," the prefect announced as the men rose to their feet. "Ullen's family would feel better if I confirmed his condition with my own eyes. They fear he is already dead."

"Of course, Prefect Orellen."

Byron retreated from the room, his thoughts grim. He returned to his shuttle to await the prefect. The hanger chief intercepted the pilot and informed him of additional passengers. Byron noted two scientists and a security guard on the list, all destined for the alien site. He would have to make several stops before he could visit Mevine.

Entering his shuttle, he surveyed the condition of his ship. After a long day of ferrying men back and forth from one location to another, he'd collapsed in his quarters on Tgren late last night. Byron had forced himself to rise early this morning and scrub the streaks of blood from the shuttle floor in anticipation of the prefect's ride to the Rennather. His ship was now clean, but he'd run out of time to visit Mevine. Byron still wanted to check on his friend.

At least I didn't have to clean the ship by myself, he thought, a smirk crossing his face. Athee had arrived shortly after he began and scrubbed the floor at his side. The bloodstains were a grim reminder of yesterday's tragic event, but somehow, her presence had made the job bearable.

Byron's three new passengers arrived first. He helped them secure their belongings and fasten flight harnesses. The prefect had protested the confining device, transferring his fury over yesterday's incident to the harness, his first flight into space, and at any individual within earshot. Byron hoped their return flight would be more pleasant or at least quieter.

Orellen arrived moments later, his security guard in tow. Byron greeted the man as he entered the shuttle. The prefect hesitated, his eyes on the other three passengers. Byron caught a flicker of annoyance, which did not surprise him. It was the anxiety in the man that caught his attention. For all his irritated bluster, Orellen was afraid to ride again within the confines of the main compartment. Clenching his fists, Byron decided to offer the man something far more appealing than the cargo hold.

"Sir, would you prefer to ride up front?" he asked, gesturing toward the cockpit. "Your niece always enjoys the view from the co-pilot's seat."

Orellen cast him a suspicious look before gazing into the cockpit. Byron sensed curiosity. The prefect turned to his guard and told the man to take a seat with the others. Byron assured the Tgren was properly fastened in his harness before returning to the cockpit to assist Orellen. The man was absorbed with the view outside the main window. The prefect did not protest the restraints this time. Byron took his seat and prepared for liftoff.

"My niece has spoken highly of your training sessions," the prefect offered as the shuttle passed through the second set of doors.

"She's an outstanding pilot, sir," said Byron, his gaze fixed on the stars beyond the hanger bay.

"Yes, she is, but I was referring to your psychic sessions together."

Orellen's interest in the matter surprised him. "She has learned to master her abilities quite well, sir. Her telepathic skills are exceptional. In addition, Athee has assisted with numerous jumps and understands the concept of teleportation to my satisfaction."

The shuttle entered space, curving away from the Rennather. Byron reached for the teleporter and its energy pulsated in his mind. Visualizing his destination, his mental powers matched that of the unit. Byron performed the jump without error. Emerging over the valley, he heard the prefect gasp. He struggled to contain the smirk that appeared on his face. At least teleportation impressed the man.

"My niece can do that?" Orellen asked in astonishment.

"Yes, sir. She's performed the maneuver on her own on many occasions."

The prefect shifted in his seat, his attention on Ktren as they approached the city. "Shame she'll have no use for that talent."

Yeah, it is a shame, Byron thought. It would be many years before the Tgrens achieved that level of space flight.

He dropped the prefect off first before flying to the alien ruins. Crews had set to work on cleanup this morning, and battered equipment lay strewn across the ground outside the cave entrance. At some point today, he and Garnce would return the damaged items to the Rennather. It seemed he would endure another long, hard day.

Assuring the senior security officer that he would return soon, Byron flew to the Tgren city. If he didn't visit Mevine this morning, he wouldn't have an opportunity to see him until tonight.

Byron found the young man pouring over his computer pad notes. Mevine offered a broad grin and gestured to his pad.

"I didn't lose any data," he said, relief radiating from his thoughts.

"That's good," Byron replied. "Considering the state of the equipment I just observed at the site, you're fortunate."

"I'd noticed a similarity between the alien symbols and the Tgren's written language. I'd entered the data and run the information through all encryption codes minutes before the explosion. I thought I'd lost all of it."

"But you didn't?"

"No, sir. And several of the Tgren letters match new alien symbols, so I may be on to something."

Byron smiled and offered his friend a nod of congratulation. He noticed a small basket on the bed beside Mevine. Peering inside, Byron realized it was full of Tgren sweets. He pointed at the basket.

"Who brought you the treats?"

Mevine glanced at the basket and grinned. "Athee. She said it would make me feel better."

And maybe put some weight on your frame, Byron thought. "That was nice of her."

"Want a piece?" the young man said, offering the basket to Byron.

"No, those are for you to enjoy."

Mevine leaned back against his pillow. "They said I can leave this afternoon. But no one is to stay overnight at the site. Officer Seheller said we were to seek lodging at the Cassan facility in town."

I wondered why there was so much activity in the building this morning, Byron thought.

"I wish I could've secured a room last night," Mevine said with a frown. "I heard it's already three men to a room and they're sticking latecomers in a downstairs office."

Byron shifted his position and exhaled a deep breath. He liked his privacy, but his friend's plight tugged at his conscious.

"If you need a room, you can stay in mine," he offered.

"Sir, I can't do that!"

"You'd rather sleep in an office with a dozen other men?"

"No, but..."

"Mevine, are you refusing the generosity of a senior officer?"

Spoken with authority, Byron's question had the desired effect. The young man stared at him in surprise. Mevine wrestled with the idea a moment before Byron sensed his compliance.

"No, sir," he murmured.

"Good, then it's decided."

Mevine's brows came together. "Sir, I haven't earned the right to share a room with a senior officer, certainly not one as prestigious as you."

Byron smiled and patted his arm. "You're not. You're sharing a room with a friend."

The tension drained from the young man's face. He thanked Byron repeatedly.

"I need to return to the site," said Byron, overwhelmed by Mevine's outpouring of emotions. "Let me know when you're released, all right?"

Byron returned to the alien site, his thoughts preoccupied with the young man's reaction. Mevine soaked up friendship like he was dying of thirst. Had no one ever expressed kindness toward the boy? Had Mevine never experienced the camaraderie of a good friend?

I didn't have a real friend until I met Bassa, Byron thought. Considering how much that one relationship had changed his life, the least he could do was mentor Mevine.

He approached the thin landing strip. Byron caught site of a Tgren plane overhead, hugging the mountainside. It pulled away from the rock and performed a tight arc. He set the shuttle down and glanced up once more at the plane. Barreling down on his location, the craft's wings dipped from side to side. The small plane skimmed low as it flew over the shuttle, its rumble loud enough to shake his ship. Byron grinned and shut off the shuttle's engines. Only one Tgren pilot performed that maneuver.

As he exited the ship, the tiny plane rolled to a stop not far from his shuttle. Byron waited while the pilot cut the engines and emerged from the aircraft. The ever-present wind caught Athee's hair as she approached, pulling it away from her face. She offered a grin and Byron responded in kind.

"Waiting for me?" he teased.

"I was surveying the mountain for rockslides or any other visible damage," Athee admonished, slapping her gloves together. "It appears the blast was confined to the control room. It didn't damage any of the rock plates."

Byron nodded. "That's good news. I just visited Mevine. He's doing better. I appreciate the basket of treats you dropped off for him."

"Hopefully he's eaten some of it."

"I think you've finally discovered his weakness. Maybe the boy will gain a few pounds while on Tgren."

"Officer Byron!"

He turned toward the speaker. His eyes caught the large stack of burned and twisted metal that was once science equipment. Byron's gaze continued to drift to the pile of damaged items as the science officer informed him it all needed to be returned to the Rennather. It would require several trips to transport all the equipment.

"And I'm sorry, Officer Byron. We can only spare one person to help load the shuttle," the man announced.

Byron's shoulders sagged. Two men working on that pile would require all day to load the damaged equipment. He was about to protest when Athee's voice rang in his head.

I'll help you.

You helped me this morning. This will be some damned heavy lifting.

I don't mind.

Byron knew it would do no good to argue the point further. Besides, he preferred her company. She bolstered his confidence and reminded him of forgotten joys. He just couldn't reveal how much he enjoyed Athee's presence. His feelings toward the Tgren woman were already far too transparent.

Outfitted with heavy gloves, the three of them began loading the shuttle. Byron located several thick cargo blankets. He used the padding to protect the floor and walls. Soot and debris fell off the damaged equipment, covering both the shuttle's main compartment and those carrying the loads. Byron discouraged Athee from lifting the heavier items although she was more than willing. The Tgren woman's frame was slight, but it contained an amazing amount of strength and stamina. Her consistent work ethic kept Byron plodding forward, determined not to drop before his petite helper.

At last, the pile of equipment whittled down to nothing. Byron secured the final piece, his muscles protesting the effort. He wanted nothing more than to wash off the black soot and enjoy a decent meal. The hanger crew would attend to this final load and Byron decided they could clean the shuttle as well. He did not feel like scrubbing his ship twice in one day.

Returning to the main compartment, he found Athee sweeping sand and grit out the open hatch. She paused in her efforts as he approached and leaned against the shuttle wall. Her face boasted several dark smudges where she'd wiped her face with a dirty sleeve. Feeling the itch from soot in his hair, Byron suspected his appearance fared no better.

"One more trip," he announced, his voice as tired as his body. "And tomorrow, if anything remains, Garnce gets the honor."

Athee blew a long strand of hair away from her face. "How did he get out of it today?"

"He's been busy ferrying people back and forth," replied Byron, grasping a handle overhead. "Claimed there was no need for both shuttles to get dirty."

"And you bought that excuse?"

"I didn't feel like dealing with Garnce today. He would've made this job miserable for all of us."

He brushed aside his hair and glanced at his helper. Athee gripped the broom in both hands and offered a tired smile. Byron managed to return the gesture, grateful for her assistance.

"Want a good dinner when you return?" she asked.

Byron laughed. "You have enough energy to prepare a meal?"

"No, but I have enough energy to locate one."

"You're on, then."

He returned to the Rennather, renewed energy coursing through his body. Byron informed the hanger crew they had less than an hour to unload and clean his shuttle. His stomach already rumbled from lack of food. Byron didn't want to delay the prospect of a good meal any longer than it took him to clean up and report to the commander.

Korden cautioned him to remain on alert. Any evening transports would fall to Garnce unless they were overwhelmed with requests. After a day of backbreaking work, Byron was relieved. It provided some uninterrupted time with Athee as well. It surprised him how much he looked forward to sharing a meal with her this evening.

Damn it, she's getting to you, he thought as he entered the hanger. When did you become so gullible?

Sir?

Mevine's hesitant voice was just above a whisper in his mind. *Yes, Mevine?*

You wanted to know when I was released. They're transporting me to the Cassan facility in a few minutes.

I'm heading back to the surface now, Byron answered. He reached his shuttle and the crew chief informed him it was clean and ready for flight. *I'll meet you there.*

Yes, sir. Thank you.

And then maybe I can finally eat, he thought.

Mevine was waiting in the central hallway when Byron arrived. The young man's bag was slung over his shoulder and his good arm lay wrapped around several rolls of bedding. He straightened his back as Byron approached. The movement caused two blankets to slip from his grasp.

"I'll get those," Byron announced, retrieving the bedding from the floor. Mevine would never make it up the stairs without assistance.

"Thank you, sir," the young man stammered.

Byron led the way to his room. The smell of food emanating from the kitchen and small dining hall taunted his senses. He'd notified Athee of his arrival time, explaining the need to get Mevine settled in his quarters. She'd agreed to meet him at the facility and he expected her in a few minutes. If dinner resided more than five minutes from the facility, Byron was certain he'd drop from starvation.

His quarters were small, but there was room for Mevine's makeshift bed. Byron helped him unroll the padding and blankets. Noting the boy's trembling shoulders, he asked Mevine if he'd eaten.

"No, sir, I haven't."

"I'll show you to the dining hall then," said Byron. "And we're off duty, Mevine. Drop the sir."

"Yes..." the young man said, his mouth closing before the word could escape. Byron smiled and patted his good shoulder.

"Come on."

Once on the first floor again, Byron directed Mevine down a short hall. The sound of voices and clanking dinnerware was obvious now. "All the way to the end. You can't miss it."

Mevine hesitated, his brows pulled together. "You're not eating?"

"I'm taking my meal elsewhere tonight," he answered, giving Mevine a gentle push toward the dining hall.

His friend's eyes displayed puzzlement. Byron kept his expression neutral, hoping to avoid an explanation. To his dismay, Mevine's face broke into a mischievous grin. An image of Athee escaped the young man's thoughts.

"Go on!" Byron said, unable to suppress a guilty smile at Mevine's lucky guess.

He stepped outside and squinted at the final rays of sun poking over the horizon. The Cassan security guard nodded and stood at attention as Byron strode past the man. After yesterday's incident, the Cassan facility was now guarded in case of Tgren backlash or protest. The people of Ktren had remained calm and civil thus far. Byron hoped the trend would continue. They didn't need a riot.

Athee waited at the bottom of the steps. Attired in a dark green tunic and matching, calf-length pants, her appearance was a vast improvement over this afternoon. After viewing himself in the mirror during his final trip to the Rennather, Byron suspected she entertained similar thoughts about him.

"Hungry?" she asked, smiling in eager anticipation.

"I'm starving. And if I have to travel farther than two blocks, you're in trouble."

"Good thing it's just around the corner."

As promised, their walk was short. Athee led him into a single story building covered in vines with tiny blue flowers. The interior boasted a similar design painted on the walls, with a kitchen to their left and several round tables to their right. In addition to small bulbs in the ceiling, candles residing on tables and affixed to the walls bathed the room with an inviting glow. A large set of double doors opened onto a covered courtyard out back. Byron noticed more tables surrounding a small fountain. However, what struck him was the smell. The most delicious aromas drifted from the kitchen, causing him to salivate in anticipation of a flavorful meal.

Athee greeted the owners, who cried with delight to see the young woman. She requested a table in the courtyard and Byron noticed the curious stares of the other diners as they passed. He wondered if it was the presence of a Cassan or the identity of the man accompanying the prefect's niece that drew attention. He pretended not to notice and followed Athee to their table.

Two glasses of Jtal were placed before them. Byron allowed his companion the honor of ordering. She promised he would enjoy her selection.

"I'd eat anything at this point," he told her, lifting the glass to his lips.

"The food here is excellent. You won't be disappointed."

Byron stretched his sore legs. "I appreciated your help today."

"It was no problem," she answered, clasping her fingers together on the table. "I'm tired, but hard work never scared me."

"Surprised you're not tired of my company."

Athee beamed, her eyes bright. "Not at all."

Feeling self-conscious, Byron reached for his drink. The sentiment is mutual, he thought.

"How is Mevine?" she asked.

"No worse for wear and eager to return to work."

"That was nice of you to let him stay in your quarters."

"He refused at first, but I told Mevine he had no choice. Besides, the boy would've been miserable crammed in that tiny office with a dozen other men."

"He really admires you."

Spoken with conviction, Athee's observation caused him to smile. "I know. He admitted he wanted to be a pilot because of me, too. Probably a good thing he chose another path."

"I can't picture Mevine as a pilot," Athee said with a laugh.

"He'd never make it through training," Byron stated. "No, Mevine's better as a linguist. Just needs some confidence."

"Is that part of the reason you're friends with him?"

Byron shrugged. "I know how he feels. It's tough when no one believes in you."

"Was Bassa the first to believe in you?" she asked.

His eyes dropped to his drink. Athee already knew Bassa's name. She might as well know the importance of his friend.

"Yes," Byron admitted.

Her hand came into view and Athee's dainty fingers wrapped around his. Byron looked up and she smiled.

I believe in you, she thought.

Athee's open mind revealed the depths of her certainty. It had been years since he felt such genuine faith. Resisting the urge to shield, Byron smiled and returned her gentle grasp.

Thank you.

He caught more stirring in her thoughts, but the arrival of their dinner broke the connection. The enticing smells were overwhelming and Byron's thoughts shifted to his empty stomach. After a long, hard day of work, this meal would taste like pure bliss.

Conversation continued while they ate and focused on lighter topics. Recalling the festival, Byron realized he enjoyed Athee's company even without the possibility of physical pleasures lurking in his mind. Her spirit was intoxicating. He forgot the day's troubles in no time. She was a genuine person, something he didn't encounter often, and Byron wanted to relish the experience. They lingered at the table long after their empty plates vanished and the building emptied of patrons.

Night had fallen when they stepped onto the street. Athee stretched her back and stifled a yawn.

"I feel the same way," Byron told her. After a good meal, he was ready for sleep. He hoped Mevine didn't snore, or the lad would discover his bed in the hallway.

Officer Byron!

The commander's mental voice startled him. *Sir?*

I need you to collect Officer Seheller and return to the Rennather at once.

He was exhausted, but not about to question the order. Not when Korden's tone suggested a dire need. *Yes, sir. I'm on my way.*

"What's wrong?" said Athee. She taken several steps before realizing Byron was not at her side.

"I need to return to the ship," he explained. "Are you all right walking home by yourself?"

"Of course. What happened?"

"The commander didn't say." Byron grasped her hand and gave it a squeeze. "Thank you for dinner. Best part of my day for sure!"

He returned to the Cassan compound. Officer Seheller met him on the steps and suggested they take one of the transportation carts. Byron despised the awkward vehicles, but he was too tired to run all the way to his shuttle. Seheller had apparently driven on several occasions and guided the noisy cart through the streets in record time.

Once on the Rennather, they were told to meet the commander in his office. They discovered Korden, Anceptor, and the senior security officer waiting. The heavy mood in the room, not to mention the commander's grave expression, alerted Byron that something was indeed very wrong.

"Men, we just received word that we'll soon have company," Korden stated. "Long range scanners picked up a large craft in quadrant 637-118 bearing down on our location. At its current speed, it will arrive in less than two days. A flagship has been dispatched to intercept. Until we hear otherwise, we are to assume hostile intentions."

Byron's exhausted mind snapped into focus at once. The Rennather was armed, but it wasn't strong enough to defend the entire planet.

"Why would an alien vessel target Tgren?" the security officer asked. "These people aren't a threat to anyone."

"Perhaps they seek Tgren's resources," Anceptor offered.

"Or perhaps the appearance of this vessel isn't a coincidence," stated Korden, shifting his attention to Seheller.

"You think it's connected to the alien site? But why now? It's been there over a thousand years."

"Maybe the events preceding the explosion triggered it," Byron announced in a low voice.

Everyone's attention shifted to Byron. Seheller began to disagree but the commander's voice drowned out his protest.

"That is a very real possibility. Officer Seheller!" said Korden, turning to the scientist. "I want to know everything your team has accessed so far, especially the information on Detrena's computer pad. I want to know why that alien device exploded after scanning the Tgren, and if it did indeed send out a distress signal. Understood?"

"Yes, sir."

"No more equipment goes to the surface, either. If we're forced to evacuate, we won't have time to retrieve more than our personnel without starting a panic among the Tgrens."

The news unsettled Byron. "Are we going to warn them, sir?"

"When we know more, we'll meet with Prefect Orellen. No need to alarm his people without just cause. In the meantime, we'll form a contingency plan for evacuation and focus on the data from the alien site." Korden punched two buttons on his computer and peered at the screen. "The flagship will reach the vessel by morning. Once they've reported their findings, I'll call a meeting with all officers and the prefect. Another flagship should arrive here tomorrow as well. High Command is taking no chances."

Korden raised his eyes to Seheller. "I know your men have been through a lot, Officer Seheller, but I need to them to work around the clock if necessary. Time is of the essence and we won't concern the Tgrens until the time is right."

"Yes, sir."

"Dismissed, men."

Byron allowed the others to exit first. He paused in the doorway. *Sir, may I ask which flagship is joining us tomorrow?*

The Firenta, Korden answered before turning to his computer.

Satisfied with the answer, he joined Seheller in the hallway. They proceeded to the hanger in silence. The news was potentially devastating. If the vessel was hostile, the Rennather could retreat and avoid confrontation, but what about the Tgrens? They couldn't take everyone in Ktren with them, although Byron knew one person he'd refuse to leave behind. Athee wasn't just valuable to High Command. She mattered to Byron as well.

As he started his shuttle's engine, Byron's shoulders drooped. The flagship Firenta? Damn, it'll be good to see Ernx and Nintal again, he thought. Just wish it was under better circumstances.

Chapter Twelve

Byron's mind roused to consciousness. He fought the sensation, unwilling for the day to begin yet. His body felt stiff and ached from lying in one position too long. If he fell asleep again, the soreness would vanish.

A strange sound dissolved his tenuous hold on slumber and his mind grew alert. Suppressing a moan, Byron rolled on his side. He opened his eyes, adjusting his vision to the early light of dawn. His gaze fell at once on the figure stretched out across his floor. Mevine was sprawled on his back, his good arm wrapped possessively around his computer pad. He wasn't snoring, but his foot twitched in a spastic, uneven rhythm.

Everything about you is a bundle of nerves, Byron thought, rubbing his eyes.

Sleep was now out of the question. He needed to rise anyway. Once the Rennather received a report on the alien vessel, Byron would be expected to transport the prefect to the ship. Perhaps the Firenta would be in orbit by that time. A flagship was far more impressive than a mere exploration ship. It would remind Orellen of the Cassan's superior power and strength and perhaps keep the man in his place during the meeting.

As he dressed, Byron contemplated waking Mevine. The science team needed to discover if the alien ship was tied to the ruins. Seheller had ordered his men to work late, desperate to discover an answer. Mevine had remained downstairs for a long time, but decided to continue his work in Byron's quarters to shut out all distractions. Asleep not long after crawling into his bed, Byron had no idea how long the young man remained conscious and glued to his computer pad.

He's still recovering from injury, Byron thought, reaching for the door. I'll let him sleep a little longer.

Several men were awake, although it was difficult to tell if it was a result of rising early or a lack of sleep altogether. Byron secured a bowl of food and wrinkled his nose when he realized the lumpy substance was half-baked. Compared to his meal last night, this food was inedible.

He devoured half of his breakfast before depositing the remainder in the trash. It was time he roused Mevine and forced him to eat. The lad was so absorbed with his work, he wouldn't notice the poor quality of the food.

Byron passed Seheller and another science officer in the hallway. Enough of their conversation reached his ear to realize the men were discussing the data on Detrena's computer pad. Mevine had not mentioned the deceased officer's device last night, which surprised Byron. Curious, he paused and waited for an appropriate moment to speak. Seheller noticed him and silenced the other man with a hand gesture.

"Any progress?" said Byron.

His junior officer frowned. Seheller answered without hesitation. "We've discovered a code that we believe triggered the events of two days ago. It appears the scanner sought to verify certain conditions within the Tgren man." Seheller pressed his lips into a thin line and placed his hands on his hips. "When the scanner couldn't locate the correct criteria, it malfunctioned. And sent out a distress call."

"What did it seek?"

"Of that we're not sure," the senior officer answered, glancing at the other man. "Pezta has worked on it for two days, trying to break the code."

Pezta nodded and straightened his shoulders. "Right now, I believe it was a lack of technological development in the Tgrens," he stated with confidence.

Something about the man rubbed Byron the wrong way. His prideful attitude implied superiority. Byron was grateful his friend lacked that quality. Mevine's doubts threatened to overwhelm him on occasion, but that uncertainty caused him to strive harder to discover the truth.

"Is Mevine working on the code as well?" he said.

Seheller was surprised by his question, but Petza's expression bordered on indignant. "Mevine?" he demanded, wrinkling his long nose. "The boy doesn't even have a year's experience in the field. He'd slow down our progress."

Byron decided there was no reasoning with the man. He shifted his attention to the senior scientist. *Officer Seheller?* he entreated in a private thought.

"Officer Pezta, thank you," Seheller said, patting the man's shoulder. "Please keep working on it."

The man nodded and offered cold eyes to the pilot. Byron's brows came together in his most authoritative scowl. Pezta did not answer to him, but Byron still outranked the man. The science officer balked and dropped his chin. Byron followed the man's angry steps as he retreated down the hall.

"Byron, Pezta is my best analyzer, and his team is top-notch," Seheller said in a low voice. "I know you're fond of Mevine..."

"Yes, because I see a young science officer willing to work until he drops," Byron replied, not afraid to press the matter. He'd worked with Seheller for many years, He doubted the man would take offense. "He's passionate, determined, and modest enough to question his own conclusions. Considering the gravity of our situation, I'd think you would want every man possible working on that code."

Seheller's thoughts reflected doubt and he squared his chin in defiance. Byron allowed his shoulders to relax, affecting a less threatening pose.

"Sir, I know Pezta will object, but give the boy a chance," he said in a calm voice.

"Pezta will be furious and impossible to work with for weeks if I assign Mevine to the project," said Seheller, rubbing his forehead. He sighed and nodded his head. "But we need to find a solution soon. I'll give Mevine the task of breaking the code."

Byron's face broke into a gracious smile. "He'll appreciate it."

"You see through the politics and keep it simple, Byron," the man replied, patting the pilot's shoulder in a fatherly gesture. "Now to inform Mevine..."

"I'll tell him to report to you at once."

Mevine was still sleeping when he returned to the room. Byron tried to wake him gently, using thoughts to prod his mind. He had to grasp Mevine's shoulder and speak his name aloud to garner a response. The boy awoke with a start, his eyes wide.

"Come on, Mevine, time to get up!" Byron said.

His friend moaned. The lad rolled to his left side, uttering a cry of pain as his weight shifted to his injured arm. Byron grasped his right hand and pulled Mevine into a sitting position.

"Officer Seheller has a special assignment for you," he announced, retrieving the computer pad from the floor.

That prompted a response from Mevine. With assistance, he struggled to his feet. Byron handed him the computer pad, forcing the young man's fingers to lock around the device. He was about to speak when Korden's voice echoed in his head.

Officer Byron! I need you and Officer Seheller in my office now, the commander ordered, placing heavy emphasis on the final word.

On my way, sir. Byron thought.

"What's my assignment?" Mevine asked with a yawn.

"Officer Seheller has that information," Byron cried, grasping the boy's good shoulder and pushing him toward the door. "But if you don't go talk to him right now, you'll have to wait until we return from the Rennather. Now go!"

The young man fumbled with the doorknob a moment before throwing open the door. Mevine vanished down the stairs, his rapid footsteps reverberating within the stone staircase. Byron located his personal computer pad and followed his friend to the first floor. Once Seheller had informed Mevine of his new assignment, he and Byron departed.

When he fired up the shuttle's systems, Byron noticed a large object on the radar. The Firenta's in orbit, he thought. I hope the other flagship sent good news.

Byron jumped the shuttle into space and a jolt of surprise escaped the science officer's thoughts. The Rennather was no longer the largest object in the sky. A flagship a hundred times greater in size dwarfed the tiny exploration vessel, its long frame stretched across the view out the cockpit window. Byron noticed a squadron of Cosbolts below them and regret tugged at his heart. Burying the sensation, he followed the formation on the radar until the squadron vanished behind the Firenta.

The senior officers gathered in Korden's office. One look at the commander's face told Byron the news was not good.

"Commander Tencor is joining us on visual com," Korden announced, gesturing to his computer screen. The unit's adjusted angle provided the Firenta's commander with a clear view of the room. The man's grizzled features suggested many years of service and a hardened attitude to match.

"We received a report this morning from the flagship Cortella," Korden announced, his expression grim. "They intercepted the alien vessel and requested open communications, which received no response. After a thorough scan revealed external weapons and a thick exterior plate, the Cortella assumed a defensive pose. The alien ship ignored all warnings. The commander ordered a laser blast across her bow. The vessel responded with an electrical blast unlike anything we've ever encountered."

Several of the men shifted their feet. Byron's grip on his computer pad tightened as he considered the implications. Going up against an unknown adversary was always dangerous, and the alien's weapon sounded all too familiar.

"Not unlike a disrupter blast?" Anceptor said, giving voice to Byron's concerns that it shared traits with the Vindicarn's deadly weapon.

"No, but that electrical blast reduced the ship's shields by half," answered Korden, his words causing a silence to fall over the room. "The Cortella is now following the alien vessel at a safe distance, scanning for weaknesses and any sign of life. Other than the one discharge, there's been no response. However, High Command issued an order that the ship is to be treated as hostile."

"Two more flagships have been dispatched to intercept," Tencor announced, his deep growl resonating within the small room. "We are to hold position here and prepare for their arrival. The craft is still on a trajectory to reach this planet by tomorrow afternoon."

"We have yet to plot the exact location," Korden said, glancing around at those present. "Although I suspect its destination is the alien site."

Which places it directly over Ktren, Byron thought, his stomach churning.

"Officer Seheller, have you anything new to report?"

"Sir, I've a full team working on the data from the master control," the officer answered. The man's voice sounded stressed and tired. Byron did not envy Seheller's position as he repeated Pezta's theory and possible cause of the device's destruction.

"So the approaching alien ship may be a direct result of our tampering with this device?" demanded Tencor.

"It appears the two events are connected," Korden admitted with a sigh. "If we can discover what triggered the beacon that summoned this ship, we might be able to stop it."

"Is the alien site transmitting now?"

Seheller cleared his throat, his eyes on the computer screen. "Sir, we've detected no transmissions from the site. In fact, every system has shut down completely."

"Then how do you intend to stop the alien craft with no form of communication?" Tencor exclaimed with indignation.

"There has to be a way to communicate with this craft, sir..." Seheller offered.

"Commander Tencor, we've requested complete scans of the alien vessel from the Cortella," Korden offered, coming to his science officer's rescue. "If this ship and the ruins are of the same origin, then there will be similar features. We may be able to communicate using our own systems."

"Sounds like a long shot to me, Korden," the Firenta's commander observed.

The commander leaned against his desk. His wrinkled brow and stretched jaw muscles revealed to Byron the man's heavy thoughts. They'd served together for more than fifteen years and had faced some rough encounters. Nothing compared to the situation developing over Tgren. It affected everyone involved, but Byron's superior bore the weight of the situation. In his opinion, the commander was doing his best to cope with the crisis.

"We're sending our findings to High Command," Korden announced. "I'd like to set up a conference with Command on the Firenta, so we all understand the situation."

"Of course," answered Tencor, his voice calmer, but no less intense.

Korden rubbed the back of his neck. "And it's time we involved the local authority, too. I'll request Prefect Orellen's presence during the conference."

When the connection with the Firenta ended, Korden sank into his chair. Questions arose in Byron's mind and he sensed those around him shared his concerns. Before he could form an intelligent comment or question, Anceptor's voice broke the silence.

"The prefect will not take this news well," he observed.

A smirk pulled at the corner of Korden's mouth. "No, safe to say, this will probably destroy all relations between our people." The commander's hands came down on his desk and he rose to his feet.

"Officer Seheller, the moment we have the schematics of that alien ship, your team will be granted full access. Continue working on the master control data, but find me a way to communicate with that ship.

"Officer Byron, return to the planet to collect Prefect Orellen. I'll contact him directly and set up the conference in one hour. After that, be prepared to begin the evacuation of our people. If that ship cannot be stopped, no Cassan is to remain behind."

The commander continued to give orders as Byron's thoughts lingered on his potential assignment. He wasn't leaving Athee on the surface either.

Chapter Thirteen

Athee ran up the steps of the state building and burst through the front doors. A security guard jumped, but he did not move to intercept the prefect's niece. She raced past him and down the hall toward her uncle's office.

The conversation with Byron still echoed in her mind. Athee had known something was wrong after his hasty departure last night, but never imagined an alien craft would be bearing down on her home planet. Not since the Bshen War had panic so gripped her heart. Only this time, they had no way to confront the enemy.

The prefect's doors stood open. Athee skittered to a stop just inside his office. Her abrupt arrival startled the occupants. She ignored the glares from the two diplomats and approached her uncle. He raised his hand, his attention returning to the men. Athee stopped within a few feet of his desk, her body trembling as she waited for Orellen to finish his business with the diplomats. The moment they were out of the room, she stepped closer and grasped the edge of his desk.

"Uncle, Byron just told me what's happened!"

Orellen arose and began to gather his papers. "Yes, it appears Tgren is the target of an approaching alien ship, against which we are defenseless."

"But there's a Cassan warship in orbit now, and several more on the way."

The prefect slammed his fist on the desk. "And we would not be in this predicament if it weren't for the Cassans!"

Athee leaned back, her eyes wide. "No, but they aren't abandoning us either. They intend to fight. That has to count for something."

Her uncle's chin dropped. He gripped the edge of the desk and she sensed Orellen wrestling with his anger. Moving closer, she grasped his arm.

"Uncle, I know the Cassans will defend us."

"They'll defend their precious compound," he growled.

Athee's fingers clasped with his and she gave his hand a firm squeeze. "I heard the truth in Byron's thoughts, Uncle," she said in a low voice. "They're staying to defend Tgren's people, not just the compound."

Orellen released a deep breath and lifted his head. Athee used every ounce of persuasive talent to convince her uncle of the Cassans' sincerity. She had to still his agitated thoughts. He needed to remain composed if they were to survive this crisis.

"It still places us in a predicament."

"Which is why you need to remain calm, Uncle."

"And you came to settle my nerves? I'm sure that's not the only reason you are here right now," he asserted. His thoughts were composed now, although still racing with urgency.

Athee leaned back and straightened her shoulders. "I want to go with you to the Cassan ship," she stated.

Orellen retrieved a stack of papers and faced his niece. "If Officer Byron allows it, I don't have any objections. You've travelled into space far more often than me."

"Yes, but I need for you to insist that I go."

"Why?"

Athee rolled her eyes. "It's a long story."

Orellen held up his hand. "I don't have time for a long story."

There was a sound at the door and a guard entered the room. "Your transport is ready, sir."

"If you're coming, let's go," the prefect informed her, moving toward the door.

Byron was waiting for them at the shuttle. He flashed an inquisitive look as Athee followed her uncle into the ship.

My uncle insisted, she offered. *Really!*

The Cassan shook his head. *You're sneaky.*

I can't just sit and wait, Athee thought, her nerves still on edge. *Not with that ship bearing down on us.*

Or with a Cassan flagship occupying your sky?

Athee did not respond. It wasn't the whole truth. However, she couldn't deny her curiosity regarding the warship. When would she get the opportunity again?

Byron closed the hatch. He turned to face her and focused on something behind Athee. Glancing over her shoulder, she realized her uncle and his guard were still standing. She recalled the delighted account provided by her uncle when Byron allowed him to ride in the cockpit. Athee wondered if he expected that privilege now. The four exchanged nervous glances, waiting for the first person to lay claim to the coveted co-pilot seat. Orellen reacted first.

"I need to focus my thoughts," he announced, moving toward the first empty seat in the main compartment.

Athee decided not to protest his decision and slipped into the cockpit. She slid into the co-pilot's seat and fastened her harness. When Byron joined her, he flashed Athee a scowl that was offset by a smirk tugging at his lips.

Now let's see if Commander Korden buys your excuse.

He will if you don't say anything, she admonished.

Byron didn't respond and concentrated on lifting the shuttle into the sky. Once they were airborne, he leaned back in his seat.

I'm glad you're here, though.

Athee turned to face him. The pilot's gaze remained fixed on the view outside the cockpit. Byron's expression revealed trepidation, and it had nothing to do with the approaching alien ship. Considering the gravity of their current situation, Athee decided not to question the man. He never supplied a direct answer anyway.

Byron leveled the ship and she felt the hum of the teleporter. *Besides, you didn't want to miss this,* he declared.

The patchy clouds vanished. Athee gasped as a monstrous ship filled their view. She leaned forward, pulling hard against the harness, and peered up as the shuttle flew beside the vessel. The Cassan flagship appeared impenetrable. Athee knew nothing of the alien ship approaching Tgren, but she couldn't imagine it measuring up in terms of size or defense. This mighty craft seemed capable of destroying a planet.

Impressive, isn't it? thought Byron, angling the shuttle away from the ship.

Athee made no attempt to hide her foolish grin. *It's incredible. You used to serve on one of these ships?*

Many years ago.

She continued to stare open-mouthed until they passed the end of the flagship. Athee's attention shifted, and she realized they were approaching the Rennather.

I need to pick up Commander Korden and a few other passengers, Byron explained, guiding the shuttle into the hanger.

When the others boarded, Athee sent a quick reminder to her uncle. She listened to his exchange with the commander and smiled to herself when Korden did not protest her presence. It was too late to return her to the surface regardless.

Awe filled her chest as Byron landed in the wide bay of the Firenta. The mechanism used to draw the ship into the hanger was fascinating. She listened with interest to the gentle whirring sound. They moved forward again after the first doors closed and Athee's eagerness grew as the final set of doors opened. They revealed a cavernous maw large enough to house the entire city of Ktren. A small cry escaped her lips as she viewed her first flagship hanger.

Beside her, Byron chuckled. *Bigger than you expected?*

It's immense! Athee thought, ogling the massive hanger. Ships larger than Byron's Darten filled her view. The wider, more rounded vessels were lined in neat rows staggered across the flight deck. She glanced at the row on her immediate right and noted the long canopy adorning the tops of the ships. Peering closer, she realized two seats rested underneath.

Feeling her excitement swell, Athee turned to Byron. *These are Cosbolts?*

Yes. They are the core of the Cassan fleet.

The shuttle came to a rest. Fingers racing across the control panel, Byron shut off the remaining systems. *Wait here,* he instructed.

Athee unfastened her harness and remained in her seat. Outside the cockpit window, she noted several security guards waiting. They saluted the visitors and two men escorted the shuttle's passengers away from the vessel. She felt confusion as her uncle proceeded with the others across the hanger. He was leaving her behind. Athee rose to her feet as Byron returned.

"We're not going with them?" she said.

Byron shook his head and retrieved his computer pad. "I wasn't invited to attend, which means you weren't, either."

Athee glanced out the window, her eyes on the figures as they disappeared through a large doorway. "We're to sit and wait?" she said with disappointment. Something touched her arm, and Athee glanced at Byron.

"Not when we have over an hour to kill," he announced with a wink. "Come on. I've friends on the Firenta I haven't seen in years."

Eager to see more of the ship, she followed him out of the shuttle. *It's all right if I accompany you?* she asked, pausing as she eyed the waiting security officer.

After the last time I left you alone in a shuttle? You're coming with me, he replied, turning to the guard.

Athee clenched her teeth, unable to respond to his teasing. She had no plans to repeat that mistake. While Byron spoke to the guard, she peered at the nearest Cosbolt. Standing in the shadow of the fighter, she felt dwarfed by the size and obvious strength of the ship. It would crush her tiny plane.

"I've requested to see the crew chief," said Byron, moving to her side. "As soon as I've confirmed the Firenta has replacement parts for my Darten, we'll locate my friends."

She nodded, her eyes never leaving the Cassan ship. "It's so much larger than your fighter."

"The Darten is built for speed and agility. The Cosbolt is all about firepower and endurance. It's our elite fighter; the first into combat. Only the best fly this ship."

Athee glanced at Byron, alerted by the tone of his voice. "And you were one of the best?"

"I was," he stated without inflection.

The hanger chief arrived and Byron arranged for replacement parts for his Darten. He then requested the location of Squadron Leader Nintal. The chief indicated they would find the man on the simulator levels.

The guard isn't coming with us? Athee asked, glancing over her shoulder. The Firenta security officer remained by the shuttle.

As a senior officer, I am your escort, Byron announced. *So don't get me into trouble, all right?*

Once outside the hanger, they entered a large telepod. The ones on the Rennather were much smaller and Athee scanned the device from top to bottom. When Byron chuckled, she elbowed his arm.

This may be ordinary to you, but it's still new to me, Athee chastised.

Then by all means, enjoy.

He led her out of the telepod and down a wide hallway. Unusual sounds echoed from two open doors up ahead. Athee could hear multiple motors and hydraulics in use. Her curiosity grew as they approached the wide doorways. Byron paused and glanced at the numbers over each door.

This one, he announced, turning to the right.

Athee trotted to keep up with the Cassan, but her gait slowed as she viewed the large room. The rows of machines confused her and she stared at the closest device. What appeared to be the cockpit portion of a Cosbolt was secured to a rolling base and several hydraulic arms. It listed to one side before the nose dipped lower. Athee noticed that she couldn't see inside the cockpit. She wondered as to the purpose of the machine.

It's a simulator, Byron announced, startling Athee. She noticed he was waiting and she increased her pace.

What do you mean? she thought as she rejoined him. The noise from each machine was minimal, but with so many operating at once, it created a steady disturbance.

Byron pointed at the nearest one. *A computer creates a scenario with images inside and the roll of the craft adds to the realism. Simulators are used in training while the crew becomes familiar with the craft and on flagships for practice and to prepare for difficult situations.*

Athee offered an absent nod, still feeling confused. Byron patted her arm.

I'll show you one before we leave. Come on.

She followed him up a short flight of stairs and into a small control room. Two men watched through the large window overlooking the room. A third man hunched over the console, monitoring the machines. The man nearest the door glanced up as they entered. His broad face broke into a grin.

"Byron!" he cried, moving toward the pilot.

Athee caught Byron's delight as he clasped the man's outstretched hand. He thumped his back before turning to the other man, who responded in kind. They were obviously pleased to see Byron.

"Damn, it's been ages," the second man said, slapping Byron on the arm.

"You've been avoiding us," the first man added, a mischievous smirk on his face.

"Apparently I didn't hide well enough," declared Byron.

None of the men's thoughts were guarded. Similar images flashed through their minds and Athee realized they were old friends. Her mentor's open thoughts surprised her. Byron showed no traces of his reserved nature now and seemed at ease in their presence. That aspect alone amazed her. He let down his shields for so few people.

The first man's gaze shifted and his eyebrows rose when he noticed Athee. "I see you're keeping better company these days."

Byron motioned her forward. "This is Senior Officer Ernx, Cosbolt pilot," he said, indicating the first man.

She sensed curiosity as he shook her hand. Ernx was shorter than Byron and the lines around his mouth suggested he was a few years older. However, the gleam in his eyes revealed a man with many youthful qualities.

"And this is Senior Officer and Squadron Leader Nintal, Cosbolt navigator."

The second man was taller and more stoic, with an air of authority. His short cropped hair added length to his muscular face. He returned her handshake and stepped back, placing his hands behind his back. The man's scrutinizing thoughts penetrated her very being. Unnerved, Athee edged closer to Byron.

"We served together on the Sorenthia many years ago," he told her. "Men, I'd like to introduce you to Prefect Orellen's niece, Athee, and one of Tgren's best pilots."

"Welcome aboard the Firenta, Athee," stated Nintal, addressing her with respect.

I bet she's one of Tgren's best looking pilots, Ernx thought.

Athee beamed with mischief. The man had addressed his comment to Byron, unaware that she could hear his mental voice. *Thank you, Officer Ernx,* she replied, affecting a gracious pose.

The man's eyes grew wide and the smile vanished from his face. Byron laughed at his friend's reaction.

"The Tgrens are developing psychic abilities," he said, offering her a wink, "and Athee's are the strongest we've tested so far."

"Damn!" said Ernx, shaking his head and glancing at Nintal. "Guess I better watch what I think."

"You should've read the report on this planet before we arrived," scolded his navigator.

"Well, my apologies, Athee. I didn't realize you possessed telepathy."

She nodded in acceptance of Ernx's apology. Athee shot Byron an inquisitive glance.

He straightened his shoulders and took a deep breath. "That's not all," he said. "She's a jumper."

This time both men registered surprised. Nintal's face grew longer, wiping away the man's solemn expression. Ernx's mouth fell open and his stunned thoughts escaped his mind without inhibition. Their scrutiny intensified as the men's minds processed this information and broadcast their contemplations.

Women didn't teleport. Only Cassan men possessed that ability. And jumpers were incredibly rare. That a woman enjoyed Byron's rare gift...

Sensing indignation, she straightened her shoulders. A reassuring thought from Byron settled her irritation.

"Damn! You're kidding, right?" Ernx stammered, finding his voice.

"No, I'm not," Byron answered.

Athee glanced at the pilot, surprised by his calm reply. His smug expression did not hide the gleam in his eyes that meant he was speaking with his mind as well. She didn't catch the exchange, but somehow she knew he'd come to her rescue.

The rolling thoughts of disbelief and resentment subsided. Regaining control, the men began to question Athee. Byron fielded most of the questions, providing her a moment to gather her wits. Thoughts of amazement continued to drift from Ernx's mind, but she felt she'd gained a measure of respect from Byron's friends.

"Officer Nintal?"

The navigator turned to the man at the controls. "Yes?"

"The simulator run is ending, sir."

Byron gave Ernx a light shove with his elbow. "Why aren't you participating? I'm sure you could use the practice."

The man's indignant thoughts were offset by his playful grin. "Look who's talking! Why don't you have a go?"

Athee's heart skipped a beat at the prospect of seeing his skills in the cockpit of a Cosbolt. Byron smiled and shook his head. Upon seeing the pilot's reaction, Nintal's brows came together.

"You should," he stated. "We're the last squadron until after the midday meal."

Byron affected disinterest and glanced at Athee. "I promised we'd at least take a look at the simulators. As soon as your squadron departs, we'll do just that."

He said goodbye to his friends, ignoring Ernx's final jab regarding the simulators. Feeling disappointed, Athee waited with Byron in the control room while the squadron exited. She wished his friends possessed stronger powers of persuasion. Perhaps she could talk him into one flight. Even if it wasn't the real thing, she still wanted to see him pilot the giant fighter.

Leading her to the nearest machine, Byron began explaining how it worked. Seeing the simulator up close increased her comprehension of the device, but it was still confusing. How well could it replicate actual flight when fastened to the floor inside a large room? From the outside, it presented a bumpy ride at best. Afraid of offending her escort, she feigned intrigue as she listened to Byron's monologue.

When he let her slip into the navigator's seat, Athee's interest sparked. She'd viewed the interior of his Darten, but never enjoyed the privilege of sitting in the ship. The main panel control was compact and arranged differently from that of the shuttle. Eager to understand, she asked the purpose of every unfamiliar button and screen.

Byron answered her questions without hesitation. He explained how the connection between pilot and navigator was vital to flying the ship. Athee was in awe of the symbiotic relationship. It really was two people flying as one. She longed to share that moment with her mentor.

"Can we try it?" she said, unable to contain her enthusiasm any longer.

Byron laughed. "You don't know the first thing about flying a Cosbolt."

"I know enough to fly the shuttle," she protested. "And you said it can be flown by one person if necessary. I'll let you handle the controls."

"Athee, do you realize how much training is required to master this fighter? They don't just throw anyone into the cockpit."

"I think I can fake it. Besides, it's not like I can crash the ship."

"No, but..."

She realized he was stalling. "And I'm sure you remember how to fly one."

"That's not the point," Byron replied.

"Well, what is the point?"

"I just can't, all right?"

Athee slapped her thighs in exasperation. "Can't or won't?"

Byron frowned in disgust and looked away. He closed his mind, but not before she caught the flicker of a stray thought. She perceived a moment of tragedy that still haunted Byron. Athee recalled her conversation with Mevine and realized the source of his reluctance. He'd not set foot in a Cosbolt since he lost his navigator almost twenty years ago.

Athee tried to touch his mind but met with resistance. Byron's mental shields remained locked in place. Lifting her hand, she lightly clasped the fingers that clutched the cockpit's outer shell. Her grasp grew stronger and he finally turned toward Athee.

"I know why you no longer fly Cosbolts, and I understand," she said, her voice low.

Beneath her fingers, his grip on the metal tightened. Even with his mind closed, the strength of the emotions that surged through Byron reached Athee. Her chest tightened as her own feelings of loss swirled in response. The approaching alien ship could take away all she held dear. Either of them might die in the process. This might be her only chance to share a flight with Byron.

"You flew with me that day, through the canyons," she said, holding her voice steady. "I really want to know what it's like to fly with you. Please?"

He stared at her a moment, the muscles in his face tight across his cheeks. Something flickered in his eyes and Byron sprang to his feet. Startled, Athee lifted her body from the seat in an attempt to follow Byron. She hesitated as he raced up the stairs and into the control room. Through the glass, she could see him talking with the officer on duty. When she saw him exit the small room with two helmets in his hand, Athee let out a chirp of excitement. He was going to fly a Cosbolt!

"I requested a very short freestyle run," Byron announced as he handed her the helmet. "No targets and no objective. Try not to navigate us into the side of the Firenta."

His tone was severe, but Athee believed it was due to resignation rather than anger. She wiggled the helmet onto her head and at once noticed the old, overused odor that lingered inside. The faceplate bore signs of wear as well. Byron waited while she fastened her harness, adjusting her helmet once, before he slid into the pilot's seat.

Still fiddling with her position in the seat, Athee was startled to see the canopy closing. It snapped into place, plunging the cockpit into near darkness. The control panel came to life and she gazed in awe at the glow of colors. She scanned the gauges and hoped she'd remember their uses.

Bright lights appeared on the canopy and she jumped. A ring of lights illuminated, disappearing into blackness down a long tunnel.

That's the simulation, Byron explained. *We're in the launch tube now. Are you ready?*

I'm ready.

Athee grasped the throttle out of habit. Silly, Byron is flying this ship, she thought, releasing it and resting her hands over the proper controls.

"Launch in three...two...one..."

The jolt of acceleration pressed her back into the seat. The lights of the tunnel raced overhead. Athee felt a surge of adrenaline as the ship increased speed and shot out into the darkness of space.

That felt so real, she thought, gazing with wonder at the stars.

Remember your job. What is the location of the Firenta?

She glanced at the main screen and noted the ship directly behind their vessel. *Behind us!*

Don't tell me. Show me.

Feeling their connection, Athee projected an image of the flagship and its location. She caught Byron's approval at once.

That's the primary job of the navigator, he thought. *Maintain awareness of all objects and convey that information to the pilot.*

That must be difficult when many ships are flying.

Byron chuckled. *It's even more crazy during a battle when ships are jumping in and out.*

The ship pulled to the left. The star pattern changed as Byron circled and placed the Firenta in their view.

We'll do several passes over the ship, he announced. *That will help you maintain perspective.*

He flew in low over the Firenta. Athee felt torn between the view outside the cockpit and her screen. The shuttle's radar also displayed space in three dimensions, but not with such clarity. She could see every small protrusion and curve of the flagship. Noting the proximity of its surface as the Cosbolt dropped lower, Athee conveyed that information to Byron.

Good! he thought, pulling away from the ship.

Swinging wide, Byron flew past the engines. Athee had a quick look at the rear of the ship before stars filled their view once more.

That was incredible! she thought, allowing her delight to radiate into his mind.

Let's do it again then.

They made another pass over the Firenta. This time Byron darted in between the higher structures of the flagship. Athee felt the sharp motion as their Cosbolt tilted from side to side. On the outside, the movement of the simulator seemed rough. Inside the cockpit, their flight was smooth. She cried out with delight as he completed another pass.

This time, you select our course, he thought.

Me?

Yes. I'm going to maintain a constant altitude and you tell me the path to follow.

Athee took a deep breath. *I'll do my best.*

Don't worry, I won't let us crash, he thought with a sense of amusement. *And I'll keep the speed slow and steady.*

Flying low, Byron made another approach. Athee could see the uneven landscape of the ship and it looked like an obstacle course. Tearing her attention from the real view, she focused on her navigational screen. Noting a large bulk rising in their path, she suggested he veer left. Byron obliged and the Cosbolt flew around the tower of metal. Plotting their course, she navigated them through the obstructions, relying only on her display. Byron followed her direction with ease. They emerged into open space once more.

I did it! Athee thought, the knots in her shoulder muscles loosening.

Just like flying through those canyons, Byron replied.

Except you're the one flying.

You were navigating, so we were both flying.

Athee grinned, pleased with that assessment. *It must be wonderful to share this experience with another.* Still connected with Byron's mind, she sensed a fleeting thought of regret.

Byron circled around and soon the landing bay came into view. *Now let's land this ship.*

Athee doubted she had much to do with the actual landing, but the Cosbolt entered the bay at the correct angle and speed. Byron touched down the runners and reversed the engines. Immediately the ship's speed decreased. It came to rest on a marked panel. The systems shut down and the view vanished from sight.

Now you've flown in a Cosbolt, he announced as the canopy retracted.

And you've finally flown one again, Athee thought, shielding her words from Byron.

Byron emerged first and assisted her out of the simulator. He helped Athee with the helmet and pulled the device from her head. Free from her confines, she flashed him a bright smile.

"That was incredible," she announced, still giddy from the flight.

"Glad you enjoyed it."

Athee grasped his arm and gave it a gentle squeeze. "Thank you. If we die tomorrow, at least I got to share that joy with you."

Byron cocked one eyebrow. "Let's hope it doesn't come to that."

They returned to the shuttle. Byron confirmed the crate of requested Darten parts resided in the cargo hold before joining her in the cockpit. He slumped into the pilot's seat and leaned his shoulder against the backrest. Athee swiveled to face him.

"What's going to happen tomorrow?" she said. The joy of the simulator ride was now fading and the weight of approaching doom filled Athee's mind.

Byron sighed and rubbed his forehead. "I don't know. Depends on if the other flagships can turn away the alien ship. Or if our scientists find a way to stop it."

"And if they can't?" she said, rubbing her fingers together.

"Then we'll have to prepare for the worst."

His words sent a chill down her spine. Her entire world might cease to exist tomorrow. It was all happening too fast.

"A year ago, we didn't even know there were others out there," she said, mulling over the rapid changes. "Now we're about to have ships filling our skies."

"I'm sorry," Byron offered, leaning his elbows on his knees. "I suspect your people would be better off if they'd never met us."

Athee frowned at that thought. "No we wouldn't. Eventually, we would've discovered that alien site and poked around until we blew up the control room on our own. Then no one would be here to help us."

Dropping her hands to her lap, she forced her face to brighten. "And I wouldn't have met you."

He returned her smile, an unusual gleam in his eyes. To Athee's surprise, he reached over and grasped her hand. Clasping it with both hands, Byron rubbed her fingers with his thumb, his gaze transfixed on the process. Lifting his chin, he met her eyes. His mind unshielded, Byron's thoughts projected affection. Her emotions stirred, grasping at the possibility that he cared for her as well. They were now close enough to kiss. Athee held her breath, waiting for him to make the first move.

Byron's eyes unfocused and he leaned back. "Our passengers are returning," he announced, releasing her hand. "Go ahead and fasten in."

Concealing her disappointment, she reached for her harness. Why couldn't they enjoy just five more minutes of privacy?

Byron stepped out to greet his passengers. Athee secured her harness, her fingers fumbling with the straps. She glanced out the cockpit window. Her uncle was deep in conversation with the commander, and judging from his rapid hand movements, he was agitated. Reaching out to touch his mind, she discovered a whirlwind of thoughts. Unable to focus on a single topic, Athee crossed her arms in indignation. The conference's resolution would have to wait until they reached the surface.

Byron transported his passengers to the Rennather first. Before the commander departed, Korden told Byron he was to return after dropping off the prefect. Athee contemplated joining her uncle in the main compartment, but stayed in her seat. Her curiosity remained, and she listened again for her uncle's mind. Now that he was no longer engaged in conversation, his thoughts were clearer. Her fingers wrapped around the armrests when she caught the word "evacuation."

Byron slid into his seat and Athee turned at once to the pilot. *We're evacuating Ktren?* she demanded. The proposition of moving the entire population to another location seemed daunting.

Yes, he thought. *No one is to remain.*

But where will we go?

I believe your uncle has selected a location.

She caught his disturbed thoughts and found it difficult not to press for more details. Fighting her growing impatience, Athee bit her lip in frustration. She wanted answers.

Byron wasted no time returning to Tgren. The moment the shuttle touched the ground, Athee unfastened her harness. She dashed into the main compartment and confronted her uncle.

"We're evacuating? To where?"

Orellen removed his harness and rose to his feet. "To the foothills of the Red Canyons," he said.

"The Red Canyons?" she cried. "The Dven Caves are closer."

"We could not house the city's population in those caves," Orellen stated, moving toward the open hatch. "Nor do we want to be below ground."

"Do you realize how long that will take?"

"Yes, I do! Which is why we must begin at once."

The prefect exited the craft, his long strides carrying him down the ramp in two steps. The guard followed, but Athee paused at the open hatch. She pivoted on her heels and faced Byron. The pilot's expression exhibited stoic resolution. Despite the urgency of the situation, she was reluctant to leave his presence.

Byron grasped her shoulder. *Go. We've a lot to accomplish today.*

Athee nodded, feeling numb. She exited the craft, her heavy steps kicking dust as she crossed the flight line. Moving everyone in Ktren to the Red Canyon was a monumental task. It would require dozens upon dozens of flights to transfer the population. She and the other pilots would spend every hour flying, probably right up until the alien ship arrived.

Jolted by the reality of that thought, she paused to watch the departing shuttle. *Byron, will I see you before...?* she thought, tears coming to her eyes as the ship lifted into the sky.

Yes, he answered. *I promise.*

Clutching her fists at her side, Athee closed her eyes. As long as she would enjoy his company again, she'd maintain hope.

Chapter Fourteen

Byron returned to the surface with Officer Seheller and a regiment of security officers. Once the prefect announced the evacuation, including the reason behind the order, there could be trouble. Korden wanted to ensure their people and equipment were removed without incident.

Officer Seheller ordered his team to begin packing equipment. Little remained at the alien site and the only Cassans present were a small security team. Garnce was to drop off reinforcements before flying to the city to assist with the evacuation. Judging from the amount of people and equipment in the Cassan facility, Byron suspected it would take all day.

When he asked Seheller who was returning to the Rennather on the first flight, the man offered a short list.

"I need as many strong backs as I can get to pack all of this equipment," Seheller explained, placing items in a padded crate.

"I'm adding one more to your list then," Byron replied.

He searched the downstairs offices until he located Mevine. He was struggling to set a heavy piece of equipment into a sturdy case. Byron came to his rescue and slid the machine into place.

"What's yours?" Byron demanded, fastening the case.

"Well, I was using this translator," Mevine stammered, placing a hand on the case and glancing around the room. "And of course there's my personal computer pad."

"That's it?"

Mevine blinked. "Technically, yes."

Byron grasped the handle and hoisted the heavy case. "Grab your computer pad and follow me," he ordered.

Without waiting to ensure Mevine would comply, he exited the room. The whole building buzzed with activity. Several men brushed past him in the hallway, their bodies uncomfortably close. Byron reached the foot of the stairs and glanced behind him. As expected, Mevine followed the pilot.

"Where are we going?" the young man asked as they ascended the stairway.

"To our room to pack."

Reaching the second floor, Byron grabbed the door handle to his room and pushed hard. Bursting into his quarters, he set the case by the door and reached for his bag.

"But there's so much equipment to organize," Mevine protested.

Byron threw open the doors to a small wardrobe and reached for his flight suits. "Yes, and Officer Seheller wants the strongest to remain to pack. Which means you're leaving on the first flight."

A flash of indignation erupted from Mevine. "I can still help!"

Tossing his suits on the bed, Byron whirled and grabbed the boy by the shoulders. "Mevine!" he said in a voice meant to illicit total compliance. The lad might want to stay and help, but their cause was better served with Mevine working to find a solution from the safety of the Rennather.

"The Tgrens are going to panic when they hear of the alien ship. They may turn on us. Do you understand?"

Mevine's mouth opened. He stared at Byron. Obviously, the thought of a Tgren riot had not crossed his mind. Pressing his lips together, the young man nodded. Byron eased his grip on Mevine's shoulders and calmed the agitated thoughts in the boy's head.

"I want to be sure you reach the Rennather safely, all right?" he asked, his tone less severe.

"Yes, sir," Mevine answered.

Patting his right arm, Byron released Mevine. "Now come on, we need to pack."

With only one good arm, Mevine could not carry both his bag and the case. Byron handed over his lightest bag, confirming his friend could carry it before shouldering the other two. Grabbing the heavy case, he ushered Mevine into the hall and surveyed the room one final time. Satisfied they had gathered all personal belongings, he closed the door. Byron followed Mevine down the stairs.

Officer Seheller, how long before the first load is ready for transport? he thought.

One cart is almost full, the man replied. *The officers will be ready in a moment.*

The sound of a siren pricked his ears. Byron picked up the pace, his rapid footsteps prompting Mevine to move faster. The wailing siren grew louder as they reached the exit. The lonely and desperate cry rang throughout the streets of Ktren. His nerves jangled in response to the sound.

One cart was already full of equipment. Byron directed Mevine to the second cart, noting the passage of several running Tgrens. The street bustled with activity as people and carts moved with purpose. Fear hung heavy in the air. Byron used it to fuel his adrenaline. He needed to be alert and prepared for anything.

A small battalion of Tgren guards arrived just as three science officers joined them. One of the men conferred with a Cassan guard before ordering his troops to surround the carts. Byron shoved Mevine onto the cart and took the seat beside him. Once the other Cassans were settled, he told the man driving the cart to depart.

The procession plodded through the streets of Ktren. Their speed was hampered by the presence of Tgrens scurrying to reach their destination, many driving similar carts. The siren continued to wail, bringing a heavy fog of unease to the otherwise pleasant city. Mevine fidgeted in his seat and Byron sensed apprehension in his young friend. He resisted the urge to calm the lad. They weren't safe yet.

More than one Tgren flashed the Cassans a resentful scowl as they passed. An older man shouted an unintelligible threat, but he didn't approach the carts. A stray rock flew over their heads, missing Mevine by a hair. Byron didn't catch sight of the perpetrator until a second rock struck the side of the bench. Their Tgren guards chased away the young man and he ducked down a side street.

The procession turned another corner, and Byron noticed several men placing boxes on a small cart. The Tgrens looked up as the first cart rolled past their position. Even at that distance, Byron could not miss their scowls.

"You brought this upon our city!" one man said, pointing at the Cassans on the second cart. The other men gathered at the Tgren's side as he approached. "You and your damned technology, poking about in our business."

"Stand back," ordered a Cassan guard, placing himself between the angry men and the cart.

With an enraged cry, the Tgren who'd spoken shoved aside the guard. His companions joined in the fracas and the Cassan went to the ground. The other guards immediately moved to intervene, pulling the attackers off the fallen man.

The man who'd started the fight staggered against the side of the cart. He grasped the vehicle and looked up at the passengers. Byron's muscles tightened as the Tgren's gaze fell on Mevine. The man snarled at the boy and grasped the front of his shirt. Wrapping an arm around Mevine's chest, Byron grasped the back of the seat and placed his booted heel on the man's chest. The Tgren fell backward and only Byron's hold on Mevine prevented his friend from tumbling to the ground as well.

The attacker leapt to his feet and Byron reached for his weapon. The sound of a laser blast, followed by Tgren gunfire, caught everyone's attention. Byron did not turn his head, but through peripheral vision, he noted two guards with weapons pointed in the air. The man who'd seized Mevine hesitated, distracted by the sound. When his attention returned the science officer, Byron pointed his weapon at the man's head.

"Don't," Byron said, his voice calm. The Tgren froze, his teeth clenched.

"All of you, move back," ordered one of Orellen's men, waving his weapon at the men.

Mevine's attacker remained where he stood as the carts rolled past. Byron put away his weapon and slowly sank to his seat. Mevine sat up straighter and adjusted his tunic, his fingers trembling. Byron patted the boy's good shoulder in assurance and turned his attention to the street.

For the most part, the presence of Orellen's guards kept the natives at bay. It was still a tense journey, lasting far longer than necessary. Byron breathed a sigh of relief when the carts rolled through an empty hanger and onto the runway.

Garnce's shuttle sat next to Byron's and several guards surrounded the craft. The sound of rumbling engines caught his attention. He noticed a line of small Tgren fighters rolling out of the largest hanger. He resisted the urge to confirm Athee's presence among the pilots. Byron would worry about her safety later.

Pulling up alongside his shuttle, the men at once began to unload the carts. Byron instructed Mevine and another science officer injured in the blast to stow their gear and remain out of the way until the ship was loaded.

You can ride in the co-pilot's seat, he told Mevine before he could protest.

Byron began grabbing equipment. The Tgrens stood guard while the Cassans unloaded the carts. Byron made three trips into the cargo hold of his shuttle before he realized Garnce had not budged from his cockpit.

Garnce, we could use your help, he thought, scowling at his fellow pilot through the cockpit window.

This is grunt work, the man replied.

Indignation rose in Byron's chest. *Get off your ass and help! That's a direct order, pilot.*

The man grumbled in protest, but rose from his seat. Byron hauled a large case to the cargo hold and secured it in place. When he returned for another load, he caught Garnce hoisting a box from the second cart. Scowling, the man carried it into his shuttle. Byron shook his head, annoyed by the pilot's attitude. He would not tolerate apathy today.

As he secured his passengers, a commotion outside caught Byron's attention. He glanced out the open hatch and noted two Tgrens arguing with those escorting the carts. He realized they wanted the carts and were protesting the Cassan's use of Tgren property. The argument escalated into a shouting match within seconds. One man shoved a Cassan security officer and he stumbled back against the cart.

Alarmed, Byron emerged from his shuttle. Before anyone could intervene, two Tgren guards stepped between the man and the officer. The Cassan stood erect and faced his attacker.

The Tgren lunged forward again, lips pulled into a snarl. The local guards caught the man before he could reach his intended target. Byron watched the scene unfold with a sick feeling. Tensions would only increase as the day progressed.

"Officer Byron, we'll keep several men stationed for your return," the closest security officer called.

Nodding at the man, Byron stepped back into his ship. *I'll let you know when we leave the Rennather.*

He closed the hatch and hastened to his seat. *Garnce, prepare for takeoff,* he informed the pilot.

Beside him, Mevine shifted in his chair, but did not speak. Byron quickly ran through the systems and lifted the shuttle into the air a moment later. He noted the departing Tgren planes as they launched into the sky and followed their trajectory toward the canyons. The traffic over Ktren was almost as congested as within the city. Sending a message to Garnce, he jumped the shuttle.

The view outside the cockpit changed and the comforting sight of the Rennather materialized. The muscles across his chest relaxed. There would be many more trips today, but his friend was safe. Once the Cassans were all secure on the exploration vessel, he would focus on retrieving one more person from the surface. Byron hoped Korden would acquiesce to his request to bring Athee to the ship.

He glanced at Mevine and the science officer met Byron's gaze with wide eyes.

That is why I wanted you off the planet, my friend.

Checking the position of Garnce's ship, Byron guided his shuttle into the landing bay. Once through the double set of doors, he navigated the vessel into the middle of the main bay. Setting it down with a gentle tap, Byron shut off the engines. He opened the hatch from the cockpit and the sounds of hanger crew entering the ship filled his ears. Unfastening his harness, he rose to his feet. Mevine struggled for a moment with his harness and Byron offered his hand. Pulling the slight boy to his feet, he patted Mevine's good shoulder.

"Come on, we've work to do," he announced.

"Sir?"

Byron hesitated and eyed Mevine with curiosity. The young man straightened his back, affecting a rare pose of confidence.

"Sir, thank you for returning me safely to the ship."

"You're welcome," Byron answered, offering a brief nod.

"And I never properly thanked you for saving my life after the explosion..."

Mevine's voice faltered. A flush of red crept across his cheeks. Byron could hear the crew moving crates out of the cargo hold. He needed to assist with the equipment, if only to prevent damage to his ship. He couldn't leave Mevine in such a state of agitation, though. Byron approached the science officer and grasped his good arm.

"That's what friends are for, Mevine," he said, reassuring the lad with his thoughts as well. "Now, come on, boy genius. You've a code to crack."

The young man's eyes brightened. "Yes, sir."

Retrieving all Cassan personnel required four shuttle trips. Garnce's last load comprised of security officers from the city and the alien site. The evacuation was far from complete, though. Byron had time for a quick bite of food before the shuttles returned to the surface, each carrying several security officers. Korden had pledged Cassan assistance in transporting the people of Ktren to the Red Canyons. Byron hoped the Tgrens would appreciate this act of good will.

Coordinating with Ktren's guards, the two shuttles landed near the loading planes. Dozens waited for a ride to safety, clutching sacks, bags, and small children. Byron opened the hatch and coaxed those closest to his ship to board. The men and women approached with hesitation, even with the Tgren guards encouraging them to climb aboard the shuttle. It took several minutes to persuade the first batch to enter, and longer still to stow their baggage and secure each harness. Byron realized his patience would wear thin by the end of the day. He sent a stern warning to Garnce. The last thing they needed was an incident during transport.

The larger Tgren planes were also ferrying passengers to the evacuation site. Byron selected a secure spot to emerge from their jump to avoid a potential collision. The scene below them was mass confusion as people attempted to erect shelters among the canyons. He'd noted a caravan of carts traveling toward the site as they departed Ktren and estimated their arrival would occur under the cover of darkness.

He suspected the shuttles would continue to fly until nightfall as well.

The sun continued to drop and soon cast shadows across the landscape. Darkness covered the land as Byron prepared to return for one final load.

Just seven Tgrens and a small load of cargo, the security officer in Ktren informed him.

Good, because I'm beat, he thought, lifting the shuttle into the sky. *Garnce, return to the Rennather. I've got this one.*

With pleasure, the pilot answered.

Byron landed near a small knot of people, grateful for the hanger lights flooding the runway. No planes were in evidence now, although he suspected fatigue as much as inability to see as the reason. His stomach had ceased to rumble hours ago and all Byron craved was his bed.

The security officers assisted with the passengers. Too tired to do more than watch, Byron leaned against his shuttle's exterior as the men and women entered the ship. He noticed three men from the hanger approaching the shuttle. Byron didn't move from his position until the light revealed their identities. He stood at attention as the prefect and two guards drew near.

"Prefect Orellen," he said in greeting, his husky voice revealing his fatigue.

"Officer Byron," the man replied.

Now that Byron could see his face, he realized the prefect's features displayed a similar exhaustion. The lights cast deep shadows across his face, accentuating the aging grooves in his skin. Orellen glanced at the passengers as they boarded and nodded.

"Please tell Commander Korden we appreciate your assistance with the evacuation," he offered.

"Yes, sir. How many of your people remain?"

"Less than sixty, and most of those are guards. They are patrolling the streets to ensure no property is damaged and everyone received notification of the evacuation. I am staying until I'm certain no one remains in Ktren."

"We'll return in the morning to assist," Byron offered.

"Appreciate that. Let's hope there aren't many stragglers," said Orellen, his eyes on the last Tgren as he entered the ship.

His inhibitions running as low as his energy, Byron decided to make a bold move. "Sir, after the last of your people have reached the safety of the canyons, I would like your permission to take your niece to the Rennather."

The prefect's attention shifted to Byron. "You wish to take Athee to your ship?" he asked, his thick eyebrows poised high on his forehead.

"Yes, sir. She'll be in no danger. The Rennather will break orbit and depart before the alien ship arrives."

Byron waited for the man's response. Orellen eyed him with skepticism, his hands clasped behind his back. To his surprise, he sensed acceptance of the idea.

"You guarantee her safety?"

Straightening his shoulders, Byron presented his most confident look. "With my life."

Orellen nodded, his eyes straying to the waiting shuttle. "I'll contact Commander Korden to ensure that happens."

Byron felt relieved, but wanted to be sure Athee's uncle believed him. "I promise Athee will be safe with me."

"Of that I have no doubt, Officer Byron." The prefect's attention returned to the pilot, his expression somber. "We will see you in the morning."

Byron wished the man a good evening and entered the shuttle. Checking the harnesses of his passengers, he returned to the cockpit and prepared the ship for one final flight to the canyons. As he lifted the shuttle into the air, his mind replayed the exchange with the prefect. The man's agreement to his proposal meant he trusted Byron with Athee's life.

Maybe I've finally earned his respect, he thought.

Bleary-eyed from a lack of sleep, Byron staggered out of the dining hall. In his haste, he'd hardly tasted the food. He entered the closest telepod, and his stomach continued to protest the rapid consumption of his meal. The commander would offer a sharp reprimand if he was late to the officers' meeting, though.

To his credit, he was not the last to arrive. The commander scanned those present, his thoughts shielded and beyond Byron's reach. Korden began the moment Seheller slid into his seat.

"Men, the Rennather will break orbit as soon as the evacuation of Ktren is complete," he announced, hovering over his computer screen. "We will monitor the situation from a safe distance and be prepared to jump if necessary.

"Officer Byron, how many more on the surface require transport?"

"The prefect informed me around sixty, sir," he answered, hoping that number had not risen this morning. "We should be able to move them in three trips."

Korden nodded and leaned on his desk. "The situation is grim," he admitted, his brows pulled tight. "The three flagships engaged the alien vessel early this morning. I'm afraid the results of that encounter were not favorable. One flagship lost her shields completely and received substantial damage. The other two ships hope to restore their shields by the time they reach this galaxy. However, despite the intensity of the attack, the alien vessel received minimal damage and lost none of its speed."

The weight of the news fell on the room with a nauseating thud. Byron felt sick to his stomach and wished he'd forgone food this morning. If three flagships couldn't stop the invader, what options remained?

The commander tapped his computer pad. "A recovery vessel was also lost, but only three Cosbolts were destroyed. Either they are too small and fast," Korden said, shaking his head, "or the alien vessel doesn't view the fighters as a threat."

"If the flagships couldn't penetrate the hull, then I doubt fifty squadrons of Cosbolts could inflict much damage," Anceptor observed.

"There is talk of loading several drones with explosives and detonating them beside the engines," offered Korden, dropping his chin. "This tactic would have to be performed before the alien vessel reaches orbit, though."

"And if that doesn't work?" someone asked.

The commander raised his head and focused on his chief science officer. "That is why I hope you have some good news for us, Officer Seheller."

The man shifted in his seat and gripped his computer pad tighter. "Sir, I don't have a solution just yet, but I can tell you what we've discovered so far. I'll begin with the data we've translated," Seheller said, leaning back in his chair and licking his lips.

"It appears the Tgren race was an experiment."

"A what?" demanded the security officer.

"An experiment? By whom?" another man asked.

Byron stared at Seheller in stunned disbelief. The entire population on Tgren was nothing but an experiment? He'd heard of other races tampering with genetics, but not on a planet-wide scale. It was beyond the abilities of all the known races.

Korden held up his hand for silence. "Elaborate."

Seheller nodded. "The Tgrens are not indigenous to this planet. They arrived in an alien craft, the remains of which we uncovered near Ktren. Once released, the Tgrens were allowed to develop at their own rate. From what we can tell, they were one of many such experiments."

"Were they under observation?" Anceptor asked, leaning forward.

"We don't believe so. Not active observation. From what we've translated so far, it appears the race that planted the Tgrens was interested in how long it would take them to reach full development."

"In what? Technology?" demanded the commander.

The science officer slumped in his chair. "We don't know yet. But the device that scanned Ullen was attempting to verify that development, and the Tgren did not possess it."

The commander's cheeks drooped and he sank into his chair. Byron leaned back in his seat, at a complete loss for words. Had they indeed unearthed the alien device too soon? Was the Tgren race now doomed to extinction?

"We also compared the schematics of the alien site's technology and that of the approaching vessel," Seheller continued, his voice unusually loud in the still room. "Sir, they are of the same design."

"Have you determined the purpose of the alien ship?"

The man straightened his shoulders, his eyes on the commander. "The sensor data that we've collected indicates that the ship houses a device similar to the one on Tgren. We believe its first course of action will be to scan the area around Ktren for the appropriate level of development."

Korden drummed his fingers on the desk. "And if it doesn't find what it seeks?"

"My people are still working on the final translation," Seheller offered, swallowing hard. "But we think it might consider the experiment either tampered with, or a failure, and shut it down."

"You mean annihilation?" demanded Anceptor.

"It's a possibility," the science officer conceded, his voice low.

As voices rose, protesting this development, the commander called for silence.

"Seheller, it's imperative that your team discovers what this ship seeks," Korden stated, his deep voice overriding all others. "I want a brief report I can forward to the flagships immediately."

"Yes, sir."

"Dismissed!"

The men rose to their feet and Byron sent the commander a private thought. *Sir, if I could have a word before I depart?*

Officer Byron, I need to speak with you as well.

Commander Anceptor and the security officer lingered, asking questions. Byron waited with a growing sense of impatience. He was pressed for time, but refused to leave without stating his plea for the removal of one Tgren from the planet. He hoped Orellen had conveyed his request, which would validate Byron's proposal to ensure Athee's safety. If Seheller's assessment proved correct, he was not about to leave her on the surface to face certain death.

As the two officers exited the room, Byron approached the commander. "Sir, I'd like your permission to grant Athee sanctuary on this ship and remove her from Tgren before the alien ship arrives," he said in an urgent voice.

"Officer Byron, I received a similar request this morning from Prefect Orellen," Korden stated, gazing at his computer screen. "Considering her importance, I am inclined to accept his request."

A weight lifted from Byron's shoulders. "Thank you, sir."

"You have your orders. Dismissed."

Chapter Fifteen

Notifying Garnce of their departure, Byron dashed to the hanger. The two shuttles launched a few minutes later and teleported to the surface. The sun had cleared the mountains, filling the valley with bright rays of light. The clear morning was a sharp contrast to the darkness approaching Tgren, and Byron felt his chest tighten. Why did the morning have to be so bright and cheery while those inhabiting the planet were on the brink of destruction?

Sixty-three people remained in Ktren. He and Garnce performed two trips to the canyons and returned for the final load. The prefect greeted him as the hatch opened.

"I believe this is everyone, Officer Byron," he announced as he entered the ship. "I sent word for Athee to meet us upon our arrival."

Byron ushered the man into the cockpit while he secured the other passengers. Confirming Garnce's readiness to leave, he lifted the ship into the air. The prefect did not speak during the short flight. Byron had detected his heavy mood the moment the man entered his ship. Orellen might be unaware of the approaching ship's purpose, but he knew the situation was grim. Byron didn't voice his concerns. The Tgrens didn't need to know today might be their last.

As he set the shuttle down on the dusty canyon floor, Byron caught sight of Athee among those waiting for the prefect. He shut off the engines and opened the hatch by remote. Tossing aside his harness, he turned to assist Orellen to his feet. The man grasped his forearm, forcing Byron to meet his eyes.

"You keep her safe," he ordered, his voice but a hoarse whisper. "And if something happens..."

"I'll keep Athee safe. And we'll find a way to defeat this enemy," Byron answered, mustering conviction he did not feel.

Orellen nodded and released his arm. The prefect exited the shuttle and was greeted with a firm embrace from his niece. The man stepped aside while the other passengers disembarked, maintaining his hold on Athee.

Byron confirmed nothing remained in the cargo hold before returning to the open hatch. He caught the Tgren woman's distress at once. She struggled in her uncle's arms, wiggling in an attempt to break free.

"Uncle, I'm not leaving you!" she cried.

"Athee, I am ordering you to return with Officer Byron to the Cassan ship," he responded.

She continued to squirm, pulling away from the prefect. Alarmed she might break free, Byron trotted down the ramp and placed his hand on her shoulder. Athee flashed him a desperate look, her face twisted with agony. Determined her anguish wouldn't sway him, Byron presented a firm expression. His thoughts enforced his resolution to take her to the Rennather. Uttering a desperate cry, she faced her uncle again.

"I can't leave you now," Athee cried.

"You have to go."

She attempted to break free, but to no avail. Uttering an anguished cry, she threw her arms around Orellen's neck. Byron released her shoulder and stepped aside. The prefect hushed Athee, his eyes closed.

"You go with Officer Byron," he said in a soothing voice. "You'll be safe with him, understand?"

"What if I never see you again?" she gasped. "You're my only family!"

Orellen patted her back. "We'll see each other when it's over. I promise."

Releasing Athee, he nodded at Byron. Grasping her shoulders, Byron pulled her free and guided her up the ramp. A wave of panic burst from Athee as they entered the shuttle, and Byron wrapped an arm around her middle. Hitting the button that controlled the door, he closed the hatch. Athee cried out as the door sealed and her uncle vanished from sight.

In the confines of the ship, her agony broadcast loud and clear. The sensation pounded at Byron's temples. He blocked the memories Athee's tortured thoughts brought to the surface of his mind. He had to keep a clear head.

Maintaining his hold on the distressed woman, he led her into the cockpit. She ceased to struggle and dropped with resignation into the co-pilot's seat. Byron fastened her harness before sliding into his seat and preparing for liftoff. He signaled to Garnce and the two shuttles rose in the air. Turning away from the canyons, he placed a suitable amount of distance between the ships and the Tgren encampment. Tapping into the teleporter's power, he jumped to the Rennather's location.

Secure at last in the exploration vessel's hanger, Byron shut off the engines and powered down the systems. The ship fell silent, allowing ambient noises from the hanger to penetrate the hull. The deep hum of the Rennather's engines permeated the shuttle's walls, vibrating the air. Unfastening his harness, Byron glanced at his unwilling passenger. Athee had not moved or uttered a sound. The woman continued to stare out the cockpit window, her breathing slow and steady.

Sliding out of his seat, Byron reached for Athee's harness. She offered neither resistance nor assistance with the procedure. Her demeanor appeared calm, but he could hear the tumultuous feelings raging inside the woman. Dropping to one knee, Byron spun her chair and forced Athee to face him. Her body began to tremble. She bit her lip as if to forestall the tears that now filled her eyes. A gasp escaped her lips and Athee covered her face with her hands.

This time, Byron couldn't just watch her cry. Wrapping an arm around her body, he pulled Athee closer. Without any inhibition, she grasped his neck and clung to the pilot. Byron didn't know what to say and focused on calming Athee with his mind. He held her close as the tears gave way to short gasps for air.

"Officer Byron, did you acquire the prefect's niece?"

Korden's voice discharged with force from the com system. Reaching for the control panel while maintaining his hold on Athee, he pressed the button. "Yes, sir. Shuttles are secure in the hanger."

"Very good. We're breaking orbit now."

Byron's attention returned to Athee. She wiped her eyes with the back of one hand and took a deep breath. Raising her chin, she met his gaze.

"Come on," he enticed, grasping her hands.

How will we know what's happening? she thought, her mental voice heavy with distress.

Byron rose to his feet. "We'll watch from the bridge, all right?" he said, gesturing for Athee to stand.

Leading her from the cockpit, they exited the shuttle. Byron maintained a hold of Athee's hand as they strode across the hanger. She couldn't run now, but his touch had a soothing effect on the woman. Selecting the closest telepod, he transported them to the bridge.

The control room bustled with activity. The commander noticed their presence, his eyes meeting the pilot's for a brief moment. Korden nodded but did not order Byron and Athee from the bridge. Stepping away from the entrance, Byron selected a vantage point out of everyone's way. Athee curled one hand around his arm and clung to the railing with the other, her grip tight on both. She stared at the elongated window, her gaze occasionally straying to the many screens surrounding the natural view. The large screen on the bottom revealed the view from behind as the planet began to shrink in size. The Firenta was already lost to the naked eye.

They observed the scenario in silence. Athee's thoughts were troubled and filled with anguish. It was almost beyond comprehension that they might witness the destruction of every person on her planet. Byron couldn't imagine losing everything he'd ever known on such a massive scale. When the day drew to a close, Athee might be only Tgren in existence.

"Commander Tencor on the com, sir," an ensign called.

Byron glanced toward Korden. The commander nodded at the man and leaned on the display table.

"Commander, we have reached our vantage point," he stated in a loud and resigned voice. "We will monitor the situation from here."

"Very good. We will break orbit shortly and intercept the alien vessel," Tencor answered. "The Cosbolt drones are ready and all three flagships will release their fighters in one hour.

If the drones don't stop that ship, we'll engage the enemy until our shields are exhausted."

"Understood. Good luck, Commander Tencor."

Athee released his arm and grasped the railing with both hands. Byron rested a hand on her lower back, hoping to provide some measure of comfort.

What will happen then? she thought. *What happens when that ship reaches Tgren?*

Dropping his chin, he shielded his thoughts. It didn't matter, though. Athee already knew the fate of her people.

Everyone will die, her mental voice whispered.

You don't know that, Byron asserted. *I've faced worse odds. There's always hope.*

She turned to face him, her lips pressed in a thin line. Byron detected a deep need for assurance as Athee edged closer. Fighting the conflicting thoughts as they arose in his mind, his shields dropped and Byron reached out to the young woman. He wanted nothing more than to comfort Athee.

Grasping the hand wrapped around his arm, Byron attempted to provide assurance. Athee pressed closer, her thin frame trembling. He felt her mind reach out, seeking solace. Byron allowed a connection. Balling his free hand into a fist, he forced his thoughts to remain optimistic. The Tgren woman drew strength from Byron, and he pressed his convictions even harder. Athee needed him, and that fact was strangely comforting to Byron.

His mind's shields lowered, another voice entered his thoughts.

Officer Byron! What's your location?

Frowning at the interuption, he leaned away from Athee. *We're on the bridge, Mevine.*

We?

Athee is with me.

Mevine's emotions spiked with excitement. *Athee is here? Sir, that's incredible.*

What do you mean? Byron asked, meeting Athee's concerned glance.

I know what the alien ship seeks!

What are you talking about, Mevine?

Sir, I'll be there shortly to explain.

"Commander?" Seheller's voice rang over the com. "We may have a solution. I'm on my way to the bridge."

Athee gasped and reached for Byron's arm. Puzzled by Mevine's cryptic words, he shook his head. Together they pivoted to face the main entrance.

A moment later, Seheller and Mevine burst into the room. The young man noticed Byron and Athee, and his concerned expression gave way to elation. He bounded over to his friends while the senior science officer continued toward the commander.

"Sir, I cracked the code!" Mevine gasped, brandishing his computer pad. "We were wrong about the alien device."

"What do you mean?" said Byron, reaching out to take the pad.

"It wasn't seeking a level of technology."

"Officer Mevine!"

Seheller's reprimand caught the young man's attention at once. "Commander, my apologies," he stammered.

Byron felt Mevine pull on the computer pad. However, he wasn't ready to give up the device yet. The screen displayed the alien encryptions, but his friend's translation interested him more. Mevine tugged again and Byron glanced up as Commander Korden approached. The man's brows were drawn together. He did not sense disapproval of conduct as much as interest.

"If it's not technology, what do the aliens seek?" Korden demanded, closing the distance.

Releasing his friend's computer pad, Byron straightened his shoulders. Mevine clutched the device close and cowered as the commander hovered over the lad. Officer Seheller joined them and came to his junior officer's rescue.

"Sir, Officer Mevine just finished with his translations and discovered the objective. We believe it's the development of psychic powers."

Korden's focus remained locked on the young man. Hands trembling, Mevine held out his computer pad for the commander to examine. Scanning the screen, Korden glanced at the boy.

"You're sure of this translation?" he stated.

"Yes, sir," the young man offered, glancing at his superior officer. Seheller nodded and Mevine swallowed. "When the device scanned the Tgren, it sought to confirm the development of psychic powers. But he hadn't achieved the appropriate level yet, which is why it malfunctioned and sent a distress call to the alien vessel."

"Sir, that same device is located here," added Seheller, holding up his computer pad.

Byron leaned closer and noted the schematics of the approaching ship. The science officer pointed to a small section located on the underside of the vessel.

"If our calculations are correct, the ship will descend on Ktren and scan again for mental development."

"But Ktren is empty," Byron asserted, straightening his shoulders. "What will it do when it can't locate any Tgrens?"

Seheller met his gaze and a look of fear crossed his face. "It will either scan the surrounding area or..." His voice trailed off and he glanced at Athee.

Byron locked his shields into place. He wasn't about to reveal the possibility of total annihilation. Mevine was not so quick, though. Byron caught the young man's thoughts of destruction as they transmitted unchecked. Before he could send a word of warning, Athee gasped and grabbed his arm.

"Or it will destroy every person on the planet?" she cried, glancing from one man to the other.

No one spoke. Byron sought to comfort Athee, but her mind was a jumble of violent emotions. He could think of no words to settle the young woman. Sighing, he dropped his chin to his chest.

"It won't if it detects a developed mind," Mevine offered, his voice but a hoarse whisper.

As evidenced by a lack of response, the idea behind those words eluded the others. However, Byron caught Mevine's insinuation.

"What are you suggesting?" he demanded with indignation. "That we place Athee in its path?"

The young man stepped back, and Seheller moved to his junior officer's side.

"The device seeks the full psychic capabilities of its experiment," he stated. "No one else in Ktren tested as high as Athee. She possesses almost all of the elements..."

"Almost?" exclaimed Byron, growing more agitated.

"What elements, Officer Seheller?" Korden asked, his authoritative tone slicing through the tension.

"Sir, Officer Mevine discovered five psychic elements in the equation," the man replied.

Byron clenched his fists. "Athee only possesses four."

"That we know of," interjected Mevine, casting a guilty glance at the senior pilot.

"Officer Byron," said Seheller in a loud voice, "our tests only cover four aspects, but there are other mental abilities. Considering the strength of her known powers, we can only assume Athee is fully developed in all areas."

"And you want to risk her life on an assumption?" Byron demanded.

Korden held up his hand. Brows pulled together, he faced his senior science officer. "Is this an option, Officer Seheller? I need to know your level of conviction."

The man hesitated and glanced at his junior officer. "Officer Mevine is convinced. I support his theory."

Exasperated, Byron turned away from the group. He was angered by Mevine's suggestion. The device had all but destroyed Ullen, rendering the man brain dead. He was not about to allow Athee to suffer a similar fate.

"What do I have to do?"

Athee's question, laced with resignation, startled Byron. "No!" he said, grasping her shoulder.

"Those are my people down there," she protested, narrowing her eyes.

"We don't even know if this will work."

"But I have to try," Athee replied, shrugging off his hand. She turned to Mevine. "What do I need to do?"

Seheller cleared his throat. "You'd need to be in a position where the device can scan your mind. A small transport should be able to fly you close enough to activate the scan."

Athee licked her lips and nodded. "I'm willing to try."

"Let me contact Commander Tencor," announced Korden.

The commander gave orders to hail the Firenta and returned to the display table. Frustrated with the situation, Byron grabbed the woman's shoulders.

"Athee! Do you realize what might happen? Ullen is brain dead now. What if that happens to you?"

"I've got to try," she answered. "What if this is our only chance?"

"Damn it, I promised your uncle I'd keep you safe."

Then help me! Don't abandon me now, she thought.

Her soft plea was laced with fear. Byron flexed his fingers, still unwilling to acquiesce to her direct involvement. Athee's hands grasped his arms and he felt her tremble. Sensing his own vulnerability, Byron released her. Narrowing his eyes, he nodded. Athee's expression reflected her gratitude, and she managed a faint smile.

Irritated by his decision, Byron glanced around the room. Seheller had joined Korden at the display table as they awaited a response from Commander Tencor. However, Mevine had not moved and stood a few feet away. Byron's frown deepened and he channeled his anger toward his friend.

How could you make such a suggestion? he thought as he approached Mevine.

Officer Byron, please!

Byron grabbed the young man's shoulders. *What if she dies?* he demanded, digging his fingertips into Mevine's bony shoulders.

He didn't flinch, but Mevine's body shook. He clutched his computer pad to his chest, fear and pain emanating from his mind. Too angry to care, Byron stared hard at Mevine as he towered over the science officer's slight frame.

Sir, I wouldn't have suggested using Athee if I wasn't sure, I promise, Mevine thought, his mental voice filled with desperation. *I know how much she means to you.*

Mevine's words were punctuated by a hoarse, audible gasp. Byron continued to stare at his friend, his jaw working has he processed the lad's statement. Sincerity and a deep urge to please his friend dominated Mevine's thoughts.

I hope you're right, Byron thought, releasing the young man.

Commander Tencor's voice reached his ears. Turning away from Mevine, Byron joined the others.

"Unfortunately, that alien vessel is shooting down anything larger than a Cosbolt, Commander Korden," the man was saying, "and once we launch those drones, I predict all ships will become targets."

Reaching the table, Byron glanced down at the display. The image of the Firenta's commander occupied the center screen.

"We could return the Tgren woman to the planet's surface," Korden offered, leaning both hands on the table.

"I've seen the damage reports from this morning's encounter," Tencor said, his tone curt. "Neither flagship boasts full shields yet and my weapons officer doubts the drones will do more than slow the vessel. If you really believe we can stop this ship by another means, then we need to take action before the drones are launched."

Grasping the edge of the table, Byron lowered his head. His chest tightened as he realized there was only one solution.

Sir, I need to get her to the Firenta now, he said in a private thought to Korden. *A Cosbolt could take her close enough to activate the scan. But I need to be the one to pilot that fighter.*

The commander glanced his direction and nodded. "Commander, Senior Officer Byron will arrive shortly. Since it will require a Cosbolt to get the Tgren woman close enough to trigger the scanner, I recommend that Officer Byron pilot that fighter. He's skilled enough to fly solo."

Pushing off from the table, Byron grabbed Athee's arm before he changed his mind. *Sir, please request the accompaniment of Officer Nintal's squadron,* he told the commander as he brushed past Mevine.

Consider it done.

Leading Athee out of the control room, he located the closest telepod. Pulling her inside, Byron envisioned their destination

You're flying me to the alien ship? she thought, projecting disbelief.

Yes. Damned if I'm letting anyone else fly that Cosbolt.

Athee's hand slid into his, and their fingers entwined. *Thank you,* she answered.

They ran to the shuttle and prepared for takeoff. He requested exact coordinates for the Firenta, intending to appear just outside the hanger. She'd already jumped to the alien vessel's location and joined the other two flagships. With the drones set to launch soon, Byron realized they didn't have much time.

Chapter Sixteen

The shuttle emerged from its jump on target and Byron landed in the Firenta's bay. He and Athee were out of their harnesses by the time the shuttle came to rest in the main hanger. Several officers were waiting when they emerged. A man with a hanger insignia stepped forward.

"Officer Byron, we have a Cosbolt waiting," he stated, signifying they were to follow him. "You can suit up in our flight room."

"And Officer Nintal's squadron?" said Byron, concerned his request had been denied.

"They are preparing for flight now."

The man led them to a room full of flight suits. It took a moment to locate the appropriate size and gear for Athee. She was tall, but slender. Suits were designed to fit a larger male figure. When they found the correct size, the man laid the suit across the bench. The hanger officer turned expectantly to Byron and Athee.

Byron frowned. "Out!" he ordered. Athee did not require an audience while she changed.

The man was surprised, but he didn't linger. As soon as they were alone, Byron gestured to the suit. "I'll turn my back so you can change."

He looked away while she stripped out of her Tgren flight suit. He scanned the rows of flight suits, desperate for a diversion. After their mad dash to the Firenta, the lull felt unnerving. Byron tried to focus on their upcoming flight. His mind drifted to the possible outcomes. What if the alien device failed to scan Athee's mind? What if it continued on its path and reached Tgren? Those thoughts were minor compared to his real concern. What if the scan rendered Athee brain dead?

Glancing over his shoulder, Byron realized Athee was dressed. She fumbled with the snaps around the neck and he moved to assist her. Fastening the straps on the collar, he assured the suit was secure.

"I'll help you with the helmet when we're in the cockpit," he said in a controlled voice.

Athee nodded and adjusted the sleeves. Byron checked her collar again and she held still, her body rigid and eyes forward. His eyes met hers and he hesitated. Her mind swirled with apprehension, but the mission itself was not Athee's dominant thought. She feared she might never see him again.

Gazing into her eyes, Byron realized he shared her trepidation. This Tgren woman had invaded his world, demanding a large portion of his attention and energy. He'd fought it at every turn, unwilling to share his life with another. Faced with uncertainty and a mission that might eliminate Athee from his existence, Byron now found he treasured their time together. He treasured her being part of his life. And he didn't want to lose that wealth now.

Acting on impulse, he pulled Athee close and kissed her. A level of surprise that bordered on shock flowed from the woman. It was replaced at once by complete surrender. Shields down, Byron experienced a connection unlike any he'd ever encountered. Her previous feelings of affection resurfaced, filling his mind and confirming his suspicions. Athee's admiration and devotion ran deeper than mere infatuation. She loved him.

Slowly breaking their physical connection, he stared at Athee. Her eyes were wide with wonder as she gazed at him. His hand still rested on her neck, and Byron reached up with his thumb to stroke her cheek.

I will not lose you, he thought, determination pounding at his senses. Her hands clutched his flight suit even tighter and her spirits rose.

Now, let's get this over with.

Moving with purpose, he retrieved their equipment from the bench. Byron handed Athee her helmet and gloves. With a nod of resignation, he led her from the room.

The hanger was full of activity. Following the hanger officer to their ship, Byron noted several rows of Cosbolts entering the launch tube. Nintal's squadron would provide cover, although he hoped to approach the alien vessel undetected. With any luck, it would not perceive the Cosbolts as a threat and would ignore the fighters.

Turning his attention to their escort, Byron's gaze fell upon a lone ship. He eyed the vessel with trepidation as they approached. His final flight in a Cosbolt, so many years ago, flooded his mind and his chest tightened. He could not allow this mission to end with the loss of another navigator.

They ascended the stairs and Byron waited while Athee climbed into the cockpit. She wiggled her fingers into the gloves and he placed the helmet on her head. Satisfied with the seal, he patted her shoulder. Byron leapt into the pilot's seat, burrowing into the padded cushions.

Nintal? he thought, reaching out to his friend.

My squadron will be ready for you, the navigator answered, his mental voice ringing with confidence. *We won't let you down.*

That's why I requested you, my friend.

Byron felt the touch of Nintal's pilot. *Successful mission, Byron!* Ernx added, his thoughts radiating optimism.

I will not fail, Byron thought as he powered the ship. Nor will I lose another friend.

He ran through the systems check, including the functions of the navigator. Taxiing the ship into position for launch would fall to him as well. He would pull double duty for most of this flight. Despite their successful simulator run, Athee knew nothing when it came to navigating a Cosbolt. He couldn't expect her to function in that role with any proficiency. Considering the gravity of the situation, she would be in no state to offer assistance, either.

You all right back there? Byron thought, reaching out to his passenger.

Yes. Glad we had a chance to practice yesterday.

You let me worry about the ship's functions, he thought, lowering the canopy. It sealed with an audible whoosh.

I can still navigate! Athee protested. *It'll give me something to do.*

Her tension beat at his senses. Byron wished her first flight in a real Cosbolt was under different circumstances. Athee would've really enjoy this moment.

Don't be afraid. I'm with you.

"Officer Byron?" a voice called over the com. "The schematics of the alien vessel have been uploaded from the Rennather."

Accessing the ship's computer, Byron pulled up the layout of the ship. The section containing the scanner was highlighted. He studied the screen for a moment, contemplating their best approach. The device was contained within a deep recess. They needed to get the ship's attention in order to activate the scanner. It was possible the device wouldn't engage until the alien vessel reached the surface, but Byron pushed that thought to the back of his mind.

Pressing his head against the seat, he glanced out the cockpit window, awaiting the signal to move the ship. Athee's anxiety continued to broadcast without inhibition. Unnerved enough by his first Cosbolt flight in close to twenty years, Byron decided to calm his passenger with a diversion.

Feel the teleporter? he thought, tapping into the device's power.

Her thoughts joined his as they connected with the unit. The inaudible hum of the teleporter pulsated in his chest. His ability to perform multiple jumps provided a closer bond with the device. Since she shared his skill, he knew Athee felt it as well. Jumpers were rare. Byron doubted two had ever occupied the same cockpit. Their unique talent escalated their partnership to unimaginable levels. If he and Athee were a real Cosbolt team, they'd be invincible.

The com buzzed to life. "Officer Byron, move into position."

The ship rolled forward under his guidance. Byron paused while the launch tube opened and he slid the Cosbolt into the shaft. When the second door opened, his hand tightened around the throttle.

Prepare for launch, he told Athee.

"Three...two...one..."

The ship raced through the tunnel and burst into space. Athee's exhilaration filled the cockpit. Byron permitted a brief smile to cross his lips. Angling his trajectory, he joined the other Cosbolts.

"Wide formation," Nintal ordered.

Taking his place among the ships, Byron followed the squadron's flight path. Athee projected the position of the other ships, and he confirmed their placement. The purpose of the Cosbolt's controls might elude her, but she understood navigation.

As they rose over the Firenta, Byron got his first look at the alien craft. Its diminutive size surprised him. It wasn't much larger than the Rennather. Yellow strips of light ran the length of its oval shape, illuminating the dark blue surface. The scanner's location placed it on the underside of the curved nose and poised at an angle. The rest of the bottom's surface was flat as if designed for landing.

Let's prevent that from happening, he thought.

The squadron approached the alien vessel and reduced speed. Byron spied the other two flagships, each maintaining a safe distance from the craft. Lining up his ship to cross under the nose, Byron followed another Cosbolt as they prepared to make their pass. The lights on the underside of the alien vessel grew bright and pulsated with life.

"It knows we're here," Nintal informed his squadron. "Everyone stay sharp."

Edging the nose of his Cosbolt higher, Byron confirmed the exact location of the scanner. He reached out with his mind to reassure Athee and she signified her readiness. Gritting his teeth, Byron flew under the alien vessel.

The lights overhead were bright and filled the cockpit with an eerie glow. A second later, the Cosbolt emerged on the other side. Byron let out a bark of disgust.

It didn't scan our ship, he thought, conveying his words for all to hear.

Try getting closer, said Nintal.

Any closer and I'd hit the damn thing!

Athee's surprise mirrored his own. *Were we too fast?* she offered.

Byron glanced back as the squadron circled around the ship. Speed could very well be a factor. The alien ship and his

Cosbolt were both moving at a rapid rate. Perhaps he needed to match the vessel's speed in order to get its attention.

Byron, I've been informed we're running out of time, Nintal announced. *We get one more pass before they launch the drones.*

Clenching the throttle, he made a quick decision. *I need to rise up from below and pace the craft.*

You'll have to maintain a constant speed. And watch your position.

Touching Athee's mind, he detected her willingness. *We can do it.*

You be damned careful! ordered Nintal.

Following their leader's instructions, the squadron adjusted its flight pattern. Soon the alien ship filled the view over the canopy. Byron increased his speed until they were directly below the vessel's nose. Maintaining their forward thrust, he nosed the Cosbolt up toward the craft.

Help me get into position, he instructed Athee.

Byron, are you sure?

Yes. I trust you.

Locking with her mind, he adjusted their heading according to her directions. Athee guided them closer and the vessel's surface drew near. The indention that housed the scanner was directly overhead; its size suggested the Cosbolt would almost fit within the recess. Hands sweating inside his gloves, Byron brought the ship closer until the glow from the lights were almost blinding. The curve of the alien ship enveloped the Cosbolt. One wrong move and they were both dead.

Why isn't it responding? Athee thought.

I don't know! Its sensors must detect the ship.

It needs to detect me. Come on, I'm here! she thought, her mental voice bursting forth. *You must hear me. Please.*

Her mental voice cracked and Athee gasped.

Don't destroy my people!

The force of her final cry caused Byron to wince, but it elicited a reaction. The lights of the alien vessel dimmed, and Athee caught her breath. A shaft of pale red light touched the nose of the Cosbolt. Byron held their position as the light traveled across the ship's surface. He fought the urge to flinch as it entered the cockpit. Focused on the light, his arms trembled as he clutched the throttle with all his might.

The shaft paused for a moment and he realized it was scanning his mind. Warmth filled his head, causing his hair follicles to tingle. There was no other sensation outside of the faint heat. Failing to find what it sought, the beam vanished from view as it moved to the other occupant of his ship. Their minds still connected, he listened for Athee's reaction.

A blast of pain burst from her mind. Byron's eyes closed as his shields locked into place, protecting him from the searing fire. He squinted in desperation, his body trembling from the shock. The throttle shook in his hands as he fought to maintain control. He had to sustain their position and complete the process.

Holding steady, he confirmed the Cosbolt's placement within the recess of the alien ship. His mind still reeled, but he couldn't lose contact with Athee. Byron reached out and touched only agony. Ignoring the burning sensation, he held fast to her mind. He couldn't lose Athee now.

Suddenly their connection was severed. Frantic, Byron felt for his passenger and tried to establish a bond. He groped for a stray thought or spark of consciousness, but detected only a void. He could no longer touch Athee's mind.

Athee! he thought.

His call met only silence. Athee's mind was empty. Cold fury flooded his thoughts, sending a shockwave down his spine.

No!

Byron's mind touched the teleporter. Without altering his course or pulling away from the alien ship, he jumped the Cosbolt.

The Rennather's landing bay filled the view outside the cockpit. Commander Tencor would protest his choice of destination, as the Cosbolt belonged on the Firenta. Byron didn't care. The exploration vessel was safer.

Incoming wounded! he announced, broadcasting his thoughts to every open mind on the Rennather.

Pulling back on the throttle, Byron threw the engines into reverse. The Cosbolt's runners touched with a rough jolt as he landed the ship. The heavy fighter's momentum carried it to far side of the bay and he brought it to a rest moments before striking the far wall.

Officer Byron! the commander exclaimed, his thought loud in Byron's head.

I need medical personnel in the hanger immediately! Athee's mind isn't responding.

He continued trying to reach her as the Cosbolt was pulled through the double doors. The computer confirmed she was still alive, but her mind resembled an empty void. The thought of losing Athee cut deep into his soul, causing a wave of panic in Byron. Heart pounding in his chest, he removed his helmet and gloves and waited with growing impatience as the Cosbolt was towed into the hanger.

Unfastening his harness, he opened the canopy before the ship even came to a halt. Pulling himself upright, Byron realized the hanger crew was still scrambling to locate a platform tall enough to accommodate the Cosbolt. Unwilling to wait for an exterior foothold, he threw his torso across the divide between navigator and pilot. His hands grasped Athee's limp body as it lay crumpled in the seat.

"Athee!" he called, shaking the woman.

When she did not respond, he pried the helmet from her head and tossed it across the hanger. Adjusting her body's position, he rested her head against the back of the seat. Wrapping his hand around her neck, Byron felt her weak but persistent pulse. However, her mind displayed no signs of life.

Ripping off one of her gloves, he grasped the woman's hand. "Athee, come on. Wake up. You've got to wake up."

His mind projected his words as well, desperate to reach Athee. If she'd merely passed out from the experience, her brain would still be active. She couldn't answer, but he'd still be able to touch her mind. He probed deep into her thoughts, desperate to discover any indication of life within the woman.

Byron couldn't detect any brainwaves, though. No thoughts stirred in her head. Her mind was empty.

Pulling his body closer, Byron pressed the side of his head against hers. "Athee, please answer me," he gasped, squeezing her hand. "Please wake up. I don't want to be alone anymore."

Feeling tears come to his eyes, he squeezed them shut. The ache of loss gripped his heart, and he uttered a soft sob. She was gone.

Athee...

He pressed his cheek against hers, fighting the agony that threatened to consume him. Damn it, I can't do this again, he thought. I can't live without her...

Something stirred within Athee's mind. Byron grasped at the sensation, abandoning all inhibition. The ripple grew in intensity, and he clung to the thoughts as they strengthened. Suddenly, Athee's mind exploded back to life. Byron uttered a tearful cry of joy.

Athee, wake up now, he thought, leaning away to view her face. Byron adjusted his hold on her neck and gave her hand a gentle shake. *Come on, wake up.*

Her eyelids fluttered and he sensed she was regaining consciousness at last. Uttering a gasp, Athee opened her eyes. Byron greeted her with a relieved gasp of his own.

Welcome back, he thought, stroking her cheek with his thumb.

Her brows came together. *What happened?* she thought, her mental voice hovering above a whisper.

The scanner knocked you out. I couldn't even hear your mind.

Did it work?

I don't know. Byron pressed his forehead against hers. *I'm just relieved you're still with me.*

A loud noise caught his attention. Byron discovered a platform resting against the fighter. Medical personnel scurried up the ladder, arms pumping in frantic strokes. The lead man reached them and knelt down to examine Athee.

"She's awake now," Byron announced, the words cascading relief down his back.

The officer checked her eyes and nodded. "We need to get her to medical for a full evaluation," he cautioned, reaching for her other hand.

"No!" said Byron. He leapt from the cockpit, his torso sliding off the divide. "I'll get her."

Removing her other glove, he assisted Athee to her feet. She all but fell out of the cockpit, but he caught her in time.

Securing his hold, Byron scooped her up in his arms. She managed to place her arms around his neck, her body limp. The medical officers stood aside as he descended the stairs with care to the hanger floor.

She felt good in his arms. Drawing strength from the sensation, Byron held her even closer. He refused to set her on the gurney and announced he would carry Athee to medical. The two officers protested, but he kept moving toward the exit. The hanger boasted a larger-than-normal amount of personnel. Byron didn't slow his pace to take stock of the onlookers. His only concern was Athee's well-being.

Byron stayed with her while the medical officers performed numerous tests. Her mind registered on every level and appeared fully functional. Other than exhaustion, Athee had sustained no permanent damage. Relieved by the news, he suggested she sleep for a while.

I'll be right here when you awaken, he thought when she opened her mouth to protest. *I promise.*

Athee smiled at him and Byron squeezed her hand. She adjusted her head's position on the pillow, burrowing even further into the medical bed. She drifted into unconsciousness, her mind slipping into sleep mode. Her thoughts stopped projecting and fell to a soft murmur. Exhaling a deep breath, Byron allowed his muscles to relax. At least this time, Athee would awaken.

And I'm not losing contact with you ever again, he thought, his hands wrapped around her petite fingers.

Chapter Seventeen

Her body slowly roused. She wasn't yet ready to leave the comforts of sleep. Wrinkling her nose, Athee buried her face further into the pillow.

As her mind grew alert, she became aware of her surroundings. Subtle background noises reached her ears. A deep hum vibrated in her chest and an assortment of strange smells assaulted her nose. However, it was the presence in her head that snapped Athee out of slumber. Grasping her pillow, her eyes flew open.

Byron's wry grin greeted Athee. Still clad in his flight suit, the pilot rested on a stool beside her bed. He reached for her hand and gently untwined her fingers from their death grasp on the pillow. He didn't speak, but his comforting thoughts drifted through her mind.

How long have I been asleep? she thought, enjoying the sensation of his hand curled around her own.

Not long. Maybe an hour?

Wiggling her other hand free from the covers, Athee grasped his fingers. Byron leaned closer and enclosed her hands within his, thumbs rubbing her skin in a slow, rhythmic motion. His mental shields were absent and she was surprised by the level of affection residing within his mind. Drawing strength from his tender thoughts, Athee sought to quiet the one concern nagging at her heart.

What about the alien ship?

His smile grew. *It's currently on its way into deep space.*

The good news brightened her spirits, but something tugged at her thoughts. Athee struggled to focus on the wisps of information and images fluttering in her mind.

What's wrong? Byron thought, his grip on her hands growing tighter.

I'm trying to remember, she thought, grasping at the reflections in her head. It was like recalling a hazy dream. Anxiety began to churn in her stomach. *When that ship scanned me, I caught a glimpse of the beings who sent that ship.*

What did you see?

It wasn't so much a visual image as just a sense of purpose. Mevine was right. That ship was seeking proficiency of mental powers. We were an experiment. That alien race was trying to confirm our proper development. And if the ship hadn't scanned me, if the appropriate level wasn't discovered near the site...

But it did scan you, Byron thought, reassurance flowing from his mind.

My people could've been wiped out!

Byron lifted a hand and placed it alongside her cheek. *But they weren't.*

Athee stared at him, trying to process his words. Byron's thoughts were calming and a smile tugged at his lips. It dawned on Athee her worries carried no merit now. The ship was no longer a threat. Releasing all apprehension, she allowed her muscles to relax. Her people were safe, and that was all that mattered.

Athee pulled herself into an upright position. Byron adjusted the pillow at her back and grasped her hand once more. She grinned, feeling triumphant.

We did it, she thought.

Byron opened his mouth as if to protest that statement. He nodded instead. *Yes, we did it.*

She sensed more stirring in his thoughts and cocked her head. Byron's chin dropped and he stared at her hand.

I thought I'd lost you.

His words were tinged with anxiety, an emotion rarely exhibited by the stoic pilot. Disturbed by his distraught feelings, Athee squeezed his hand. She'd feared death, but for reasons beyond the confirmation of her own mortality. Dying meant she would leave unresolved feelings behind. Athee craved validation of the words she longed to utter. She'd almost lost the chance to say them. If she didn't speak now...

Byron, I love you.

Lifting his chin, Byron fixed her with a penetrating stare. *I love you,* he thought, his words causing her fingers to tighten their grip in response. *And I'm not about to risk losing you again.*

Leaning closer, he grasped her head and planted his lips on her forehead. The accompanying thoughts of genuine affection filled her senses. No longer inhibited, Athee allowed her own feelings to flow freely into his mind. Byron leaned away, his eyes closed and a faint smile on his lips. Byron's fingers stroked her hair, his touch full of purpose. Opening his eyes, he met her gaze.

I know I'm not an easy man to get along with, he thought. *And I'll not deny I value my privacy. I've existed in survival mode for most of my life, but I'm tired of it. I'd like to enjoy life. The only way I can do that is with you.*

Athee's heart beat faster. To hear Byron confess that he shared her desires overwhelmed her senses. She wanted nothing more than to spend her days in his presence. She had ached for a sign from this aloof Cassan for so long, anything that indicated he cared, and now Athee was enjoying a full declaration of adoration. Unable to contain herself, she smiled as tears came to her eyes.

Byron... she thought, trying to formulate an appropriate response.

His expression grew even more serious. *Athee, I want you to be my mate.*

Jolted by his unexpected words, Athee's mouth fell open. Abandoning all pretext of restraint, she leaned forward and threw her arms around his neck. His hands pressed against her back and she delighted in the sensation. Byron's physical touch was accompanied by an open connection with her mind stronger than their moments together in flight. Athee didn't fully understand bonding, but if it meant his thoughts would always be available, she relished the idea. At last, she'd gain some insight into this reserved, but genuine man.

A sound reached her ears and Byron pulled away. A medical officer had entered the room to check on Athee. She responded to his questions in a polite manner. However, the interruption annoyed her. Couldn't this have waited just five more minutes?

Don't worry. We've plenty of time ahead of us.

Pleased with that thought, her muscles relaxed.

Informing Athee she'd be discharged soon, the man departed. As he stepped out of the room, she noticed someone in the hallway. The person appeared to be hiding behind the doorframe, afraid to enter. She glanced at Byron and he winked.

"Mevine, I said you could enter!" he called.

The young man stepped into view, his shoulders down, and he peered anxiously into the room. Byron gestured him forward. Mevine took a few timid steps toward the bed.

"I...I wanted to be sure you were all right," he stammered. His balled fists moved with a nervous quiver at his sides.

Athee smiled to quiet his fears. "I'm fine."

"No permanent damage," Byron added, resting his hand across hers. "Technician even said she can leave medical soon."

Mevine's expression was one of relief. "That's good news."

He shuffled his feet and glanced down. His troubled thoughts, straightforward and unshielded, tugged at her heart. Athee waited for Byron's friend to compose himself. Mevine's brows came together and his shoulders drooped further.

"Officer Byron, Athee, I am really sorry I put you in such a dangerous situation. I was just so sure of my calculations that I didn't stop to think that you might get hurt or even die. I just wanted to apologize..."

"Mevine!" said Athee, exasperated by his self-defamation. "You saved my people."

He paused, mouth ajar. Brows coming together, the young man shook his head. "You're the one who took the risk. I didn't do anything..."

"Except break the code and come up with a solution," said Byron, finishing his sentence. "That makes you a hero."

Mevine's eyes grew wide. His fingers uncurled, hanging limply at his sides. Shock and disbelief rippled from his mind as he stared at them.

In Athee's mind, Byron chuckled.

"Remember what I told you? That you'd do something heroic on this assignment? You should've believed me." He leaned back on his stool. "And I'm sorry I was so harsh with you on the bridge. I should've trusted you as well."

His friend smiled at last, his anxiety subsiding. Byron continued to reassure Mevine and apologized again for berating the boy. Athee sensed Mevine's distress stemmed as much from his perceived loss of a friend as from the possibility of her demise. The science officer was very devoted to his idol. Aware of Byron's feelings, she realized he was just as devoted to Mevine.

Athee remained silent, content to listen to their conversation. She focused on Byron's hand curled around her fingers, enjoying the warmth and sense of connection it provided. More than once, she caught Mevine's attention shifting to their hands. His obvious interest amused Athee. Whether out of shyness or respect for Byron, he left the room without commenting on their physical contact.

When cleared to leave medical, clean clothes were brought to her room. The Cassan outfit hung loose on her frame, billowing from her arms. Athee decided it would suffice for now. She needed to retrieve her Tgren flight suit from the Firenta at some point.

"We need to return the Firenta's missing Cosbolt as well," Byron announced with a grin when he entered her room. He picked up her Cassan flight suit and flung it over his shoulder.

"Are you in trouble for bringing it here?" she said, adjusting the fall of her sleeves.

"Korden explained to Commander Tencor that my primary goal was to ensure your safety. The Rennather's location meant it was out of harm's way; thus it was the logical choice."

Athee straightened her shoulders, tired of fussing with the material. Byron grasped her shoulder, his thoughts possessive.

"And I wasn't trusting your life to strangers."

Giving her arm a squeeze, he gestured toward the hallway. "Come on, let's get something to eat. We'll return the Cosbolt later."

He led her from the room and into the hall. Athee glanced at the other rooms as they passed. Most of the beds were empty, but she noticed two occupied by sleeping men. She paused at the second doorway when she caught sight of the man's face. The dark complexion and black hair could only belong to a Tgren.

"Is that the man I helped carry out?" she asked, grasping the doorframe. Byron's hand pressed against her lower back.

"No, I'm afraid he didn't make it. That is Ullen, the scientist who was scanned by the alien device on your planet."

Athee stared at the man. His head was bandaged, as was his chest and right arm. Every computer screen above his bed was lit up with bright lights, their function beyond her comprehension. A mask covered his mouth and numerous tubes snaked from the machines to his body. She reached out to touch his mind but felt nothing. The sensation distressed Athee.

"His mind was wiped clean by the device. He's alive, but essentially brain dead," Byron said in a gentle voice. "After you were scanned, I feared the same thing had happened to you."

Glancing at Byron, she noted his solemn expression. Her gaze returned to the man and Athee felt a strange sensation. Something stirred within her mind. Following the subtle guidance, she approached the man's bed.

Looking down at Ullen, she noticed something puzzling in his appearance. His body exuded no heat. Glancing at Byron, Athee noticed a warmth surrounding him that was absent in the Tgren. Puzzled by the differences, she leaned closer to the man in the bed.

"What is it?" Byron asked, moving to her side. He'd obviously picked up on her conflicting emotions.

Athee shook her head. Stretching out her hand, she rested her fingers on the man's right temple. The coldness seemed to permeate the very depths of Ullen's mind. However, the absence of brain activity didn't stem from an empty mind. His thoughts seemed frozen and unable to respond.

"He's not brain dead," she announced.

"How can you tell?"

"I hear him."

Closing her eyes, Athee focused on Ullen's mind. It was as if his brain lacked a pulse. A body without a heartbeat died. However, the man's mind was still alive. It just needed a jump-start. If she provided a strong enough jolt, it might bring his thoughts alive and shatter the frozen barrier. She simply had to concentrate...

A sensation similar to teleportation seized her chest. Recalling her endless hours of training with Byron, she tapped into that energy. Concentrating on Ullen's mind, Athee poured the burst of energy into reaching his trapped thoughts.

Hear me!

Her efforts impacted his brain with the equivalent of a lightning bolt. Ullen's mind responded with a ripple of thought extending outward as it traveled. Similar to the effects of the morning sun rising on the desert, the flower of his mind opened and bloomed. Within seconds, only warmth emanated from the man.

Athee opened her eyes. She felt Byron grab her arm.

"Athee! His mind's active again."

She removed her fingers from his temple. Ullen's eyelids fluttered in an attempt to open.

"We need a medical officer in here immediately!" Byron bellowed, his fingers still wrapped around Athee's elbow.

Taking a step back, Athee continued to stare at the man as he returned to consciousness. Now that she was no longer connected to Ullen's mind, she could sense Byron's stunned disbelief. Straightening her shoulders, she met his wide eyes.

How did you do that?

I'm not sure...

Two medical officers ran into the room. One bent over Ullen while the other checked the monitor. The Tgren started to struggle and pulled at his mask. Confusion filled his mind and Athee reached out to comfort the man.

It's all right. You're aboard the Cassan ship. You were brought here because of injuries received at the alien site.

Ullen peered up at her and she smiled in assurance. He became still and allowed the medical officer to readjust the mask. The man at the monitors gasped.

"His brain's functioning again. I've never seen anything like this."

"You healed him," Byron announced, as stunned as the medical personnel.

Both officers ceased their examinations and stared at Athee. "But how?" one stammered, his voice filled with awe.

"I sensed his mind was still intact but...frozen," she explained. "Ullen needed a jolt to restart his brainwaves."

The man at the monitor shook his head. "I've never seen this done before. I don't even know of a race capable of healing the mind."

Byron twisted her body to face him. "The fifth area of psychic ability?" he asked in a hushed tone.

The implications of such a talent struck Athee with force. The power to reach a silent or injured mind would be invaluable. If she possessed the ability, then other Tgrens were capable as well. Lifting her chin, she winked at Byron.

"At least we know what it is now," she stated.

"We need to inform the commander," he replied.

"Officer Narunva will be interested as well," the medic offered.

Athee smiled, delighted by the discovery. Byron's hand dropped to her fingers, securing a tight hold.

"We'll inform everyone after we eat," he declared. *I don't know about you, but right now, I am starving!*

Athee laughed and agreed with his plan. If they didn't eat first, they might not find another opportunity for hours. Glancing one more time at Ullen, she allowed Byron to lead her from the room.

As they exited the medical facility, he cast a suspicious glance her direction. *Any more surprises I should know about?*

Athee flashed a wicked grin. *If I told you, then they wouldn't be surprises, would they?*

Chapter Eighteen

Byron announced his presence and was given permission to enter. He strode into Korden's office with a bounce in his step.

"You wanted to see me, sir?" he said, standing at attention.

The commander looked away from his computer screen. "Take a seat, Byron," he instructed, leaning back in his chair.

The absence of a formal title with his name piqued Byron's curiosity. After serving together for fifteen years, the commander's relationship with him resided at a level different than with other officers on the ship. Korden and Anceptor had returned a few minutes ago from diplomatic negotiations on the surface. Byron assumed he was about to receive privy information. Eager to hear the latest developments, he slid into the chair across from Korden.

"The Tgrens have agreed to allow us to build a base here," the commander announced. "It will serve many purposes, the list of which continues to grow. One of its primary directives will be further research on the alien site. Now that the alien equipment is functioning again, High Command wants a full analysis. They want to know more about the race that created that ship, as well as the possible connection to other races, including our own."

"Think we were an experiment as well?" said Byron, arching an eyebrow.

Korden offered a light shrug. "It' a possibility. That's why High Command wants a science team stationed here. Those already present will receive first consideration, of course. I doubt we could drag those men from the site after the events of the past month."

Recalling Mevine's excitement, Byron chuckled. The lad had bubbled with enthusiasm when he heard power had returned to the alien site. Now that his friend had a handle on the alien code, he was eager to translate every piece of information he could discover. Mevine wanted nothing more than to remain on Tgren for as long as the fleet would permit.

"It would crush Mevine's spirit if he had to leave now," observed Byron.

Dropping his hands into his lap, Korden smiled. "That young officer is not in question. His assignment here is guaranteed."

"What other teams will be assigned to the base here?"

"Several squadrons of Cosbolts, along with a team of psychic and medical officers will be stationed on this planet. We will continue to test and train the Tgrens on the use of their psychic powers. High Command hopes to bring Cassans who've lost their abilities to the facility and revive those powers."

A ripple of hope traveled through Byron. "Such as those who lost their senses during the Vindicarn War?"

"Precisely."

That was good news to Byron. So many men had lost their mental powers due to Vindicarn disrupter blasts. The chance to end the silence in their minds would be worth the long journey to Tgren.

"We have one more day of negotiations before the Rennather departs for Cassa. The diplomats will remain for another week, and the Firenta will continue patrolling the area. This sector will become a rotating flagship assignment."

"We'll have a base to defend," Byron observed. "So, we're going straight home?" The Rennather still had two months remaining in her schedule.

"We'll be missing half of our crew," the commander said with a chuckle. "Plus we'll have two very important passengers traveling to Cassa."

Byron permitted a smugness to tug at his lips. Athee had already received clearance to return with him to Cassa. However, the identity of the second person eluded him. One possibility crossed his mind and concern swept through his thoughts.

"Prefect Orellen isn't coming with us, is he?"

A grin tugged at the corner of Korden's mouth. "No, I'm afraid we won't enjoy that pleasure. One of his officials tested as high as Athee in psychic ability, and the prefect has cleared the man's passage to Cassa."

"Good," said Byron, relaxing further in his chair. "He can play test subject for our psychic scientists then."

"High Command still wants a full evaluation of Athee, though. Teleportation is a rare trait in a woman."

"Any word yet on my request?"

Korden's fingers strummed the edge of his desk. Byron sensed resistance to his proposal from High Command and his defenses tightened. He'd made a promise to Athee.

"I believe they are taking it under consideration."

"I would think a Cassan-Tgren Cosbolt team stationed here would represent a step of faith and strengthen diplomatic relations."

"I stressed that point. And placed emphasis on her excellent flying skills and ability to perform multiple jumps. However, Athee's citizenship might prevent her from entering the program."

"Is that the primary objection?"

"According to Chancellor Dentex, yes. He said the other issues were negligible as far as he was concerned."

Byron pressed his lips together. He'd discussed returning to Cosbolt service with Korden, and his commander was in favor of the plan. Assignment to Tgren wouldn't be difficult either. It all hinged on his potential navigator. Byron would not fly without Athee as his partner. If citizenship was the only obstacle…

"Then please inform Chancellor Dentex of the elimination of that objection."

Korden frowned. "How so?"

"By the time we leave Tgren space, Athee will be my mate, and a Cassan citizen by default."

The commander's eyebrows rose. It was a rare moment that Korden exhibited genuine surprise. Byron had stunned the man with his announcement. He'd not discussed it with his senior officer, citing the events and hectic schedule of the past two weeks as his excuse. If it lent strength to his request that Athee train as a navigator, then Korden needed to know Byron's intentions. He also doubted the commander would allow her to stay in his quarters unless they were bonded.

"That certainly changes the situation," Korden admitted. He fixed Byron with a penetrating stare. "You're sure of your decision?"

"Yes, sir, I am."

The commander leaned forward, pressing his elbows on the desk. A slow grin spread across his face. "Finally meet your match, Byron?"

"I'd rather think of her as my equal," he replied.

"Is the prefect aware of the arrangement?"

Byron laughed as he recalled Orellen's response. He'd expected resistance, and the man's initial thoughts confirmed his prediction. However, Athee's overpowering enthusiasm had negated those feelings. With little protest, the prefect had acquiesced to his request.

"I think it's the only reason he agreed to Athee's passage to Cassa."

Korden nodded. "Then I will notify Chancellor Dentex of this arrangement."

"Thank you, sir."

"Byron, I will miss your presence on the Rennather, but I am glad you are finally moving on with your career. And your life," the commander announced, his voice carrying an edge. "I think you have made a wise decision, on all accounts. With Athee as your navigator, you will make an exceptional squadron leader here on Tgren."

"Thank you, sir. I've appreciated the opportunity to serve you on the Rennather."

Korden smiled, and Byron sensed genuine appreciation and friendship in the man's thoughts. He'd always remained on good terms with the commander, maintaining respect for Korden's level of authority; however, he'd never considered him a real friend. Byron realized that in the passage of time, he'd forgotten how to develop a true friendship. Athee and Mevine had shown him the way again. The return flight to Cassa would provide an opportunity to solidify his friendship with Korden. He'd have time to rectify the situation

A little dense, but I'm still learning, Bassa, he thought.

His door panel chirped, announcing a visitor. Byron grabbed the last two boxes on the floor and jammed them into his crate. Dropping the lid, he rose to his feet. Adjusting his flight suit, he brushed aside his recently trimmed hair and signified for his guest to enter. Byron was surprised when the panel slid aside, revealing not one but two visitors.

"Ernx, Nintal! What are you doing here?" he asked, gesturing them into his quarters. Both men exchanged handshakes with Byron.

"One of our shuttles was transporting goods to your ship, so we hitched a ride," Ernx explained, leaning against the small corner table. "Couldn't let you leave without saying goodbye."

"Especially since we rarely get to see you anymore," added Nintal, his accusing tone offset by the smile tugging at his lips.

"Well, soon you'll know where to find me."

Ernx's face broke into an enormous grin. "Yes, we heard you're recertifying as a Cosbolt pilot and returning to Tgren."

"That's the plan. And I've been told there's a chance I will be placed in charge of the six squadrons assigned to Tgren."

"Byron, that's great!"

"Congratulations," said Nintal.

Ernx slapped him on the arm. "Glad you've decided to fly a Cosbolt again. I mean, I know why you didn't want to fly after the war, but you're too damned good a pilot to quit forever."

"Thanks," Byron admitted, glancing at the floor. "I made a promise though."

At the sound of footsteps, he looked up just as Nintal's hand came down on his shoulder. The navigator gave a quick squeeze with his fingers, his expression serene.

"And I believe Bassa would say you've fulfilled that promise."

Byron nodded in agreement. For almost twenty years, he'd flown for an exploration ship. It was an adventure he would've shared with his friend if not for Bassa's premature death. Between his promise and a reluctance to fly without his former navigator, Byron had remained in exploration. As Nintal had pointed out, he'd more than fulfilled his obligation. More importantly, he was healed and ready to move forward with his life.

Patting his friend's arm, he offered a smile. "I'm sure he would," he said. Besides, I have a new promise to fulfill now, he thought.

"Is it true that the Tgren woman will train as your navigator?" Ernx said, his voice tinged with interest.

"Yes, she will," Byron admitted, crossing his arms.

Ernx let out a loud exclamation of surprise. Nintal stepped back and exchanged glances with his pilot. Defenses rising, Byron fought the urge to grow angry with his friends. After all, it wouldn't be the last time someone expressed shock that his partner was a woman.

"Damn, if that won't create a stir," Ernx observed. "Hope you're prepared."

"I can handle it."

Ernx flashed his navigator a wicked smirk. He shifted his stance and his boot heel came in contact with the crate.

"Sorry," Byron said, reaching for the crate. "I was trying to rearrange this place before I retrieved our last two passengers from the planet's surface."

"You don't have to share your quarters, do you?"

Ernx's question was punctuated by a laugh. Lifting the crate into the air, Byron set it atop another crate nestled in his closet. He closed the compartment and stared at the door, his jaws clenched tight. Turning to face his friends, Byron noted their furrowed brows. Abandoning all traces of uncertainty, he straightened his shoulders.

"Yes, I do," he said without reservation, "because I am taking Athee as my mate."

Ernx's mouth fell open and his entire body sagged in slow motion. The pilot's stunned thoughts projected from his mind without restraint. Even Nintal's composed expression succumbed to disbelief. His friends' reaction did not surprise Byron and he prepared for some good-natured harassment. Navigator and pilot exchanged glances and gasps of surprise before Ernx let out a whoop of astonishment.

"Damn, I don't believe it!" he proclaimed. "Byron, are you serious?"

Leaning his hand against the closet, Byron affected a determined pose. "Of course!"

Ernx emitted a bark of laughter and glanced at Nintal. His friend crossed his arms and shook his head.

"No offense, Byron, but I think we're just surprised you would finally choose a mate after all this time," the navigator offered.

"I'm not surprised by your choice, though," Ernx added.

"Oh?" Byron demanded.

"I could sense the connection between you and Athee the first time we met her."

Byron tightened his mental shields, embarrassed by Ernx's observation. Had he been that transparent? Would he lose the ability to hide his feelings once she was his mate? That thought distressed Byron more than the act of bonding itself.

"You won't regret it," Nintal stated, his knowing grin oddly comforting.

"So your navigator will also be your mate? You always liked to do things a little different," said Ernx. "Glad to see you haven't changed in that respect."

Sensing his friends' approval, Byron nodded. He glanced at his computer screen and noted the time.

"Well, I hate to rush off, but our two Tgren guests are awaiting a shuttle ride to the Rennather."

"I'm sure our shuttle is waiting for us as well," Nintal announced.

Byron said goodbye to his friends in the hanger. He hoped years wouldn't pass before he saw Ernx and Nintal again. Previous meetings had always evoked painful memories. Seeing his former shipmates no longer gnawed at his heart, though. Aware of the fragility of friendships, he wanted to maintain contact with those who mattered most in his life. Ernx and Nintal would always be good friends, no matter what distance separated them.

Emerging over the valley, Byron guided the shuttle toward Ktren. It would be over a year before he viewed the Tgren city again and he enjoyed the approach across the desert floor. The wind was minimal and he flew low over the colorful vegetation. The hanger crew had cleaned his ship last night, but Byron doubted all traces of the desert were gone from his shuttle. Sand from Tgren would travel to Cassa, exactly as he'd predicted.

Pressed for time, he picked up his passengers first. A small group waited near the largest hanger as he touched down on the runway. Byron powered down his ship and opened the hatch. Five men and two women approached. A small cart laden with several bags followed. Athee's arm was wrapped around her uncle's, her expression anxious. Exiting the ship, Byron waited at the foot of the ramp, his eyes on his future mate.

"Prefect Orellen," he said in greeting, inclining his head in a show of respect.

"Officer Byron," the man replied, pausing a few feet from the shuttle. Orellen glanced at the man beside him. "This is Second Official, Erndell. He will be accompanying you to Cassa."

"Sir," said Byron, nodding at the Tgren. "We are pleased to have you join us."

The prefect gestured to his guards and they reached for the bags on the cart. Byron showed them where to stow the baggage and secured his cargo before returning for his passengers. Erndell hugged the other woman, promising he would return soon. Athee was equally involved with her uncle, and Byron gestured for Erndell to board the shuttle. Once assured the man was fastened in his harness, he waited at the open hatch for his final passenger.

Athee's arms were around Orellen's neck. The prefect met Byron's eyes as he approached. The mistrust was absent now, but the man's heavy heart revealed itself in his drooping cheeks. The prefect was distraught over his niece's departure even as he envied the adventure she would experience. Orellen nodded at Byron and patted Athee's back.

"Time for you to go," he announced, releasing the woman. She clung to his hands and he beamed at his niece. Stretching out his arms, he indicated that Byron was to take her hands.

"I give her to you, Officer Byron. Please watch out for this precious young woman."

Grasping Athee's hands, he pulled her away from the prefect. "I promise to guard her with my life, sir."

Athee's emotions were conflicted. Her mind filling with resolution, she took her place beside him without protest. She offered a weak smile and Byron rested an arm around her shoulders.

"I still wish we'd performed an official ceremony," Orellen said, his expression pensive.

"Our pairing will be no less meaningful," Byron answered. "And once we've bonded, it will be more permanent than any ceremony."

Athee's smile grew and her eagerness bubbled forth. Byron squeezed her shoulders and his attention shifted to the prefect.

And thank you for entrusting me with Athee, he stated in a private thought.

The prefect straightened his shoulders, a smirk tugging at his lips. "I've learned it's best to acquiesce to a woman's heart…and to trust her judgment."

Grinning, Byron offered a salute. He couldn't agree more with Orellen.

Coaxing Athee into the ship, he closed the hatch. His second passenger took her customary seat in the cockpit, and Byron grinned as she fastened the harness. His days of flying alone were gone. To his surprise, that idea pleased him.

I need to make one more stop before we return to the Rennather, he announced to his passengers. Athee cocked her head and he winked. "If I leave without saying goodbye to Mevine, he'll never forgive me."

Byron flew a direct route to the alien site. As he approached, he called out to Mevine and requested the young man to meet them outside.

Is the Rennather leaving now? his friend answered in a wave of panic.

It will once we are safely on board. And I've a third passenger, or Athee and I would come in to see you.

I'll be right there!

Byron set the shuttle down and shut off the engines. He grinned at Athee as they unfastened their harnesses. He detected gratitude from the woman for the opportunity to say goodbye to Mevine. Byron followed her from the cockpit and he nodded an apology to Erndell.

Sorry, sir, this will only take a moment, he thought, projecting an image of Mevine.

The young man who saved us? Erndell thought. *By all means, Officer Byron, take as long as you need.*

Chuckling at the Tgren's assessment of Mevine's accomplishment, Byron opened the hatch. He held out his hand for Athee. Moving with care, he led her down the ramp. Before they could take two steps, a figure burst from the cave entrance and raced down the hill. Byron watched with concern as Mevine traversed the rocky terrain with awkward leaps and bounds. He arrived still on his feet and out of breath.

"We're not in that much of a hurry, Mevine," said Byron, reaching out to steady the young man.

"I don't want to be responsible for holding up the Rennather," Mevine gasped. "Or you."

"I think they'll cut us both some slack."

The young man took several deep breaths as he attempted to regain his composure. "You won't be back for a long time," he said with disappointment.

"Probably not for a year and a half," Byron responded. "Once we've finished with Cosbolt training, we'll return, though."

"I hope I'm still here."

"Mevine, I think you'll be here for as long as you want."

The boy smiled, his shoulders straightening with pride. Mevine's thin frame still required some work, but he now possessed an air of confidence that was previously lacking. Byron knew his friend would prosper here on Tgren.

"Besides, we intend to put in a good word for you when we meet with Chancellor Dentex."

Mevine was to receive honors for his involvement in the determent of the alien craft, but Byron wanted to be sure that the young man's father fully comprehended his son's contribution. Considering how eager the Chancellor was to meet Athee, Byron knew he had Mevine's father at his mercy. Mevine would no longer be the outcast of the family.

"Mevine," said Athee, speaking for the first time since saying goodbye to her uncle. "Thank you, for everything. You saved my people."

The young officer placed his hands behind his back and glanced down. "I just translated the code…" he began, tracing a line in the dirt with his boot.

Athee stepped forward and placed her arms around his neck. Shock radiated from Mevine. His wide eyes sought Byron. Smiling at his friend, Byron nodded and sent his approval. Mevine returned Athee's embrace with an awkward hug, surprise still emanating from his thoughts.

You did far more than you realize, Athee told him in a hushed thought.

She released Mevine. He staggered back, his expression almost apologetic as he turned to Byron. With a grin, Byron brought his hand down on his friend's shoulder.

"I'll miss you, Mevine," he announced, squeezing the boy's bony shoulder. Mevine stood to his full height and lifted his chin.

"Sir, it's been an honor serving with you. More than an honor! Sir, I never thought I'd have the opportunity to meet you in person…"

"Mevine!"

His jaw clamped shut, and Mevine stared at his idol with wide eyes. Byron gave him a light shake.

"If you call me sir one more time, or at any time during our communication over the next couple years, I'm going to fry your ass. Understood?"

Mevine nodded in agreement, and Byron's smile grew.

You're my friend, Mevine. And a damned good friend.

Without waiting for a response, Byron gave the young man a rough hug. The gratitude and adoration that poured from Mevine bordered on embarrassing. However, a peace resided within his friend. The tranquility occupying Mevine's mind was indescribable. The memory of another man's peace flashed in his thoughts, and Byron's chest muscles constricted.

He patted Mevine's head and stepped back, drained by the exchange. Byron felt Athee's fingers curl around his palm. He realized she'd overheard their exchange. They weren't even a bonded pair yet, and already she knew his thoughts.

"Stay out of trouble," Byron told Mevine.

The young man stood at attention as they boarded the shuttle. Athee released Byron's hand and returned to the cockpit. Byron hesitated before closing the hatch, his eyes on Mevine. His friend offered a mischievous smirk as the shuttle door began to close.

I'm glad you won't be alone anymore, Mevine thought.

Yeah, me too.

Byron wasted no time lifting the shuttle into the sky. He spun the ship around and caught Mevine staring up at them, his thin frame growing smaller by the second. Grasping the throttle tighter, he tapped into the teleporter and envisioned their destination.

The Rennather's hanger crew assisted with the bags. An ensign led Erndell out of the hanger, leaving Byron to escort Athee to his quarters. He offered his elbow and she grasped his arm. Without a word, he ushered her into the nearest telepod. Two crewmen followed with Athee's possessions draped across their shoulders.

Arriving at his quarters, Byron indicated where the bags were to be placed. He eyed the pile with trepidation. His closets weren't big enough to house so many bags. Opening up the nearest compartment, Byron attempted to place the sacks inside. He managed to fit three into the tiny compartment. The remaining two would have to reside elsewhere.

Frustrated, he closed the door. Byron glanced around the room. He noticed Athee by his computer and detected curiosity. Ignoring the last two bags, he approached the Tgren woman.

She stepped back and stared at him in wonder. *Is that Bassa?*

Noting the photo beside his computer, Byron placed a hand on her back and nodded. He gazed at the image, aware that it was the first time Athee had ever viewed his former navigator. Byron had kept his friend hidden from her, almost afraid to allow a connection between the two. As he gazed at Bassa's image, he realized the importance of the moment.

I wish you could've met Athee, my friend, he thought. Now I know I'll be all right.

Forgetting the bags on the floor, Byron twisted Athee's body to face him. His arms wrapped around her back and he pulled the Tgren woman close.

Time to test your final ability, he announced, feeling hunger arise in his body.

Her eyes narrowed. *If you want us to bond, you've got to do better than that.*

Byron grinned and raised a hand to stroke her hair. *I love you.*

Athee relaxed in his arms. *I love you,* she thought.

Returning her affectionate smile, Byron gave Athee a light shake. *Now, all I ask is that you remember your place in this relationship. You will be my mate and navigator, understood?*

Yes, sir!

Which makes me...? he prodded, affecting his most threatening expression.

Athee's grin grew and she stroked the back of his neck. *The luckiest pilot in the universe.*

I can live with that, Byron thought as he bent to kiss her.

The End

About The Author

Alex J. Cavanaugh has a Bachelor of Fine Arts degree and works in web design and graphics. He is experienced in technical editing and worked with an adult literacy program for several years. A fan of all things science fiction, his interests range from books and movies to music and games. Currently the author lives in the Carolinas with his wife.

http://alexjcavanaugh.blogspot.com

CPSIA information can be obtained at www.ICGtesting.com
Printed in the USA
LVOW041614060312

271867LV00008B/12/P